GIDION'S BLOOD

GIDION KEEP, VAMPIRE HUNTER
BOOK TWO

BILL BLUME

DIVERSIONBOOKS

Also by Bill Blume

Gidion's Hunt (Gideon Keep, Vampire Hunter: Book One)
The Deadlands: And Other Stories

Diversion Books
A Division of Diversion Publishing Corp.
443 Park Avenue South, Suite 1008
New York, New York 10016
www.DiversionBooks.com

For more information, email info@diversionbooks.com

First Diversion Books edition August 2015.
Print ISBN: 978-1-68230-013-8
eBook ISBN: 978-1-68230-014-5

This book is dedicated to my wife Sheri and our children Regan and Liam. I can't thank you three enough for the support in getting this book written.

CHAPTER ONE

When Gidion hunted, he kept a rabbit's foot in his front pocket, a gift from his girlfriend. He also wore his black t-shirt with the symbol of a red bat on the front, but several layers of clothing hid it from view. The idea of burying his luck made him nervous, and ever since winter had rolled around, he'd fought the weather more than vampires.

Winter wasn't keeping people away from Westhampton this night. Didn't hurt that this was also a Friday. Gidion had added this stretch of Grove Avenue and several other places in the Richmond area to his patrol route back in early December when the pickings had gotten slim downtown. A vampire would have to be pretty desperate to try his luck in Westhampton, a much nicer and smaller area than downtown. People would be more likely to miss anyone taken from here and dumped in a ditch.

A thick crowd had gathered inside the Blue Goat. Blue decorative lights were strung along the edges of the restaurant's front porch. When he started patrolling here back in December, he assumed the lights were for Christmas, but now that it was more than halfway through January, he'd decided the lights must be a permanent fixture. Dad had made some less than subtle hints that he wanted Gidion and Grandpa to take him to Blue Goat for his birthday, which was a week away.

Gidion needed to earn some extra cash to buy a birthday gift. His grandpa paid him a hundred dollar bonus for each bloodsucker he killed, but naturally, the vampires weren't cooperating. The word seemed to be out to stay away from Richmond. He was putting himself out of a job.

He'd circled Westhampton seven times and was on the eighth circuit when he spotted a good candidate. Since he'd started hunting this past summer, he'd killed a total of eighteen vampires, six of whom had made up the local coven. The rest had been nomads, and he'd learned to recognize the signs.

Some nomadic vampires made more of an effort than others, but even the best dressed usually couldn't avoid wrinkled shirts. Living out of a suitcase will do that. A wrinkled shirt gave Gidion his first tip-off when he saw a potential target cross Libbie Avenue and walk down the sidewalk towards him.

Gidion made a quick note of his description: white male, short black hair, red dress shirt beneath a black velvet jacket, black jeans. The velvet jacket screamed "vampire," and not just because he looked like he'd ordered his wardrobe from a "GQ Dracula" catalog. The jacket might impress the ladies, but it certainly wouldn't do jack to keep him warm on a night predicted to make it down to twenty-eight degrees for the low. Sure a guy might be dumb enough to tough it out, but he didn't look bothered at all by the cold.

By comparison, Gidion wore thermals, his t-shirt, a black turtleneck beneath a grey hoodie with the hood up, and a black reversible coat. His leather gloves only kept his hands warm enough to avoid them turning into meat popsicles. If his gloves got any thicker, they turned his grip to crap.

Given the cold, a guy dressed like GQ Drac should be hugging himself to keep warm. Only one thing remained to put the nail in the coffin, and the weather cooperated for that test. A westerly wind shot up Gidion's pant legs, so cold as to mock the effort of his thermals. His scent carried towards his prey.

The vampire stopped in his tracks. His head jerked up to look right at Gidion.

Touchdown.

Gidion knew what came next. Things always played out in one of two ways. Half of these vampires followed him, waiting until Gidion led them somewhere more private for the inevitable confrontation. Others ran. Hard as he tried, Gidion couldn't hold in his smile as he waited to see which way this guy went. He walked straight at him.

GQ Drac reached into his jacket. For a split second, Gidion thought he was about to get shot. Most vampires didn't carry weapons. They risked unwanted attention if someone noticed, but surely even a vampire with a gun wasn't dumb enough to shoot someone in a place this public.

Gidion went dead still, every muscle tensed and ready to jump left or right as the vampire jerked his hand back out of his jacket. GQ Drac didn't draw a gun, though. He pulled out a cell phone and snapped a shot with the phone's camera just as he turned tail to run.

The flash blinded Gidion for a split second. As soon as his eyes cleared, he saw his father's birthday present sprinting back the way he'd come.

The vampire ran straight across Libbie, not bothering to look for any oncoming cars.

A blue SUV slammed into the vampire. The driver hit the brakes with a horrid screech. The vampire rebounded off the hood of the car and rolled out into the intersection. The vampire didn't stay down. He jumped up and bolted like a cat dropped into a bath. With all the traffic stopped, he cut diagonally across the intersection, taking him to the far side of Grove Avenue.

Gidion chased him. He gave a token glance in all directions of Libbie and Grove. The SUV wasn't going anywhere, nor were any of the other stopped cars. He avoided looking at the drivers too long, not wanting to give them a good view of his face. Gidion saw at least two people already on their phones, most likely to dial 911, giving him a fleeting moment to be glad he was in the city and not Henrico County where his dad was working this night.

Something this weird might bring the cops here in a hurry. It's not every day a well-dressed guy gets hit by a car and then runs from the scene with someone after him. Anyone with at least two brain cells rubbing together could add these facts to know something was going down.

Indecision gnawed at Gidion, even as he continued his pursuit.

Before the police could get on scene, they'd probably have a direction of travel and descriptions. How much time did he really have to catch this vampire, cut his head off, run back to his car, and roll out of here before the police started searching the area? He wasn't sure how many minutes it would take, but he was pretty sure he didn't have nearly enough to get the job done.

GQ Drac led him past the off-white exteriors of the businesses along that block, down past the Café Caturra and across Maple Avenue. Gidion wondered if the vampire was injured and panicked enough that he was running blind. There were plenty of open spaces to park along Grove. Gidion hoped that meant the vampire had run past his car and wouldn't be able to drive away, but then he saw the outline of the old, dark blue VW van parked in the shadows that separated the street lights. No, GQ Drac had planned to abduct his victim in the dark, if need be—to shove his prey in the van and roll off.

He needed to catch up. Gidion hoped unlocking the car door might slow the vampire's escape. He spared a thought to what he'd do, if he even caught him in time. There were already too many witnesses, and even in the shadows two blocks from the accident scene, he couldn't fight this vampire and slice his head off without being seen. Adrenaline had him going, though, and he was determined to get a hand on his target.

GQ Drac reached the driver side door and jerked it open. No, of course he wouldn't bother locking up a piece of crap like that. Who would?

The van rumbled to life just as Gidion reached the passenger door. He pulled the door open, but the van took off before he could get a grip on the door frame or try to dive inside.

Gidion ran after the van as it disappeared down a side street. He'd hoped the vampire might stop to pull the passenger door shut. No such luck. The stylish coward was too freaked. Halfway down from Grove, Gidion abandoned his pursuit. He stopped with his hands on his knees to keep his body on its feet as he struggled to catch his breath.

The sirens of an ambulance got him moving again. He heard the slowing of the whine that could only mean that they'd reached the scene of the accident. Gidion unzipped his jacket and pulled it off as he jogged down Maple Avenue until he reached the next corner where he also pulled his hood down. He flipped the reversible jacket inside out and put it back on with the lime green color on the outside. He also kept his hood down and let the jacket cover it so no one would recognize he was wearing a hoodie. As fast as everything had happened, no one at the crash scene should recognize him like this. That was important, because he needed to see something where that SUV had hit the vampire.

The entire walk down that dark street, all he could hear was Grandpa's rough, chain-smoker voice in his head.

'You aren't gonna bat a thousand. A few get away, and some hold a grudge enough to come back for another try when you're older and weaker. They've got time on their side.'

He reached into his pants pocket to grip his rabbit's foot. Even if time wasn't working for him, he hoped his good luck charm would.

CHAPTER TWO

Gidion hesitated as he neared the intersection, just half a block away. An ambulance had made it on scene. Several cars idled in the road without their drivers in them. Some of the witnesses might have gone looking for GQ Drac, not that they'd find him. The flashing lights marking the accident were only red, no blue. That meant the police hadn't gotten there yet, but that could change any second, so he picked up his pace as much as he could without making himself look suspicious.

Even with the full head of hair that his dad coveted, Gidion longed to pull his hood back up to block the chill digging into his scalp. More than that, he wanted the anonymity the hood provided. At least wearing the jacket turned inside out made it a little safer to go back.

The ambulance was parked in the middle of the intersection. The first responders, already out of the cab, talked with a woman in a dull-colored sweater that screamed "soccer mom." She pointed down Grove, in the direction of Gidion's pursuit. He wasn't close enough to hear them, but he could guess what was being discussed. One of the ambulance crew members stepped away to say something over the radio. With any luck, that might send the police in the direction GQ Drac had gone and not straight to the scene.

Nobody had moved since the accident. Gidion passed beneath the glow of an old-timey style street lamp as he came up on the blue SUV. The Toyota Rav4 idled in the middle of the brick path that marked where pedestrians should cross. Two kids in the backseat had unbuckled themselves and were bouncing around. One of them flung himself against the back seat in what Gidion assumed was a reenactment of the vampire getting hit. Even with the windows and doors closed, he heard their giggles. He supposed that was better than the kids being hysterical.

Gidion stopped at the corner. No one appeared to pay attention to him. Even so, he stayed put, pretending to rubberneck as he tried to figure out whether the thing he was looking for was here.

The Rav4's passenger side had suffered the most damage, giving it the automotive equivalent of a black eye. GQ had smashed the headlight to bits and dented the top of the hood. The car looked drivable, though.

Gidion stayed on the corner as he studied the intersection, starting with tiny shards of the Rav4's headlight. The glass glittered, reflecting the street light and the red emergency lights. He found what he was looking for midway between the Rav4 and the ambulance: the red, rectangular shape of GQ Drac's iPhone.

The tightness in Gidion's chest relaxed. He thought he'd seen the vampire drop the phone, but he feared he'd imagined it. Now that he'd switched from Chase-the-Bad-Guy mode to What-the-Hell-Just-Happened mode, he realized how bad it would have been if that vampire still had his phone. The vampire seeing his face created enough problems, but the nomadic vampires getting their hands on a picture of him endangered him far more than a first-hand account describing him. By comparison, getting shot at would have been better.

He needed that phone. Not only would it potentially give him plenty of information on other nomadic vampires, but it might help him track down the one who got away and finish the job.

Odds favored that GQ Drac was a hotel vampire. Even with the wrinkled shirt, he looked too neat and tidy to be roughing it in the back of that van. When a guy's diet involves popping open a person's throat, he's gonna get messy. That meant he needed a shower or a bath. One creative guy who'd been camping in the trunk of his Buick had kept an army's worth of flushable moist wipes in the back seat of his car. Gidion wondered how many times that vampire had holed up in a public restroom and flushed his mess into the sewer.

The ambulance crew looked more focused on where GQ Drac

had gone versus the scene itself. Could he stroll into the intersection and pick up the phone without being noticed? He'd learned early on there was an art to going places he didn't belong. It was amazing how often people didn't give a second thought if he just walked with purpose. He didn't care for his chances with something this overt, though.

He had to try, though. Dammit, he needed that phone.

Gidion stepped off the sidewalk. He swore he felt the change from concrete to asphalt even through the soles of his sneakers. He made it five steps out, halfway to the phone, when a siren whooped and made him jump.

Coming around the stopped Rav4, the red and blue light bar and headlights of a Richmond Police car blinded him. Nothing to do then but keep walking and hurry out of the cop's way.

Gidion glanced over his shoulder as the police cruiser rolled through the intersection to pull into the parking lot of a gas station across the street. If the police officer went through that phone and saw the picture the vampire had snapped, there was a chance he might recognize Gidion. Better to get out of there while he still could. He continued down Grove, getting back onto the sidewalk where the chase had started. When he reached the Blue Goat, he cut into the alley between the restaurant and the movie theater. He'd parked his car in the back.

At least the vampire didn't have the phone either. Gidion puzzled over that as he climbed into his grey Kia Soul. Getting out of the cold wind felt much better. He got the car cranked and turned the heat to full blast. His mind went through the places the vampire might go next, which hotels or populated areas. There was also a good chance that the guy might be too spooked to risk going hunting again. Even so, he decided to drive to Carytown. The van hadn't gone that way, not exactly, but it was the next best hunting ground for a vampire near Westhampton.

As Gidion drove east towards Carytown, his mind kept replaying GQ Drac's reaction. No other vampire had tried snapping a picture of him. Something had changed with the vampires, and it couldn't mean anything good for him.

CHAPTER THREE

Gidion searched Carytown for GQ Drac without success. He even rolled the dice on downtown and found nothing. He hadn't bothered with walking in the cold, though. Given the vampire's distinctive mode of transportation, Gidion settled for searching the most popular parking lots and side streets. He made it south of the river, back to his side of town. As he was cruising westbound on the Midlothian Turnpike, the music cut off in the middle of one of his favorite songs, replaced by barking. Great. Grandpa was calling.

"You didn't check in." Grandpa's voice always reminded Gidion of loose gravel.

"Sorry, Grandpa." He checked the clock display on his dash and saw it was a few minutes past midnight. He was supposed to call Grandpa every hour. He'd tried to talk him into just letting him send a text, but he didn't think Grandpa knew how to read a text sent to his cell, much less send a reply. That Grandpa could answer a phone call to his cell was nothing short of a miracle, but Gidion wagered he still didn't know how to make a call from it. This call came from his office at the funeral home. "I lost track of time driving around."

"Driving?"

Gidion explained what happened in Westhampton.

"You got lucky, boy. Walking around in those hoodies of yours with vampire blood on them is stupid. You're inviting an attack."

"That's the point." Gidion paused as he saw a vehicle with a boxlike shape coming from the opposite direction on Midlothian. As he got closer, he saw it was an SUV, not a van. Darn it. "Lot easier finding vampires to kill when they're dumb enough to come after me."

"Not if they kill you before you see 'em," Grandpa said. "If all you're gonna do is cruise around, call it a night. I'd like to go home and have a beer."

Gidion clenched the steering wheel. "It's not even past one yet, and it's a Friday night. Packing it in now would be stupid."

"Don't give me lip, boy." Grandpa chewed through the words like a bulldog. "You're like a damn Indian wearing scalps from his kills and waltzing into a saloon. Get your ass home. Wash the damn hoodies. Besides, we've got a busy day tomorrow. You're driving for four funerals. First one's at ten, so be there by 9:30. Don't be late."

Gidion jerked the phone away from his ear as a loud crack and rattle thundered over it, no doubt from Grandpa slamming down the handset. He didn't bother plugging his phone back into the car stereo. Instead, he turned into the parking lot of the Capital Ale House. These places stayed open pretty late and made some great hamburgers, too. One night, he'd come here to pick up a late dinner and ended up chasing down a vampire who'd come here hoping for a late night snack of his own. It was easier to find his prey by thinking less like a vampire and more like the people they hunted, going to the places people frequented at night.

His hopes for finding his target's VW went unfulfilled. Things were already winding down at this restaurant, not many cars in the parking lot. He went inside and ordered a burger called a Ring of Fire. He knew from experience that one had a good burn to it, perfect for a night as cold as this.

He waited by the bar and pulled out his phone to text his girlfriend.

'*Looks like my hunting is ending early tonight. You want to chat when I get home?*'

Shortly after Tamara moved to Phoenix, he'd bought a camera for his laptop so they could see each other when they talked. Up until Christmas, they'd been trading emails, texting and calling each other almost daily. She'd gotten busier this month, and his timing had stunk. They didn't get to see each other as much, since he stayed out late most nights, even with the time difference.

By the time his food was ready and he'd paid for it, Gidion's girlfriend still hadn't answered. The app showed she'd received his text, but she still hadn't sent a reply by the time he made it home.

His dog Page barked at him through the front door as he unlocked it. He struggled past her. The large German Shepherd mix sniffed at him as he walked to the kitchen. His phone chimed like a small bell, the sound he'd plugged in for when he received a text from Tamara.

"Yes!" He pulled out his phone, hoping his luck had finally turned for the evening.

'Sorry, can't talk. Out with some friends.'

"Great." So much for his luck improving.

He sent a reply back, promising to text her again soon. Page dropped flat on the floor, her tail wagging as she whimpered, her way of saying she was desperate to go outside.

"Oh, all right." She jumped around like a rabbit as he walked to the front door to put her out on her leash. While she did her business, he sat at the kitchen table to eat and went through his email. He loved this new phone. Dad had finally brought them both into the current century this past Christmas.

The most recent email came from his Dad's work account. Odd. He usually sent texts, but as soon as Gidion read the email, he understood why he wasn't texting. Dad couldn't find his cell, wanted to make sure he'd left it at home and hadn't dropped it somewhere.

Gidion went upstairs and into Dad's room. He found the black phone sitting on the bed. He brought it downstairs with him and set it on the kitchen table. As he typed an email to let Dad know he'd found his phone, the display on Dad's phone lit up. He wondered if it was one of his dad's co-workers texting him. Their consoles allowed them to communicate with an Instant Messenger program, but Internal Affairs and the 911 supervisors could read that stuff. For their personal conversations, a lot of them preferred to text.

He glanced at the message. It was from someone named Lillian. *'Looking forward to seeing you tomorrow night and meeting everyone at the Byrd.'*

The message showed in the notification since the sender had kept it short. Dad's phone never would have let him read it otherwise. Dad used two different password commands to access the phone. He believed in double-confirmation with most anything computer-related, and he had never let Gidion use his stuff.

"Wow. Go, Dad." His dad had behaved like a monk ever since Mom died more than a decade ago, which had also ended Dad's vampire hunting career. He glanced at the wedding portrait of his mom on the wall near the kitchen table. When Grandpa showed Gidion that vampires were real, he'd never said Mom was the reason Dad stopped hunting, but it didn't take a genius to connect it. He knew Dad missed her, but Gidion had been pushing him to date again. He even had a deal with his Dad to ask out his world history teacher if he got all As in her class this school year, and that's when it hit him. He looked back at the phone and that name, Lillian.

"Miss Aldgate?" His teacher was texting his dad after midnight on a Friday. Were they planning a date for tomorrow night?

Even if it wasn't a date, it was a hell of a lot more than Gidion was doing. He sent his email to Dad, not bothering to mention the text from his teacher. While he waited on Dad's reply, he looked back at his phone and the text from Tamara.

Not even one o'clock, and he was at home instead of hunting vampires. This sucked.

Dad replied about the same time Gidion let Page back in the house. He said not to bother with bringing him the phone. Told him thanks and to get some sleep.

Gidion sent a reply wishing his dad a good night. He knew better than to hope he had a "quiet night." Mentioning the Q word was a major jinx word for dispatchers. Dad said it was worse than uttering "Macbeth" in a theater.

He tossed his trash in the garbage can, much to his dog's disappointment. Page yawned as she plopped down in front of the TV to pout. She stared at him as he bundled up again. He wanted another shot at finding GQ Drac, and he had a new idea for how to find him.

CHAPTER FOUR

Clothes might make the man, but the car he drives says a lot more about him. A guy in a Lexus so pristine and shiny that it might have rolled off the dealer's lot that morning is working with a lot of cash. Someone like GQ Drac, who drives a rust-covered and dented older model VW van that looks less posh than a rat's nest, isn't going to spend his sleeping hours at the five-star Jefferson Hotel.

Using one of those hotel finder websites, Gidion plotted the cheapest hotels in the metro area. After that, he worked his way out from Westhampton where his target had kissed the hood of that Rav4. He started on the nearest major road, West Broad Street. He drove past the dark strip malls and neon-bright twenty-four hour convenience stores, looking through the lots of the hotels on his list.

When he didn't find anything on Broad, he moved outward, staying with the hotels closest to the interstates, I-64 and I-95. A little after two o'clock, he pulled into a hotel along Chamberlayne Road, just off of I-95. The hotel was north of Richmond and was surrounded by a lot of apartment complexes. If they put this place on a Monopoly board, it certainly wouldn't be anywhere near Boardwalk and Park Place.

Parked in the corner of the lot, about as far from the building as a car could get, Gidion found the VW van. His prey chose the darkest part of the lot, maybe hoping he might turn another guest into a snack and drain them in the van.

Gidion parked a few spaces away. He'd learned the hard way that his car was permanently stained with vampire blood from his kills. A vampire had figured out he was a hunter just by sniffing the car as he walked past it. That's how he'd learned vampires could pick up on the distinct scent of their kind's blood. Given how GQ Drac ran earlier, Gidion decided it was best to keep his car far enough away to avoid detection. He just hoped the wind would cooperate.

The parking lot wasn't crowded. What were the chances he could go door-to-door until he found the guy? Answer: not good. Some irritated guest might call the police. Not that it would end any better for him anywhere else, but he was all too aware he was in Henrico County, the jurisdiction where Dad worked.

A gust shook his car, and Gidion heard what sounded like a distant, muffled scream. He thought it came from the direction of the VW. The second scream confirmed it. He watched the van to see if it moved, but he couldn't tell. The van was backed into its space with a wooded area just behind it, a great place to dump a body.

He hesitated but then decided he couldn't wait. If someone was in there, then they didn't have much longer. As he jumped out of his car, the cold air hit him like a wall and sucked the breath out of him. He pulled out his box cutter and extended the blade as he ran for the van. He couldn't see if anyone was inside. The windows were covered on the inside with curtains.

The vampire had left the passenger door unlocked earlier. Gidion gambled GQ Drac didn't lock the other doors either. Deciding he didn't want to be visible from the hotel, he went for the far side of the van and jerked the door open.

Empty. The back didn't even have any seats. They'd been removed. Dark blue, vinyl mats, the kind he'd napped on back in kindergarten, covered the floor. If a vampire killed someone back here, wouldn't be hard to wash out the evidence. A dark red tool box was shoved against the back of the van, just over where the engine would go.

Gidion slammed the door shut. He wondered if the screams had been nothing more than the wind, but then he heard another, a shriek from the woods.

He ran in the direction of the woman's cry. The idea GQ Drac had decided to take his snack "camping" made perfect sense. Why clean when you can dine and dispose in one shot?

Then he heard the gunshots. He stopped in the middle of the

wooded area with the moonlight and parking lot lights hidden by the evergreens. The noise reminded him of whip cracks on steroids. For a split second, he considered they might only be firecrackers, but then he heard more screams. Just lovely. He'd gone hunting for a vampire and stumbled onto some domestic or gang fight.

More shots fired, deeper than the first and closer. He felt the sound of the shots reverberate through the air and into his chest.

He turned and ran back towards the hotel before any bullets ventilated him.

Shouts chased him. Someone or maybe several people had just entered the woods from the opposite side.

Gidion rushed back into the parking lot by the VW. More yelling came from the woods, and he picked out at least three different voices. He'd never reach his car before these guys got out of the woods.

He froze, and in that split second of indecision, he heard another gunshot. That made the choice for him. He gave up on reaching his car and dove into the vampire's van.

Police sirens followed. They raced past the hotel on Chamberlayne. They must have been close when the calls started coming into the 911 center. He heard several curses from just outside the van. He scrambled to lock all the doors. He needn't have worried. The guys coming out of the woods ran past the van and towards the hotel.

Once he'd calmed his heart and his breathing, he realized the cops were going the wrong way. He pulled out his cell phone but stopped short of calling 911. They'd see his phone number. Worse, what if Dad got the call and recognized the phone number?

These guys might have just killed someone, and he couldn't even do anything about it.

Just then, a police car pulled into the parking lot. Apparently, the police had already figured on people possibly running this way. The police car passed right by the van. Gidion ducked, praying he'd been fast enough not to be seen. A white light mounted on the police car's driver side door flashed towards the van. He stayed down, pressing into the vinyl mats. Whatever antiseptic cleaner GQ

Drac used to wipe down these mats overwhelmed his nose. Beneath that, he detected a hint of blood. He looked up and saw the flood light pass through the van's windows and then slide past to focus on the woods. Gidion waited another moment to make sure the light didn't come back in his direction. He crouched up towards the driver side window and saw the police cruiser rolling past his car, the light trained on the woods.

If he got out of the van, he could tell the officer what he'd seen. He'd gotten a good look at all three men, could give a detailed description of what they were wearing, but he couldn't risk it. Climbing out of this van and revealing himself to the officer would also raise too many questions. Chief among them would be why he was hiding in someone else's van. They'd probably run his name and date-of-birth to see if he was wanted, and it was a sure thing someone up in the 911 center would realize they'd just run Aric Keep's only son. Dad would lose his shit if he realized what Grandpa had him doing. Come to think of it, even Grandpa would light into him at this point. He was supposed to be in bed and resting for work in the morning.

He readied himself to jump from the van the minute the police car disappeared from the hotel lot, but it didn't. The cruiser stopped in the middle of the lot and kept its light sweeping over the woods. It even passed through the van windows a few more times.

His heart pounded as if he was running again. He was trapped. No way he could get out of the van and make it to his car without being seen. Add to that, he looked suspicious as hell. He was wearing all black with a hoodie. Never mind the sword strapped to his back and the box cutter in his front pocket.

He'd just have to wait out the officer. Then the flood light on the cruiser went dark. He dared to hope he'd get out of here clean, but the police car didn't pull away. Instead, the officer got out. He walked up to the Little Hearse and shined a flashlight to look inside the car and see if anyone was hiding there. He didn't take long to see Gidion's car was empty.

Then the officer headed towards the van.

CHAPTER FIVE

All sorts of solutions to hide rushed through Gidion's mind as the officer walked towards the van. He thought about hiding under the vinyl mats, but moving around to do that would rock the van and make it even more obvious someone was hiding in it. There was the slim chance he could jump out the other side and run for it, but the time for that had long since past. These officers had probably established a perimeter by now. They'd close in on him the minute he ran. On top of that, they might have a plane on the way and a canine unit.

That left him one option: crouch as low as he could go, stay still as a statue and pray this officer's eyesight was total crap. At least the side windows were covered.

Gidion positioned himself just behind the driver's seat. He saw the beam of light cut through the space between the front seats. He jerked back from that light.

Then he heard the officer's radio squawk. He couldn't make out what the voices said, but he heard the urgent tone to the words.

The blade of light vanished. Then a car door slammed, followed by the fading rumble of an engine.

Gidion pulled up just enough to peer around the driver's seat. The police cruiser raced out of the hotel lot and disappeared down Chamberlayne Road.

He sat up and took a few deep breaths. His hands shook. He watched them in fascination, then balled them into tight fists to make them stop.

Gidion jumped out of the van, scrambled into the Little Hearse and fought the urge to plant the accelerator against the floorboard.

Only once he'd gotten out of the hotel lot and onto the interstate did he floor it.

• • •

The morning arrived way too early and with the thunderous klaxon of his phone's alarm, but it was the slam of his bedroom door that sent him bolt upright in bed.

"Gidion!"

His brain took a moment to register that his father was leaning into his bedroom and staring at him. No, staring didn't really describe it. Dad glared in a way that demanded to know how someone who shared half of his DNA could be doing something so stupid. He just wasn't awake enough to figure out what fresh hell he'd managed to step into until Dad's eyes got even wider.

"Son! Turn off the alarm already. I had just gotten to sleep."

His alarm. Gidion had slept through the first three alarms on his phone. The fourth one sounded like an aircraft carrier racing its way into World War III. He turned it off.

"Thank you." Dad disappeared from his doorway. Gidion was about to put his head back on the pillow until Dad yelled from his room. "Aren't you supposed to be working this morning?"

Gidion looked back at his phone. The time displayed was 9:02.

"AUGH!"

He needed to be at the funeral home by 9:30 for the 10:00. That gave him all of three minutes to scrub the foulness from his teeth, brush his hair into submission and get dressed in a suit and tie. He had a better chance of burping up a unicorn.

A few more panicked screams followed as his usual morning routine transformed into a mad, nightmarish, multi-tasking disaster.

"Trying to sleep here." Dad's muffled complaint called through the closed door to his bedroom.

Gidion ran for the front door, passing his dog's indifferent stare from where she lounged on her favorite chair in the den. Grandpa's stare would be anything but indifferent by the time

Gidion reached work.

Milligan's Funeral Home resembled a flat group of beige brick boxes that reminded Gidion of a poorly played game of Tetris. The parking lot was already filling up when Gidion turned into it. He'd hoped to sneak in the back, through the garage, but as soon as he stepped inside, there was Grandpa all decked out in full mobster mode with his black suit and tie. He gripped his cane as if he planned to beat Gidion with it.

"You're late."

By all of five minutes, which Gidion considered pretty impressive given when he'd gotten out of bed. "Sorry."

"We'll talk about it later. Get the cars lined up." Grandpa limped down the hallway to the front of the funeral home. "Reverend 'Fast Lips' Connor is doing the first service."

Fabulous. Reverend Connor was the only preacher who always finished early. As Gidion's day progressed, that proved the exception. Almost every other service ran at least a half hour late.

By the time Gidion parked the hearse in the garage after the last funeral, it was a quarter before three o'clock. Grandpa sucked on his pipe as he sat on a stool in the garage. If he bit on the stem any harder, the pipe might snap in half.

"You remember to fill it up?" He didn't hide his skepticism, glancing at his watch.

"I did." Gidion didn't have time for this, not if he was going to go after the vampire from last night. "See?" He held up a large cup of coffee he'd gotten from the Wawa on the way back.

Grandpa grunted in a way that suggested he still didn't believe Gidion.

"This running late shit needs to stop. Are we clear?"

"I still have to sleep sometime, and these aren't the bodies you really pay me to drive around."

For an old guy who didn't look like he could bench press half his body weight, Grandpa's glare looked fit to slice a man in half.

"If you don't want to drive them, then you don't have to get paid. That clear enough for you?" Grandpa sounded like a rabid, snaggletoothed bear when he got like this and just as mean.

"Yes, sir." Gidion restrained himself from tossing in a sarcastic salute.

"Go home."

"Sunset is almost an hour away."

Grandpa slammed the end of his cane on the concrete. Despite the rubber tip, it still cracked like a bone split in half.

"I thought you needed more sleep."

Gidion held up his coffee cup. "I'm fine, and I've got—"

"No, I'm not in the mood for the bullshit." He stood and hobbled back inside towards his office. "Besides, your dad isn't working tonight."

Before Gidion could protest, Grandpa slammed the door shut.

"Fine."

Grandpa could gripe all he wanted. They'd see how well he complained when Gidion hauled in GQ Drac's corpse later tonight.

CHAPTER SIX

Much as it galled Gidion, he didn't ignore Grandpa's advice about his hoodies smelling like dead vampires. For his plan to take down GQ Drac, he needed to go undetected.

Ambushing the vampire also meant getting there early. If he moved fast enough, maybe he could get in and out of his house before Dad tried to turn tonight into a Father-Son outing to the movies or dinner.

He checked the clock on his dash as he parked in front of the house. He'd made good time getting home, but that didn't leave very long to get in and out of if he was going to reach the hotel before sunset.

Just as Gidion ran up the driveway, Dad came out the front door with coat in hand. He was dressed in a red shirt with black pants and a black vest.

"Where are you going?" Gidion asked.

Dad looked as if he'd been caught climbing out of a back window in the middle of the night. "I'm just meeting some friends at the Byrd."

"Really?" Gidion grinned as he walked past him. "You don't usually dress like that when you go to the Byrd."

Dad glared at him over the rims of his glasses. "I'm going to a wine bar afterwards."

Just as Dad was about to climb into his TARDIS-blue Corolla, Gidion shouted to him. "Say 'Hi!' to Ms. Aldgate for me!"

Dad stopped in the middle of getting into the car. His face turned as crimson as his shirt.

His eyebrows pinched towards each other as he looked at

Gidion. No doubt he wondered how Gidion knew about his date, but he didn't voice the question. Instead, Dad said, "I'll do that." Just before he closed the door and drove off, he muttered, "Smart ass."

Gidion ran inside, bathing in the glory of his small but significant victory over the parental unit.

He found Page in her usual evening spot, sprawled across his bed as if she owned it. She stretched as Gidion rubbed her tummy, but as soon as he pulled his hand away, she craned her head to look at him with wide-eyed dissatisfaction.

"Later, furball." Gidion stripped off his work clothes and tossed the suit and tie onto the bed. The storm of fabric sent Page into retreat, plopping down and walking out into the hallway.

Gidion snatched his t-shirt with the red bat on it off the floor and jerked on a pair of black jeans. His rabbit's foot went into his jean's pocket. After pulling on a dark red turtleneck, he slipped his sword on, the strap going over his left shoulder like a bandolier. This placed the sword upside down for an easy draw with his right hand. He found that much easier, pulling the short sword out from beneath the back of his jacket rather than trying to wrestle it out through the back of his collar.

Before he left, he decided to arm himself with at least one more bit of good luck, especially after all of his close calls from last night. He searched his desk, rifling through a drawer filled with a lifetime's collection of colored pencils, markers, and highlighters. About the time he reached the Crayola Age, he found what he needed. His fingers brushed against something that didn't feel like wax or plastic. The cylinder of bamboo pulled free. He brought the hollowed out stick up to his lips and blew through it, even though the sound was little more than a muffled cough. The six-inch long piece of wood was a refugee from a set of broken wind chimes that had blown free from his neighbor's house and into the back yard during a tropical storm when he was seven. The night of that storm, which was the weekend before the school year started, he'd spent the entire time hidden under the covers wishing for an extra good luck charm to get through the storm. He'd read that bamboo could generate good luck, so he kept it in his backpack for the rest of the school year. He'd earned straight As for the first time ever on every report card. He slid on his jacket and shoved the bamboo chime into the inner breast pocket.

The early evening sunlight turned a shade of fire as he ran to his car and floored it. This was going to be cutting it close. The traffic cooperated, though. He flew up the Powhite Parkway and onto I-95 in less than fifteen minutes. Another five, and he pulled into the lot of the hotel.

The eastern sky had slipped on the cover of night, but the western sun glowed too brightly for any vampire to risk going outside or to peek out a window. God bless the flammable dead.

GQ Drac's less than stylish Volkswagen van was shedding rust like dandruff in the same place Gidion last saw it. He parked in the same space as last night, a safe distance away to prevent detection. Waiting just long enough to be certain no one was watching, he walked over to the unlocked van and climbed into the back.

He stayed crouched on the floor of the van. His position gave him enough of a view between the front seats to watch for his target. He'd spent all day thinking on this plan, going over the particulars as he drove body after body to its final resting place. The idea was simple enough: stay low and hidden, surprise the vamp when he opened the door, then kill him. Sounded great right up until he climbed into this van.

Gidion wasn't accustomed to waiting, not like this. Walking down the street with a vampire following a dozen yards or more behind him until they reached a discreet location to go *mano-a-vampo* wasn't that bad, by comparison. At least that kept him moving and adjusting plans as the situation evolved. Climbing into a vampire's mobile fangshack and waiting for the guy to get in it with him suddenly felt like the most dumbass thing he'd done since he bought an issue of *The Incredible Hulk*.

He lost track of time after the entire sky went dark. The last thing he could risk was to check his phone and have the light of the display expose him.

A nervous shiver made him realize he hadn't eaten since lunch. That's when he spotted the vampire, dressed in a blinding white dress shirt and black dress pants. He was pulling a travel bag with the small wheels behind him as he walked between the cars parked near the hotel. About damn time.

Gidion pulled out his sword and set it beside him on the floor of the van. The van's interior limited his movement, so pulling the sword out now would make it easier to grab when the time arrived to lop off GQ Drac's head. He risked another glance between the front seats and over the dashboard. The vampire wasn't looking at his van to notice anyone was in it. He was too busy looking over his shoulder as he walked between two parked cars. That's when Gidion realized, GQ Drac wasn't alone. He was talking to someone behind him.

As soon as the stylish monster got out from between the cars, an equally well-dressed woman fell into step beside him.

He crouched to stay hidden. His mind raced through his options, trying to figure out in seconds how to adjust the plan he'd spent all day putting together, because the glance had been enough to tell him that he wasn't facing one vampire.

He'd cornered himself in a fight with a fanged Bonnie and Clyde.

CHAPTER SEVEN

Gidion had considered every possible scenario in this ambush—
almost. What if GQ Drac took a long time to come out of his
room? What if he spotted him in the van? What if the vampire
had a gun?

He just never imagined the bastard would have a partner.

Gidion tried to work through a new plan in the seconds left
to him, but the only thing his mind managed was a dozen different
ways to call himself an absolute, boneheaded idiot.

He considered picking up his sword or pulling out his box
cutter, to go straight for a killing blow, but he'd never behead one
without giving the other a chance to get away or tear into him. By
the time the vampires reached the van, Gidion had resigned himself
to the only thing he could do: strike hard and fast, because the
only advantage he had left was surprise. Once that was gone, he'd
be screwed.

He heard the vampires and their rolling luggage stroll up to the
passenger side of the van. The rusty door groaned as the vampire
slid it open. Gidion had positioned himself just out of view towards
the back. His hands yearned for a weapon, but for what he had
planned, he needed both hands free.

The vampire tossed his bags into the van. As he did so, Gidion
grabbed him by the arm and pulled. He'd envisioned flinging the
vampire's body across the van and slamming his head into the far
side of the interior. Didn't work like that, though. The vampire's
shin caught on the bottom edge of the door frame. The attack laid
him out on the floor instead.

Gidion moved fast enough to go for "Bonnie" and caught her

by the shirt just as she was reaching to stop GQ Drac's fall.

He'd aimed for surprise. Judging from the wide-eyed look on her pale face as he jerked her into the van, he'd hit the mark with a bazooka.

The cramped space didn't lend itself to anything fancy. Fists, elbows, and knees thrust in random disorder with mixed results. Fangs bit at air, clothing, and flesh. Gidion smelled blood before he ever felt the wounds. He dodged a few hits from each vampire which landed on the other. Gidion felt like he'd tossed himself into a bag of rabid cats fighting over a ball of catnip, denying him the chance to go for any of his weapons.

One shot to his chest nailed him right where he was carrying the bamboo stick. Pain laced throughout the left side of his torso. Yeah, that extra good luck charm was really paying off.

The metal interior worked to his advantage, though, as did his position in the pile. He might have been trapped between them, but once he got a solid grip on Bonnie, he slammed her head against the ceiling of the car.

Nails raked at his hand as Bonnie fought to get free of his grip. He slammed his elbow into GQ Drac's head, then slammed her head against the ceiling and the side of the van until the fight in her faded. The combined weight of their bodies on GQ Drac had limited his ability to get into the fight, and as Gidion flung Bonnie off towards the front of the van, that all changed.

Cold hands grabbed him by the back of the neck and shoulder and shoved him up at the ceiling, just as Gidion had done with Bonnie. Gidion threw up his arms to keep his head from taking the hit. When the first strike failed, GQ Drac went for a second try, but on the rebound, Gidion was ready. He planted his feet against the ceiling and pinned GQ Drac down with his body. He felt the breath from the vampire against the back of his throat. He slammed the back of his head into GQ Drac's face twice.

Gidion grabbed his box cutter from his jacket pocket and stabbed it into the side of the vampire's thigh and then sliced up the outside of the leg. The vampire's scream deafened him.

He lost any sense of position in the fight. One moment, he was on top of the vampire, the next second they were separated.

When faced with heavy blood loss, vampires tended to go one of two ways. Some panicked and ran for it. GQ Drac fell into the "go-feral-and-all-bloodlusty" camp. Good news: GQ wasn't going to run away; bad news: he wanted blood something fierce, and Gidion was the closest snack. Even worse, Bonnie started moving again.

The "advantage" of surprise looked lousy right about now.

GQ Drac lunged first. Gidion snatched his sword from the floor of the van and took his best swing for the throat. He hit the target, but the limited space prevented him from getting the momentum for a proper beheading. A deep gash into GQ Drac's throat sprayed blood throughout the van's interior. GQ grabbed his own throat in a vain effort to stop the blood loss as he dropped to the floor.

Having recovered from the blows to her head, Bonnie attacked. Gidion swung at her with his sword, but GQ's body bumped against Gidion's forearms before he could finish the swing.

Bonnie grabbed Gidion by the throat and slammed him down. Even with the vinyl mats for cushion, the crack of his head against the floor knocked him for a loop. He lost his grip on his sword and the weapon disappeared in the shadows of the van. His heart thumped in a chaotic rhythm, eager to run. Too late for that, though. Bonnie bit at his throat. Pain tore through the base of his neck as her teeth snapped down on him, but his jacket and hoodie prevented her from drawing blood. The mouthful of fabric just barely saved him from getting his jugular ripped open.

Her face contorted in disgust. GQ Drac flailed, whimpering in agony as his blood gushed from his throat. His hand slapped across the front of her face, fingers unintentionally jabbing at her eyes. The split second of distraction cost her. Gidion grabbed her throat and slammed her head against the window. The glass cracked. The impact also knocked the curtains off and flooded the interior with artificial light. Bonnie's eyes glazed over.

Gidion rolled her onto her back, sprawled across GQ Drac. The pair's struggles entangled their bodies, and gave Gidion the chance to finish them. He picked up his sword and slammed it down on Bonnie's throat. The killing blow required more than one strike, a few missing the mark.

He hammered with the sword, severing Bonnie's head and then hacking off GQ Drac's. He didn't stop, even after the second head rolled free, each swing excising the fear that had possessed him.

His hands shook, fingers trapped around the hilt of the sword and unable to relax. He could smell the streaks of blood running down the left side of his face. Nausea almost overwhelmed him, and only the gentle rocking of his body kept him from emptying himself.

The fog of the fight cleared from his mind. He looked up and out the front window to make sure he was still alone. No one was in the parking lot. A glance at the hotel didn't reveal any curtains pulled back to suggest someone might be watching.

He pulled up his black hood to hide his face, which was streaked with blood. He wanted to wipe it off, but his sleeves were soaked. Most of his fights took place in the open, not in the back of a van.

He left the side door of the van cracked open after he got out and moved his car. He backed the Little Hearse into the space next to the van but stopped halfway so that the back of his car was right next to the side door of the van. Transferring the bodies didn't prove as difficult as he'd feared. He didn't typically bring in two bodies, though. The back of his car was a bit cramped with the corpses. He covered them as best he could with the sports gear he kept back there for just that purpose. People saw what they expected. Even if they looked, they'd only notice the glove, baseball bats and other equipment, not the odd lumps in the dark tarp covering the bodies.

He found the keys to the VW van in GQ Drac's pants pocket. At some point, he'd need to do something about the van, take it to a self service car wash and rinse it out before dumping it somewhere. For now, he locked it to keep anyone from snooping.

He tossed the orphaned luggage into the back seat of his car. The drive to the funeral home tested his nerves. He didn't dare speed and kept just below the speed limit as he got onto the interstate. During the drive, he cracked into a case of moist wipes he kept in his glove compartment and wiped off the blood on his face and his shaky hands.

He reached his destination in fifteen long minutes without ever passing a police car. Good thing, too. Because even if he didn't get pulled over, he doubted his nerves could handle the stress.

Only after he clicked the garage door opener on his sun visor and then backed into the garage did he realize he'd been so nervous that he'd never turned on any music. He didn't get out of the car right away, even with the stink of blood and death in the back. Last time he had to pull himself together after a hunt had been his first one. Grandpa had followed his patrol that night, circling through downtown in a real hearse. If he'd needed to drive that night, he never would have reached the funeral home without getting into a wreck or pulling over to vomit. He wanted to throw up now, and the stench of blood married to the chemical odor of the moist wipes didn't help. The smell was what forced him out of the car a minute later.

He barked a laugh in surprise as his legs wobbled through his first steps from the car and into the funeral home. Routine settled in and helped him through the next half hour. The cremator took a bit to warm up, and as he waited to toss his kills into the flames, he dug through their pockets and their suitcases. They both had laptops, his-and-her Dell Inspirons. The rest of what he found wasn't illuminating, just clothes. Digging through Bonnie's panties made him feel like a pervert.

He glanced at the cell phones and wallets before tossing them into their respective suitcases. Bonnie was actually a Teanna Carter, assuming the Oregon driver's license wasn't a fake. GQ Drac turned out to be a George Hammond from New York. That the first initial matched up with the nickname Gidion had given him was just too damn perfect. The resulting laughter settled his nerves, and just in time.

"What the fuck are you doing, boy?"

Gidion spun around. His instinctive retreat pressed his back to the conveyer belt where Bonnie & GQ Drac's bodies waited on a cardboard mat to slide into the cremator.

"Good God, Grandpa!" Dammit, his hands were shaking again. He shoved them into the pockets of his hoodie to hide them. "What are you doing here?"

Grandpa hobbled forward. His cane cracked against the linoleum floor as he went to the far side of the conveyor for a better look at Gidion's kills.

"Two? You went after two of them without even fucking telling me? Are you out of your goddamned mind?"

"I was only expecting there to be one of them, and I'm fine. Thanks for asking." He managed to glare at Grandpa's face as he said that, but the fury he met there sent his eyes retreating to stare at the old man's grip on the foam handle of his cane. He realized too late that what he'd said hadn't helped his argument.

"Just fucking brilliant." He hobbled around the conveyor to the same side as Gidion. "You look me in the eyes when I'm talking to you!"

"Whoa!" Gidion backed up, less from intimidation and more from the stink of whatever the hell was on his Grandpa's breath. "Are you drunk?"

He regretted the question the instant it was in the open.

"I've had a drink, but that doesn't make me fucking drunk." Gidion recognized the slur to Grandpa's voice, though. No, he wasn't plastered yet, but he was definitely halfway up the exit ramp. "Didn't have time to finish the beer I'd started before the alarm company called me."

Gidion held in a curse. He'd been so shaken when he got here that he'd forgotten to disarm the alarm system. Grandpa had the system set for silent. He would have noticed it going off otherwise.

"Are you listening to me?" Grandpa slammed down the end of his cane with another loud crack.

"I made the kill. I admit I screwed up, got in over my head, but I made the kill." He emphasized those last words and forced himself to keep eye contact with Grandpa.

"Oh, never mind then, because that makes everything so

fucking, grade-A, happy hunky dory, doesn't it? You made the kill, and then what was your plan, Einstein? Were you gonna use a cigarette lighter to—?"

The sudden silence as he looked at the cremator was worse than the tirade. Grandpa pushed Gidion out of the way with his cane. He didn't hit him with it, just directed him to move, but the feel of that cane pressed against the side of his arm wounded his spirits. Grandpa stepped closer to the control panel and his gaze moved up and down the readings for the afterburner chamber temperature and main chamber temperature.

"Get out." The calm in his voice was unsettling. Gidion couldn't decide if he preferred that Grandpa didn't turn around to look at him. Something told him the look in the old man's face wouldn't be something he'd soon forget.

"Grandpa?"

"Just get the fuck out of here."

Gidion zipped up the suitcases and rolled them out. Grandpa didn't move, but as Gidion got into the hallway, he heard him mutter, "Thought I was done with this bullshit when your dad quit hunting."

He wasn't sure what exactly that meant, not that he couldn't make some educated guesses. Hell, he couldn't decide if Grandpa even meant for him to hear it. Only thing he knew was that he shouldn't ask about it—not now and probably not ever.

CHAPTER EIGHT

After going home to shower off the blood from his kills, Gidion drove back to the hotel to dispose of GQ Drac's van. That was a tedious mess that involved finding a place to hose away all of the blood inside it and then dumping it. The latter part turned out to be much simpler than usual. He just parked it in one of the nearby apartment complexes. Tow companies patrolled the apartments and towed cars from those lots all the time. Come morning, GQ Drac's van would be rotting in a tow lot. He cut through the woods to get back to his car at the hotel. Thankfully, he didn't run into the middle of any gunfights this time.

He made it home a little after eleven, beating Dad by more than an hour. They didn't even cross paths until it was time to get ready for church the next morning. Because Dad usually went straight to bed after work, they only made it to church on the Sunday mornings when Dad hadn't worked overnight. Dad's "weekends" rotated. He'd once tried to explain to Gidion how the schedule worked. The only thing Gidion understood afterwards was that government operations were confusing. All that meant was that their appearances at church were more of a "seasonal" event.

When they got home from church, the answering machine was blinking. Dad played the message, and as soon as Gidion heard Grandpa's voice, he retreated upstairs and closed the door to his room. He didn't catch all of Grandpa's message. The few words he heard made it clear Grandpa wouldn't be coming over to watch football.

"Gidion!"

He winced as he heard Dad call him. He cracked his door open and saw Dad walking up the stairs. "Yeah?"

Dad smirked at him. "Get changed. We're going out to watch the game."

Gidion smiled, as much from relief that Dad wasn't going to interrogate him as he was excited at the prospect of what Dad had planned. Less than a half hour later, they'd made it to Carytown and found a spot at the bar at Burger Bach. The place was decorated in wood and metal and soaked with the smell of grilled red meat that promised plenty of good eats to clog the arteries.

The bartender, a woman in a black t-shirt, placed a tall glass of apple cider in front of Dad and a bottle of cream soda in front of Gidion.

"Still got an hour before kickoff." Dad pointed at the TV, one of four behind the bar, showing all the pregame hype for the NFC Championship. "Be a shame if you got 'sugar drunk,' and I have to drag you home."

"Funny, Dad." Gidion chugged half the bottle just to be a smart ass. "Real funny."

He still remembered the first time Dad had taken him to a bar when he was ten. The "sugar drunk" line had been his joke, but Dad had been happy to remind him of it ever since. Truth be told, he still thought it was funny, but the "Teen Code" demanded he pretend to give Dad grief about it.

The experts on TV were debating the Saint's chances of beating the Packers when Dad blindsided Gidion.

"So what did you do to tick off your grandpa?"

Dad sipped his drink with all the satisfaction of a wildcat that had a mouse caught by the tail in his claws.

Gidion straightened his back to compensate for the difference in height, not that it amounted to much of an improvement. "Who says he's ticked at me? Could be you."

"Oh, it's not me." Dad didn't bother to watch Gidion to study if he was lying. He turned to focus on the football coverage. "Ol' Sailor Murph wouldn't bother calling. He'd make me call him to find out why he wasn't there if it was my fault."

Gidion grunted, not that Dad would hear it. An ass warmed every chair in the place. Even with people chowing on fries and burgers, all the chatter was deafening.

"It's the Sunday of the NFC and AFC championships, and your grandpa doesn't own a TV." Dad hit him with his cop interrogation stare over the rims of his glasses with his fingers rapping on the bar top. Crap. He wasn't gonna let this go. "So?"

Then Gidion remembered Grandpa's exact words from last night.

"Apparently, nothing you haven't done before." Gidion crossed his arms and leaned back in his chair. Yeah, take that shot Dad.

"Oh, really? What makes you so sure of that?"

"Because he said," Gidion dipped into what he liked to think was a better imitation of Grandpa than Dad could do, "Thought I was done with this bullshit when your dad..." Gidion froze for a split second. Holy crap! He'd nearly finished the last two words of that, the part where Grandpa said dad had "stopped hunting." Gidion waved his hand in the air as if to blow the thought away. "Not sure what the rest of it was, but by that point I'd been dismissed. Figured it was better to get out of there while I could and not ask him to repeat whatever he'd said."

"Probably so." Dad stared at him with that expression that insisted Gidion was full of it and that anyone with even one lonely brain cell limping into an open grave would know it. "This have anything to do with you oversleeping yesterday?"

Gidion had to fight down a smile as Dad all but gift-wrapped his way out of this mess. God bless parents who think they know everything.

"Yeah, he was less than thrilled about that."

"Can't be doing that." He drew out the last word in that tone that said Gidion knew better. "You're his grandson. If he doesn't come down on you for breaking the rules, the other people working there are going to resent you and not respect your grandpa."

"I know." Lord, he had to get this off of him. "So, how was your date with my teacher?"

Dad rolled his eyes. "It wasn't a date. I was going with a bunch of people from work, and I didn't want to go alone."

Gidion could believe that, but this was the first time his dad hadn't turned to him for his "plus one." He didn't want to press it too much, because he was actually proud of him.

"You kiss her?"

Okay, maybe he'd press just a little.

The question stopped Dad in the middle of lifting his glass for a sip. He set the glass down and fixed a look on him that would have scared a confession out of a serial killer. "No." Then he turned away and the master detective stare crumbled. As he cleared his throat, he muttered, "She kissed me."

"All right, Dad!" Gidion drummed his fists on the bar. Then he punched his dad in the arm and dipped back into his Grandpa impression. "That's the Keep blood in ya', boy!"

"Oh dear God!" Dad laughed and cringed at the same time. "Don't ever do that again."

"That's what Grandpa said when he found out about my girlfriend kissing me the first time." Gidion stopped laughing as he came within a breath of mentioning that the kiss had been after saving Tamara from a vampire. That was twice he'd nearly blown it, and in less than ten minutes. He drank his cream soda to keep himself from saying anything stupid.

He assumed filtering his life as a hunter would get easier, the idea that practice made perfect. The reverse was proving true. The longer he did it, the harder it was not to say anything. He was hunting four nights a week. The hours it made up in his life were adding up. At first, he'd been able to confide in Grandpa, but that was a bust. He'd had Tamara, too, but these days, she was more likely not to answer his texts than respond. When she did text or email, it was usually while he had his phone off and was in class.

"Do me a favor," Dad said. "Don't let your teacher know I told you that."

"Ms. Aldgate's a pretty cool lady, though. Isn't she?"

Dad nodded. "Yeah, but even I have to admit that I probably

shouldn't have asked her to go with me like that. If you don't do well in her class, that could get awkward real fast."

"I got your back. Last test, I had the highest grade in the class. I'm even doing better than Andrea."

Dad covered his mouth, not that it did anything to hide the amusement on his face. "How is 'Batwoman' doing these days?" That was Dad's nickname for Andrea, who was dating Gidion's best friend. The nickname had stuck ever since Gidion had gone with her to the Zombie Walk back in October. She'd dressed up as a zombified Batwoman. The only reason Gidion went was to hunt two vampires. He'd learned the pair was going to take part in the walk to feed on some of the participants. Andrea didn't know all that, but when she found out he was going, she'd drafted him into taking pictures of her during the Walk. Seth normally would have done it, but he was stuck at work that night.

"She's doing fine. We're meeting tomorrow after school to study for a quiz on World War II."

"Well, don't stay out too late," Dad said after their hamburgers arrived. "I'm doing an evening-midnight double, so I'll probably be gone before you get home. I want a text when you get there."

Gidion was busy eying the best place to attack his burger as he answered. "I will."

He definitely wanted to get home early. He'd been dying to get a crack at his vampires' laptops, but the risk of Dad catching him with a strange laptop had forced him to wait. He'd found all sorts of useful intelligence digging through his previous kills' recovered cell phones. God only knew what he'd find in those laptops.

His brain kept going back to the way GQ Drac had tried to take his picture and then ran. That wasn't the way a vampire responded when confronted with a hunter, and he hoped the laptop might contain some answers.

CHAPTER NINE

During lunch, Gidion and his friends preferred to hang out in West Chester High's courtyard. They had a favorite place in one of the round benches where they'd sit, eat, and talk, but winter complicated things. Cold days only offered three choices to keep warm: the cafeteria, the gym, and the library.

With Monday's high only making it up to forty-two degrees, Gidion was more than in favor of abandoning the courtyard. The wind, which the tall bushes ringing the benches did nothing to block, threatened to freeze off one of his limbs or accelerate the chattering of his teeth until they bit off his tongue.

"It wasn't that bad," Seth said as they retreated into the library.

"So says the first person through the door." Andrea cleared her throat to make it clear she was not pleased. "Chivalry is truly dead."

Gidion considered pointing out to her that he'd held the door for them but thought better of it. He'd learned not to provide Andrea with a second target when Seth had already placed himself at the end of her firing range.

Seth was just pissed they hadn't gone to the gym. He was playing on the school's basketball team these days, and he enjoyed showing off his skills. Seth got outvoted by Andrea, because you handled women the same way droids did Wookies. Let the woman win.

"Half the school must be in here." Seth didn't seem to realize saying that was equivalent to slapping a "shoot me" sign on his back.

Gidion slipped past the domestic brewing between the lovebirds to hunt for a space to sit. Finding a place for all three of them had dropped to a secondary priority. Just ten minutes into lunch, they'd already waited too late to find a table. All of the books were shelved on the first floor. That left little room for tables and chairs, especially when this place had reached the "standing room only" stage.

He searched for a place to sit on the floor along the rows of books, but that turned out to be a waste of energy. One row in the 900s was completely blocked by a pair of seniors French kissing near the European history books.

Thankfully, no one was going for the same kind of irony when Gidion reached the biology books in the 500s. He ran into Seth instead.

"No luck?" Seth pointed in the direction Gidion had come from.

"If the bookshelves stood a little lower, people would be lying on top of them." Gidion looked past him. "Where's Andrea?"

"Checking the comfy chairs." Seth didn't need to point out the odds against one of those seats becoming available.

"You see the latest issue of *Green Lantern*?" They used to meet every Saturday at the comic book shop, but ever since their friend Pete had died, they'd rarely met there. Seth had even given up his pull box.

They never directly mentioned Pete these days, and the last time they'd met at Richmond Comix, Gidion had felt nothing but guilt. Seth didn't know what really happened to Pete, how he'd gotten involved with the local coven of vampires. The vampires had turned him into a servant addicted to small tastes of vampire blood. Gidion thought he could save Pete, but freeing his friend from the vampires didn't stop Pete from killing himself. The fear of the withdrawals and whatever other "demons" Pete had taken from the experience had driven him to turn a gun on himself. Any conversation about Pete made Gidion feel worse, because he and Seth could never have an honest conversation about what happened.

"*Green Lantern*? No, I had to give them up. Just can't spare the money these days." Seth checked over his shoulder before he added, "Be glad your girlfriend lives in another state."

"At least you get to make out with yours."

Seth didn't bother hiding his grin as he asked, "You two ever... you know, while doing the video chat thing?"

"Uh, no." He held up his hands as if to push the idea away. "And, nasty."

"Too scared to ask her to try it, huh?"

Gidion sighed. "Pretty much."

Seth didn't bother to spare Gidion's dignity and laughed loud enough to get a dirty look from a few people actually here to study.

"Yeah, laugh it up. Let's see how far you get this weekend, oh Great Slayer of Chivalry."

Seth stopped laughing, but he had this knowing smirk. "Oh, I'm not worried about my chances this weekend."

"More details than I want or need, dude."

Seth pulled out his phone. "Still have more than half of lunch left."

"I'm gonna check upstairs. You?"

Seth waved off the idea. "On a day like this? I'll leave you to that."

Just before Gidion could head for the stairs, Seth stopped him. "Gid, wait! I need a favor."

"What's up?"

Seth glanced over his shoulder again. "You know how you're always asking for me to help cover you with your dad?"

Gidion felt his body go rigid. Several times, since he'd started hunting vampires, he'd asked his friends to provide an alibi so he had an excuse to be out late hunting. Technically, none of them had ever had to lie to Dad for him, but they'd agreed to. What made him nervous was that Seth was bringing it up.

"Technically, I've only done that a few times, not that often." The protest sounded weak, even to himself. "What about it?"

"Would you mind doing the same for me? I gotta do something tonight. If anyone asks, and I mean anyone, I just need you to say we did something like go to a game night at One-Eyed Jacques."

"Sure, what's the game they're doing tonight?"

The question made Seth blink. "Um…" Gidion guessed he hadn't thought this through yet.

"Hang on." Gidion pulled out his cell phone and pulled up the

Facebook page for the game shop. "Um, they don't have anything going on tonight."

"Then we'll just say it was *Magic: The Gathering*." Seth looked over his shoulder again. "Okay?"

"All right, but we don't even know how to play that."

Seth made this exasperated growl. "It's not like Andrea does either, and she's not going to go on their website. Just say we were checking it out to see if it was something we'd want to do? That work?"

Only after Gidion said, "Sure thing," did he realize what he'd just agreed to do. Seth wasn't just getting him to lie to his parents. He was getting him to keep this from Andrea.

Before Gidion could ask what was going on, Seth said, "Thanks," and walked out from between the stacks. He considered going after him, but it wasn't like he could protest now. Besides, Gidion had never offered an explanation when he was the one asking.

He tried to put what he'd just agreed to out of his head. If he was lucky, Andrea would never ask him anyway. He pulled out his rabbit's foot as he climbed the stairs and ran his thumb through the soft fur as if to summon its luck, the same as rubbing a genie from a lamp.

Seth's doubts about finding a place to sit upstairs weren't unjustified. Most of the computers that students had access to were located on the second level. That, and the second floor wasn't very big, just a wide balcony that wrapped around the library like a horseshoe.

"Come on..." He kept rubbing the rabbit's foot, but he came up with nothing on the left side. On his way to the other side, he passed another student on the hunt, coming from the opposite direction. Not promising.

The upstairs desks without a computer were dark, wooden carrel desks, the kind that had those cubicle-type blinders. They offered some excellent privacy, but for anyone hunting for a seat, it forced you to be way too obvious you were searching. Just as he was about to give up, Gidion heard a zipper.

He honed in on the source, a guy who'd just packed his bookbag and slipped it on as he stood to leave. Gidion powerwalked the five steps to the space being vacated and dropped his bag on the desk the instant the guy was out of the way, claiming it with a thud.

Gidion kissed the rabbit's foot. "Thank you, Tamara." He'd have to tell her how the good luck charm had worked.

For now, he just needed to get some research done, and as much as he liked Seth and Andrea, he was glad to have them out of the way so he could get this done.

He plugged in some earphones into his phone, went straight to YouTube, and typed in his search: *how to hack into Windows*. He was on his fourth video, still hoping to find something that sounded like it might work, when a muffled voice next to his ear startled him.

"You forget the password to your computer?"

He dropped his phone onto the desk as he jumped in his chair and squeaked.

Andrea laughed. "I didn't think your voice could go that high."

Too late, he picked up his phone and turned off the screen as he pulled out his earphones. "You trying to give me a heart attack?"

"Not my fault." She leaned against the side of the carrel to stare down at him. "You just get so intense when you focus on something. I've been standing here for a minute waiting for you to notice."

Just perfect. He looked past her, but it was just the two of them. "Where's Seth?" As soon as the question was out of his mouth, he wished he hadn't asked. Not that he had to lie right now, but the idea of lying to Andrea without knowing the reason why made him feel like scum.

She looked nice today, despite having dressed for the weather. The red sweater she wore reminded him of the bat design she'd worn on the top of her Batwoman costume at the Zombie Walk this past October.

"No idea where Seth got to. I came up here looking for him." She tapped the dark display of his phone. "So you planning to hack into the school computers? Or does this have something to do with your usual clandestine activities?"

Seth never pressed Gidion to explain why he needed the alibis. He was just too laid back to do that, but Andrea's petite nose couldn't have been more counter to her nature. She'd once made a less than subtle inquiry as to whether his girlfriend knew what he did when he went out at night by himself. He happily shut the door on her with the truth. Tamara knew exactly what he did. Hunting vampires was how he'd met her, after all.

"I'm just helping my Dad with something," he said.

"By breaking into a computer?" She didn't bother hiding her skepticism.

"Yeah." He wanted to leave it at that, but Andrea gave him that look that made it clear she wasn't going to be satisfied with a morsel. "He's got an old computer he wants to get rid of, but he can't remember the password. Wants to see if there's anything he might want before he has it erased."

"Pity. Was hoping for something much more interesting than that."

"Sorry to disappoint."

"So," she said, drawing out the word as she looked around them in a way that suggested she was trying to see who, if anyone, might be listening to them, "how are you and Tamara these days?"

"Fine." He shrugged.

"Just fine?"

He shifted in his chair. Why did the question make him feel like someone had just poured lemon juice on an open wound?

"Yes, we're fine."

She still wasn't looking at him. Instead, she stared at the top of the desk where his phone was still resting. "Well, most girls at school don't realize you're off the market. Had a few asking about you the other day."

"Asking about me? Why?"

The look she leveled at him silently asked if he'd been dropped on his head too many times as an infant.

"What?" Sometimes, he didn't understand Andrea, or girls in general.

"They want to date you, stupid."

"Well, I have a girlfriend."

"Yes, in Arizona." She scowled at him. "As far as most of them are concerned, that means you're available. They see a cute guy—the nice kind who holds doors open for them—going to waste."

"Really? And who are these girls?"

She crossed her arms and had this victorious, catlike grin. "Is that interest I'm hearing?"

"No, it's just me being curious which girls I should avoid."

Seth walked up behind Andrea, and in an act of near instant karma, scared the bejeezus out of her. "Why is Gidion avoiding girls?" Seth asked.

Andrea shrieked and then swatted Seth on the arm. "Not nice."

Gidion didn't miss the unspoken question in the way Seth looked from him to Andrea. If she noticed how tense Seth was, she didn't say. He looked out of breath, as if he'd rushed over here.

"Your girlfriend is trying to hook me up."

The answer brought a slow smile to Seth's face. "Well, it's like I've been saying, man can't live on Skype sex alone."

Before Gidion could say anything. Andrea turned to look right at Seth. "I need to run to the bathroom before class. I'll see you later."

"Sure thing."

Andrea marched off. Gidion didn't miss the stiff way she moved. She normally moved around in a more carefree manner, like she was dancing in a slow music video.

"Did she ask anything about tonight?"

The question brought Gidion's attention back to Seth.

"What? No." Gidion realized Seth wasn't smiling anymore. Hell, he looked pissed. That's when it dawned on Gidion that Andrea had left without trying to sneak a goodbye kiss or calling Seth her "Teddy Bear." "What's going on with you two?"

"Nothing. It's fine." Seth walked off. "See you later."

Gidion tried to put the whole thing out of his mind and continued searching YouTube for a way to hack into the laptops he'd taken from Bonnie and GQ Drac. It wasn't until he headed to class that it occurred to him that he was meeting with Andrea after school today to study.

Just great.

CHAPTER TEN

Gidion spent most of World History class distracted by questions about Seth and Andrea, what secrets might be found on the vampires' laptops, and the most nagging question…which girls he'd held doors for at school. He paid for the distractions, too. When Ms. Aldgate asked him a question, he didn't even realize it until she walked up to his desk to glare down at him. His only saving grace was that once she repeated the question about the Normandy Invasion, he knew the answer.

He assumed he was off the hook right up until the bell. The instant Ms. Aldgate signaled they were allowed to go, everyone scrambled to stuff their notebooks into their backpacks. By this point in the school year, they all knew better than to try to leave until she told them to.

"Gidion." Ms. Aldgate stopped him just short of zipping shut his backpack. Something in the way she spoke reminded him of Dad. If she'd gone into police work instead of teaching, Ms. Aldgate would have scared more than one perp to the ground with just her voice. Everything about this woman, from the tight bun of her long black hair to the way everything on her desk was placed at a right angle, made it clear she believed precision was a virtue. "I need a word with you before you go."

"Ouch," Andrea whispered to him just before slipping on her backpack and walking out. "Good luck."

Yeah, luck. He had that in spades lately and most of it bad. Definitely was time to invest in a new good luck charm, because the rabbit's foot wasn't doing crap for him beyond finding primo seats in the library.

Gidion slipped on his backpack and walked up to Ms. Aldgate. She stood behind her desk, rearranging items on it. It wasn't until she'd repositioned her desk calendar for the third time and her eyes shifted to the last student to file out of the room that he realized she was just stalling to make sure no one would be there to listen to them. She confirmed his suspicion when she went to the classroom door and closed it.

The whole thing reminded him of this past September. He'd just started hunting, and one of his earliest kills had been a vampire attacking Ms. Aldgate down in Shockoe Bottom. That had turned into a mess after he discovered it wasn't a random attack. Learning why they'd wanted her dead had led to him to the local coven, which he then wiped out.

"Another late night hunting?" She fixed him with a hard stare that let him know she didn't approve. Given that his hunting had saved her life, he would have expected some slack, but she wasn't a teacher known for going easy on her students.

"No," he said. "Sorry, I was just a little distracted."

"If you and Andrea weren't the two best students I have in this class, I'd consider moving you two to different sides of the room. Just understand that if I see either of your grades start to slip, I will." Before he could ask what that had to do with anything, she continued as if her point should have been obvious. She sat on the front edge of her desk and crossed her arms. The gesture let him know to keep his trap shut. "That's not why I wanted to talk to you, though. I've been thinking on this a lot, and while I'm grateful for what you did to help me last year, you need to stop hunting."

Okay, this wasn't what he'd expected her to talk about.

"That's got nothing to do with me being distracted in class. I promise."

She held up a hand for him to stop. "This isn't about class. This is about your father."

Gidion's insides froze. He suddenly wished they could go back to the discussion about him being distracted in class. "Dad doesn't know about me hunting, and he doesn't need to."

"I agree, but he's a good man." She looked down, and there was something in the way she avoided looking at him that seemed more like a student than a teacher. "We went out with some friends this weekend."

She stopped there and looked up at him. Her lips were twisted with confusion, but he couldn't make out why.

"Gidion, I like your father, and I'd like to see him again."

In spite of himself, Gidion smiled. The idea of the two of them becoming a couple had actually been his idea, after all. The way she shifted and fought back a smile of her own was downright cute. Go, Dad!

"Are you asking for my permission to date my dad?"

He started to laugh, but something in her expression silenced him.

"No, I'm asking you to stop hunting, so I can eventually date him with a clean conscience. You need to understand that I haven't gone out with anyone since I was divorced years ago. Lies have a way of ruining even the best relationship." She pulled off her glasses and rubbed the bridge of her nose. "What happens if you get hurt or killed?"

"I'm not going to."

That jerked Ms. Aldgate to her feet and sent Gidion stumbling back. "You don't know that. You wore turtlenecks and shirts with tall collars for two weeks after what happened last year. I saw the bruises to your throat from where I'm assuming you'd been choked. Don't tell me you won't get hurt, because we both know you can't control that."

"Look, my hunting has nothing to do with you now."

That only made her glare at him even harder. "I'm having to lie to your father, and I won't do that. I respect and care about you both too much. What I'm asking you to do is be honest with him so I can. Either quit hunting or tell him what you're doing. If you don't, then I'll tell him."

"What! This is—"

"I'll give you until the end of the month."

Gidion glanced at the calendar posted on the wall behind Ms. Aldgate's desk.

"That's Friday."

"That's also more than fair."

She was out of her damn mind. She had to be.

Gidion didn't wait for her to say anything else. The bell rang to signal the start of last period. He flung open the door to her room just in time to see a few students ducking into other classrooms as teachers closed their doors. Others vanished around the corner of the hallway.

As soon as he made it out into the breezeway, he realized he didn't have a hall pass for being late. He refused to go back to Ms. Aldgate to get one. His next class was P.E. Odds favored he'd be able to change clothes and get in the line for attendance before the coach marked him late.

He made it to the locker room without running into any teachers or principals. His hands shook as he changed into his gym clothes. Every option trapped him. If he told his dad what he was doing, there was no chance he'd ever get to hunt again. He could lie, tell Ms. Aldgate he'd stopped, but she'd figure it out. The first injury his clothes couldn't hide and she'd know. The option to quit hunting wasn't on the table. He refused to stop. All he had to do was think about Mom's wedding portrait, her red hair and her smile. He saw her every day. He couldn't quit and then look at that picture ever again without believing he'd betrayed her.

CHAPTER ELEVEN

The coffee mug warmed Gidion's hands almost enough to burn. When he set the café mocha on the wood tabletop, the cool air inside the café numbed his palms and fingertips. The Urban Farmhouse was more crowded than usual. By the time he and Andrea made it there, the cushioned seats and more popular corner tables were all taken. They had to settle for a table near the sliding doors that led to the patio, which even shut still made it the coldest part of the café.

Andrea tapped her pen on the side of his mug, producing a series of low pings. "For a guy drinking something with four shots of espresso in it, you sure don't seem that alert."

"No, sorry." If he hadn't already committed to give Andrea a ride home from school today, he'd probably have skipped their study session. Neither of them really needed it. Gidion doubted it would improve his chances on tomorrow's quiz anyway. If he couldn't focus now, he didn't see how he was going to tomorrow, not in the same room with Ms. Aldgate.

"This have anything to do with what Ms. Aldgate wanted?" The way Andrea said that made it seem like she already knew the answer. Even though he'd finally warmed up to Seth's girlfriend, Gidion sometimes found Andrea's nosy nature a bit much. The more a person held back from her, the more she turned all Richard Castle. Usually, he fed her a half-truth to shut her down, but at the moment, he had nothing.

"Don't worry about it," he said. She answered with a silent stare of concern, not her usual response. "Really. It's nothing." He pointed to her laptop, where she stored her notes. "Let's just get to it."

They tossed out random questions for the next hour. Not

surprisingly, she answered almost everything right. If his survival had depended on his answers, he would have resembled Hiroshima.

He even blanked on the name for the Enigma machine which the Germans used to encrypt and decrypt their messages during World War II, and he'd figured out a week ago how to use the Riddler's real name, Edward Nigma, to help him remember that one.

"I'm screwed. Wonder which of us she'll move?"

"You, of course. My grade isn't going to suffer." The confidence in her voice sounded prophetic, right up until she laughed. "Relax. You'll do fine."

He was so focused on wondering how he was going to pass the quiz that it wasn't until later that evening, after he'd dropped Andrea at her house, that he realized he hadn't told her about Ms. Aldgate's threat to separate them in class if their grades went down. If she overheard that, then he wondered how much of the rest she'd heard.

CHAPTER TWELVE

With Dad working his evening-midnight double, Gidion had the house to himself. As soon as he got in the door, he threw a frozen pizza in the oven, set the timer and ran upstairs.

Page strolled up the stairs and followed him into his room. She hopped onto his bed, doing a slow spin until she'd found just the right way to position herself. Gidion scratched her beneath her jaw before he reached under his bed to pull out a long, flat plastic tub. He kept most of the belongings he took from his kills in here, including the stash of goodies he'd taken from GQ Drac and Bonnie's luggage, van, and pockets.

He'd waited all day to get his hands on GQ Drac and Bonnie's laptops. First up was GQ's. Judging from the scratches to the black cover, that vamp put all his money into his wardrobe. The computer played that annoying default Windows greeting music as it displayed a blue login screen. This computer was still working with an older version of Windows.

The login screen showed the rather plain user name of "George."

"Not exactly the creative type." With that in mind, Gidion decided to guess the password. He tried the obvious choice first and typed "password." After that, he tried typing it with the "p" capitalized, and then the entire word in all caps. Apparently, George was a little more creative than that, after all. From there, Gidion went for variations on George Hammond's name. He only played that game for a few minutes before he got fed up with it. Fortunately, he'd prepared for this.

Gidion had spent the past two days searching online for tricks to get past the login on Windows. Not surprisingly, Google led him to the solution once he typed in a search for "forgot password to Windows Vista."

He'd considered using a few methods on YouTube, but he decided he wasn't sure how much he trusted some of the methods there. The answer turned out to be on a PC support website, and the hardest part of the process was finding a Windows Vista installation disc in Dad's office. Even though Dad wasn't using Vista anymore, he kept almost everything related to computers. He really did even have an old hard drive in the basement that he'd refused to trash on the idea he'd eventually get back into it to unload some files. Dad harbored a few hoarder tendencies.

From there, he just loaded the installation disc, went for the System Recovery Options, opened the Command Prompt and typed in the appropriate commands.

Voilà!

The login screen faded to black and then to one of those generic scenic landscapes in the desert that probably came with the computer, not that he could see much of it through the horde of icons.

"Congratulations, Gidion Keep," he said to himself. "You've probably just violated a few federal statutes, but you are now officially the master hacker!"

Page rolled her eyes without moving her head to look at him. A low groan followed. She wouldn't be impressed by anything until he'd given her a bite of pizza, which wasn't happening.

His master hacking skills didn't get much deeper into GQ Drac's computer. Most of the icons on the desktop only opened up movies saved as digital files. Going by that, GQ was a big fan of westerns and porn—girl-on-girl porn, to be exact. Not that Gidion watched any of them. Well, not for very long. Maybe only a half hour's worth.

To Gidion's surprise, GQ Drac kept his checking account on his computer, and the balance was a lot more impressive than the laptop. He supposed the expenses of a traveling vampire were limited. They didn't need food in the traditional sense. Without a house to worry about, it was all about cars, hotels, and the occasional laundromat.

Other than that, it wasn't illuminating. He might have used it to backtrack the places GQ Drac had visited before Richmond, but multiple entries for Sheetz and FasMart didn't reveal much.

Gidion had four different web browsers loaded on his laptop, so he'd worried about how many of them he'd need to search through on GQ's laptop. Luckily, ol' uncreative George used only one web browser on his computer. Gidion double-clicked on the blue "e" which went straight to AOL.com.

"Let's see who you've been trading emails with, bub." Gidion clicked on the icon which brought up the login screen. He'd expected GQ to maintain his uncreative streak and have the email address and password to auto-fill, but no such luck. He clicked on the field to see if a list of email addresses might show up in a drop list, but that didn't work either. Gidion even ran through the alphabet, hoping that typing the first letter might bring up the email address.

Gidion tried the "forgot password?" link, but without knowing the email address, it was about as helpful as Grandpa when it came to any form of technology created after the sixties.

Giving up on the email for now, Gidion went to the bookmarks. The list ran so long, the drop list couldn't fit all of the links on the screen. Clicking on a few made it clear all too quickly, they were just more of the same: movie sites and porn.

The clock was close to midnight by the time Gidion gave up on GQ Drac's laptop and went for Bonnie's. She clearly wore the creative pants in the relationship. Her laptop had come with a lime green cover, but she'd taken a permanent marker to it. The black design resembled a Celtic knot that covered all of the improvised canvas.

Cracking into her computer proved just as easy, but where GQ's desktop was chaotic repetition, Bonnie's was simple and organized. The only nudity to be found on her laptop belonged to the pictures of Greco-Roman murals and tapestries. She had several art programs, and it didn't take long to realize she did a lot of graphic artwork. The longer he went through the folders of artwork and photography, the tighter the knot in his stomach grew. This felt too human. He wondered if perhaps she was newly-turned, that all this was from her mortal life. The absence of any daytime photography made it clear that wasn't the explanation. He almost shut it down, not wanting to think on the idea that this beautiful creativity came from a beast.

He noticed a black and red icon on the desktop that resembled a set of fangs. Clicking on it opened a folder filled with videos. After all the art, he hesitated to play the videos, but curiosity won. The video opened in the media player with an image of a woman tied spread-eagle to a bed. She struggled against the ropes. A gag in her mouth turned her screams into muffled protests. The quality of the video didn't look that impressive, probably taken with a smart phone or maybe this laptop's camera.

"Great." Gidion shook his head. "More porn."

Only this didn't play out like he expected, because the woman who stepped in front of the camera was Bonnie, fangs and all.

"All ready, baby?" She leaned in towards the camera, filling the screen as she blew a kiss. "Next one will be yours."

What followed involved a knife and the slow torture and slaughter of the woman on the bed. Bonnie fed off the woman, but that was only part of the game. She taunted the woman on the bed with her words, teasing her with false hope that she'd let her go and then the lie that she'd end it quickly.

By the time Bonnie blew a parting kiss to the camera from her blood-covered lips, almost an hour had passed. Gidion's hands shook. He knew he should be disgusted and running for the bathroom to vomit, but Bonnie's sadistic game was infused with the same artistry she gave everything else. He was turned on by it more than the porn he'd found on the other laptop.

Looking through her photography and artwork had made him feel like he'd violated her, but Bonnie's video collection repaid the insult many times over.

That video couldn't be the last thing he did tonight. God only knew what dreams he'd have if he went to bed right after that. He forced himself to push forward, going for the web browsers, praying that what he found there wouldn't be as difficult to watch.

She had two web browsers loaded on her laptop, so he opted for the one that wasn't Internet Explorer. The first thing that came up was Google, and this looked promising. Up in the right corner was a small avatar with a picture of Bonnie. A link held out the hope for Gmail, so he clicked it.

The browser didn't go to a login screen. Bonnie's email account opened, no password required. "Thank you, Bonnie."

Her email offered little to interest him, mostly humorous forwards from friends, if a monster could truly have any.

One was sent from DragonSwordVA@gmail.com just a few days before Gidion killed her. The message mentioned something about an opportunity for Bonnie's "special talents" in Richmond. The email didn't specify the opportunity or which of her special talents was being referred to. After watching Bonnie's video, Gidion doubted he wanted to know, but this meant Bonnie and GQ Drac weren't just passing through Richmond when he ambushed them.

A forward from Saturday night, sent shortly before the fight in the van, caught his eye next. The email address was GHammond1949@ aol.com. Not only had he gotten into Bonnie's email, but now he had a username to work with for GQ. He'd take another crack at that after he finished with Bonnie's laptop.

The message from GQ was just two words, "Told you."

The forward came from an email GQ had received from a Gmail account with the username VampGen_EastCoast. The message was only slightly less terse than GQ's:

She needs a better picture than that shit if you expect to get paid.

Picture...GQ Drac had gone for the camera on his iPhone when they met in front of the Blue Goat. He'd lost the phone when that car hit him, but sure enough, there was an image attached. When Gidion opened it, he felt his body shiver with fear and relief.

The blue Christmas lights of the Blue Goat glowed in the background. The original email sent to this VampGen guy contained the explanation. His phone automatically uploaded any pictures taken to an iCloud account. GQ Drac came damn close to outing him, and this VampGen guy must have been willing to pay for the picture. Fortunately for Gidion and unfortunately for GQ, the picture looked fuzzy and grainy. Anyone seeing this wouldn't be able to identify his race or age.

Gidion went back to the main screen for Bonnie's Gmail account and did a search by this VampGen's email address. A long list of emails appeared, most with the same subject, "Confirmation of Tithe Received."

He'd realized these vampires were organized, but not this much. The second most common email subject was simply titled "Weekly Travel Log" and contained a list of cities. Each city included a sub-list of email addresses. After going through a few of the weekly travel logs, Gidion realized the email addresses listed identified which vampire was in which city. Sure enough, the most recent one placed Bonnie and GQ Drac in Richmond. Each city also included a number in parentheses, the number of vampires there. Some of the numbers showed up in red. Gidion assumed the red numbers meant the location had exceeded its allowance of nomadic vampires for the week. He took some pride in seeing Richmond's number staying black. He wondered how high it had to go to make it red, but the biggest number he'd seen listed since October was seven.

At the bottom of each weekly travel log was a list of email addresses not assigned to a city. Instead, the list identified nomadic vampires who had "Failed to Check In." Gidion recognized two of the email addresses, the pair of vampires he'd killed at the Zombie Walk in October. The list had gotten longer with each week. No wonder the vampires had realized a hunter was going after them, especially when so many of the missing had their last check-in while visiting Richmond.

He went back to Bonnie's inbox and scrolled down until he came to an email from mid-December. The subject made it impossible to miss, "RICCVN." The Richmond Coven had used that same abbreviation in text messages to several nomadic vampires back in

September. VampGen had sent it to himself and included everyone else using BCC, so there was no way to know exactly how many vampires received this. If the travel logs offered an indication, then possibly several hundred.

What he found in that email wasn't about the Richmond Coven, though. It was about him.

His handiwork hadn't gone unnoticed, and there was nothing vague in how they planned to deal with him.

CHAPTER THIRTEEN

The next day didn't improve matters. Gidion slept just three hours before he went to school. He'd been lucky to get that much.

The gears wouldn't stop turning in his head.

He took his quiz on World War II, but the only thought his brain could pull up was the email about him. After reading it, he'd searched Bonnie's virtual mailbox for any other details that might help him prepare. He even managed to hack into GQ Drac's email since he'd found a username to work with, but the only thing there were the same messages Bonnie received.

After school ended, Gidion went straight to the funeral home. By this time in the day, Grandpa was finishing up with the funeral services and preparing for the evening's visitations.

Gidion went in the back way, hoping to find Grandpa in his office, but no such luck. He was up front handing out assignments for the evening's visitations. Gidion knew better than to interrupt. He waited in the hallway. The dim light from the mounted lamps designed to look like candles cast the white walls and green carpet into darker hues. He didn't know Grandpa realized he was there, until he'd dismissed everyone. The old man hobbled down the hallway and past him with only a glance.

"What are you doing here?" He didn't wait for Gidion as he continued towards the back office.

"Need to talk." Gidion glanced over his shoulder to make sure they were out of ear shot from the rest of the employees.

"Maybe I'm not in the mood."

"It starts with me apologizing, if that helps."

Grandpa stopped outside his office, blocking the door with his frail body. Gidion was almost as tall as him these days, but moments like this made him feel a whole foot shorter than Grandpa.

"Your apology isn't worth shit. I know a beggar when I see one, and if you owned a hat, it'd be in your hand. What is it?"

Gidion avoided Grandpa's face. Instead, he stared at the age spots on the back of Grandpa's hand, gripped around his cane. He'd written and rewritten in his head what to say, but his reserves for eloquence came up empty.

"They've hired someone to kill me."

Grandpa grabbed him by the collar of his jacket and dragged him into the office before he slammed the door shut.

A dozen different curses, half of them in languages Gidion didn't recognize, spit out of the former sailor's lips.

"I fucking told you to lay low." He slammed his cane against the side of the desk as he walked around it to sit. "When you wiped out that coven, the thing to do was shut down for a few months. You might as well have bought a damn billboard on I-95 that says, 'Hunter here: come and get me, assholes.' How could you be so goddamned stupid?"

Gidion didn't answer.

"You seen this hit man yet?" Grandpa asked. "How do you even know they have one after you? Not that it's any fucking surprise."

Gidion explained about the laptops. He started with how he'd hacked into them but skipped all that when he realized he might as well speak Klingon. All Grandpa needed to know was what was in the email.

"Whoever sent the email organizes the nomadic vampires, like some kind of club complete with monthly dues. They know a hunter wiped out the local coven and that I've been taking out any nomad I find in Richmond. They track their members, so the body count they've figured is pretty close."

Gidion jumped when Grandpa slammed his cane on the desktop. "Get to the damn hit man already."

He resisted the urge to pace, even though it was killing him to stand still. "It's actually a woman, and that's all I know about her other than she specializes in killing vampire hunters. Not sure where she's coming from because it sounded like she was going to take a while to get here." For a brief moment, he'd hoped the message Bonnie had received about her "special talents" might suggest she'd been the assassin, and that he'd gotten lucky by ambushing her first. No such luck, though. The timeline didn't work out. Bonnie didn't get that email until a few days ago, but the email from December made it clear they'd already contacted and hired the assassin.

"They're offering a reward for anyone who can get my picture or figure out my name or where I live."

"How much?" Grandpa asked.

"Five thousand bucks with an extra 'five k' if it actually helps get me killed."

Grandpa laughed. His smile doubled the wrinkles on his face. He whooped and drummed his hands on the desk. The sudden turn in his mood was almost as unnerving as the threat of this faceless assassin.

"They're offering ten thousand dollars just for the tip." Grandpa leaned over the desk to point at Gidion. "Can you imagine what they're paying this bitch? I doubt I pay you that much in a year to drive my hearse."

Gidion just stared as Grandpa worked through his laughing fit.

"Don't you get it, boy?" He shrugged those bony shoulders of his that insisted this should be obvious. "You're worth more dead than alive."

Then his laughter cut off and the smile vanished into that scowl he'd worn for weeks now.

"You must have these fuckers pissing in their coffins. I'd be damn proud of you if that price tag didn't measure how stupid you've been."

"Are you done?" Gidion felt his fingernails digging into the palms of his fists. "Because I'd really like to not get killed, and I have no idea what they're sending my way. I don't even know if this woman is a vampire or a human."

Grandpa leaned back, the chair squeaking as he shifted. "Too late to just lay low, boy. You kicked the hornets' nest."

"So what do I do?"

Grandpa forced his way back onto his feet. "We," and he emphasized that word, "are going to throw money at the problem." He pulled his worn, leather wallet out of his suit jacket's breast pocket and placed a small stack of twenties on the desk.

Gidion picked up the cash and counted it. "I don't imagine we're going to pay this hit woman with a hundred and sixty dollars to walk away."

"No, you're going to take your car and get it cleaned. Make 'em clean the interior three times over. Tip 'em good, too."

Grandpa hobbled to the coat rack in the corner of his office. Putting on his trenchcoat and fedora made him look like an FBI agent from some sixties spy film. "After you get done with the car, go home. Put every piece of clothing that's gotten vampire blood on it into a trash bag, find a dumpster somewhere and toss it.

"You get done with that, get your ass home and shower and scrub until you smell like a rose garden."

"Great, but what are you getting ready to do?"

"Heading home. Gotta do some spring cleaning of my own, make some calls. I don't plan on my only grandson ending up in some ditch." He didn't wait for Gidion to ask anything else. He went straight for the front of the funeral home and flagged down one of his assistant directors, probably letting him know he was leaving early.

Grandpa always hinted that there were other hunters out there. Until now, he'd never given the impression he had any connections with them. Anytime Gidion suggested the idea of sharing the intelligence they'd gathered, Grandpa blew it off.

"I must be seriously screwed if he's making phone calls."

He shoved the money into his back pocket. With all the vampires he'd killed in the past few months, he doubted there was enough bleach on the planet to sterilize his car.

CHAPTER FOURTEEN

Grandpa's plan kept things quiet for a little more than a week and came with some unexpected benefits. Dad's birthday dinner at the Blue Goat turned out pleasant now that Grandpa wasn't pissed (as much) at Gidion. Grandpa even tamed his usual gripes about the food and the wait for a table.

While they were waiting to sit, they noticed one of the front windows was covered with a black curtain on the inside and outside. Dad remarked on it, too, but it was Gidion who asked the hostess what the deal was. Hanging around Andrea had taught him the benefits of giving voice to his nosiness.

"Someone spray-painted some graffiti on the window this morning." Gidion shared the news with Dad and Grandpa after they sat down.

Grandpa grunted, though it was hard to tell if it went with his response of "Damn hoodlums," or if the grunt belonged to his unspoken opinion about the menu.

"What did they paint on it?" Dad asked.

"She didn't know, but I could always go sneak a peek."

One look from Dad over the top of his menu made it clear Gidion would be risking his life if he tried it.

Dad ordered one of his favorite dishes. Pork cheeks sounded pretty nasty to Gidion, but he had to admit they were damn good. The flavor of the round balls of meat reminded him of beef from a stew. Grandpa refused to try it and got a steak.

"And how would you like that cooked?" the server asked.

Grandpa's hands shook as he handed over the menu, a sign he was getting twitchy for his pipe. Gidion wondered how far into dinner Grandpa would make it before going outside for a smoke. "Make it medium rare," Grandpa said.

Gidion had to resist pointing out that "medium rare" seemed an odd order for a vampire hunter. Dad being here meant he had to keep his trap shut.

The only time he or Grandpa said anything vampire-hunter related came when Dad went to the bathroom while they were waiting for the bill, and that was only because Grandpa brought it up.

"Everything been quiet?" There was no mistaking what he was asking about.

"Not a peep."

Grandpa answered with a long, low rumble from his throat. "Keeping your ass at home?"

Gidion nodded, fighting the urge for an eye roll. "Sitting still like this is driving me nuts. How will we even know when it's safe to stop hiding?"

"Considering you've been stirring it up for months now? You might as well find a new hobby to keep you busy for the rest of the year."

"Great," Gidion said, not sparing on the sarcasm. Andrea had talked about making their World History study sessions a daily thing. He was already too late to join the track team. He hadn't expected to be free for anything, certainly not for the rest of the year.

The server delivered the bill right then, while Dad was still in the bathroom. As the server moved onto another table, Grandpa said, "Don't give 'em anything to find, and we might not need to worry. Not damn likely, though. Keep your eyes open." He winced at the paper in front of him. "Why the hell do they have to make the print so damn small on these things?" He slid it over to Gidion and sipped his beer. "You do the math, but don't give that freak more than fifteen percent. Was slow as molasses."

Gidion gave the server twenty percent. He'd been fine. Grandpa was just a grump when it came to eating out and didn't care for guys who had ear piercings.

The rest of the evening went well. They waited until they got home to give Dad his gifts, though. Grandpa gave Dad his usual gift: cash.

Gidion was vibrating with excitement to get to the gifts, because he knew there was no way Dad would guess what he'd gotten him this year. One of the things they'd done together shortly after Mom died was watch this anime TV series called *Gatchaman*, which was about a group of science ninja superheroes. All of the team members wore these wristband communicators with a gold pentagon held in place with a light blue strap. The communicators also transformed them into their costumes.

"Where did you find this?" Dad put it on his left wrist as soon as he had it out of the box. He even struck the appropriate gesture, placing his forearm in front of his face, the same way Ken the Eagle and the rest of the team always did when they changed into uniform.

"Found it online." Gidion bounced in his chair, earning an irritated look from Page, who had resigned herself to being on the floor while Grandpa had her chair. "Was on a craft website."

The whole thing had a very "good luck charm" vibe to it. Gidion would have gotten himself one, too, but the cost of the overnight shipping to get it here in time had turned out to be way more expensive than he'd expected. He'd have to wait to get his own, no matter how badly he needed the extra luck these days.

• • •

Except for Dad's birthday, the lack of hunting all but trapped Gidion at home in the evening. He felt so stir crazy that he agreed to Andrea's suggestion that they make their after-school study sessions a daily thing.

The first Tuesday in February, they spent several hours at the Urban Farmhouse. The first hour, they worked on their homework, part of which involved random questions on the early years of the Cold War. As much as Gidion enjoyed the World War II section of their World History class, he loved the Cold War era stuff. The whole thing sounded like some kind of epic fantasy novel setting with the two big superpowers struggling for power.

"You ever see the show *The Game*?" Andrea asked.

Gidion shook his head.

"Really awesome Cold War spy series." She waved her arms all around in her enthusiasm, fueled by the café mocha she'd chugged after getting here. "I saw it on BBC America. You'd probably love it."

"Okay, I'll check that out." The conversation having turned to TV shows derailed the rest of their study time, which was fine with Gidion. They spent the next two hours doing nothing but chatting and sucking down caffeine. Gidion didn't realize how late it had gotten until Andrea's phone chimed.

She took one look at the text on her phone and then out the window at the now dark sky. "Oh, crap!"

"What's wrong?"

"I didn't realize what time it was. I'm missing Seth's game!" She furiously typed a text with her thumbs. "It's my mom. She was going to drive me to the game."

The game explained her outfit. She'd dressed in their school's colors, orange and blue. The colors worked fine for school uniforms, but they weren't Andrea's typical fashion statement, even as eclectic as she got. Today, she'd worn a tight, bright orange turtleneck sweater under a blue, denim jacket.

"I can take you," Gidion said as he packed his laptop. "Not like I've got anything else to do tonight." Not with his vampire hunting activities shut down.

"You don't mind?"

"Nah. Besides, I haven't gone to one of Seth's games in a while." He'd forced himself to some of the first few games of the basketball season, and while he didn't mind cheering on Seth, basketball just wasn't his thing.

Andrea sent her mom a text that she was all set with a ride. They made it back to campus in time for the start of the second quarter. The turnout for the game only filled half of the stands. They took some seats about halfway up the stands behind the Cavaliers' bench. The opposing team, the Monacan Chiefs, had gotten an early lead, eighteen to fifteen.

Most of the people going to the games came for specific players, at least that's how it seemed to Gidion. Anytime one of the players made a good shot, their private cheering section did their thing to cheer the loudest.

Halfway into the second quarter, Seth stole the ball from one of the Monacan players. Even Gidion had to admit it was a sweet move. Half the crowd got to their feet and shouted as Seth drove the ball down the court. Two Monacan players chased after him, unable to catch up. He reached the goal, going up for a layup that bounced off the backboard and dropped into the hoop, tying the game at thirty points.

One blonde girl who'd snagged a spot right behind the Cavaliers' bench shouted Seth's name.

"Yeah!" Andrea shouted loud enough to hurt Gidion's ears. "That's *my* boyfriend!"

"Little louder, Andrea." He made a show of rubbing his ear. "I think there might be someone in Siberia who didn't hear you."

"Good." Andrea glared down towards the bench. The opposing team had called a timeout, bringing Seth and the rest of the team back to the bench, huddled around the coach.

The game went back and forth, but in the last minutes, Monacan pulled ahead for the win.

Andrea all but dragged Gidion down the stands to make sure they had a good spot just outside the locker room door. The players took a while to come out. A group chant erupted from the locker room, signaling that the coach had finished whatever post-game pep talk he'd given them. Each player to emerge unleashed a stench of locker room-cultivated body odor. Gidion suspected there were less offensive pepper sprays and wished Seth would hurry up.

"Andrea, right?"

The question came from the blonde he'd seen cheering from behind the Cavaliers' bench. The girl's hair went down to her waist, and she was taller than Gidion, almost as tall as Seth. That placed her breasts, as big and round as softballs, just below his eye-level.

Her breasts were squeezed in tightly by a low-cut black top. He tried not to stare, but the way she flaunted them could poke an eye out.

"That's right, Seth's girlfriend." Andrea smiled back at the blonde, but Gidion didn't miss the way she did it. That was the kind of smile that accompanied a knife to the throat. "Gidion, this is Laura Heifer. She works with Seth at the movie theater."

Laura held out a hand to Gidion. "Actually, that's Hefner."

"Oh, sorry," Andrea said, her words clipped. "I would have sworn that's what Seth called you."

Gidion shook Laura's offered hand, even though he really wanted to withdraw to a safer distance. Whatever Laura had done to piss off Andrea, he didn't care to catch any stray bullets. He realized Seth had mentioned this girl to him, too, the last time they'd been at the comic book store without Andrea around. Seth had described her, saying she looked like a teenage Six from *Battlestar Galactica*. The description wasn't far off.

"Hey! You made it!" Seth emerged from the locker room dressed in Cavalier blue sweat pants. He wore the matching hoodie with the front unzipped to show his orange jersey underneath.

Andrea grabbed Seth in a tight hug that placed her between Seth and Laura.

"Hey, Teddy Bear."

Seth's lips came together in a tight line as Andrea called him by the pet name. "Uh, you remember Laura, right?"

"Oh, you bet."

If the silence that followed had a first name, it would be "Awkward."

"Why don't we go to Sweet Frog?" Andrea pointed from Laura to Gidion. "We could make it a double date, let the two of you get to know each other better."

Gidion looked up at Laura. Seriously, he was trying really hard to look up and not straight ahead. He didn't know what the hell to say to the idea, which had "horrifying" written all over it. Not that this girl wasn't tempting, but he already had a girlfriend. Besides, if he tried to make out with her, he'd look like a small lizard trying to hump a T-Rex.

"Sorry, I need to head home." Laura's bright red lips smiled at them. "Pleasure meeting you two. See you at work, 'Teddy Bear.'"

After Laura walked away, Andrea muttered, "What a slut." Whether Seth's busty co-worker had made it out of earshot was questionable, at best.

The "let the woman win" philosophy resulted in the three of them going to Sweet Frog. Gidion nearly passed on joining them, but the temptation of frozen yogurt topped with brownies and other forms of chocolate was too much for him to resist.

Andrea rested her head on Seth's shoulder in a manner best described as clingy as they hung out inside the frozen yogurt shop. The place was decorated in lime green and pink, the kind of color combo that could make a guy nauseous.

Gidion let the "happy couple" do most of the talking, which meant not much was said at all. About the only moment Andrea wasn't latched onto Seth was when she got up to run to the bathroom.

"Okay, dude." Gidion glanced up at Seth, who was poking at the melted remnants in his styrofoam cup. "I gotta know…"

"There's nothing going on." Seth put the cup down and crossed his arms. His entire face screwed up tight as he saw the skepticism Gidion found himself unable to hide. "Seriously. I just work with her. That's all."

"So Laura isn't the reason we were *playing,*" he said that last word with a show of air quotes, "*Magic: The Gathering* at One-Eyed Jacques the other night?"

"You really want to know? Then what the hell is it you do when you go out the nights we're *at the movies?*" He countered with his own air quotes for that last part. He didn't bother waiting for Gidion to answer, because they both knew Gidion wouldn't. "Bad enough I'm getting this crap from Andrea. I sure as hell don't need it from you. It's not my fault that girl is all in my business. There's nothing going on."

"Sorry." Gidion held up his hands in surrender. "It just looks bad."

"Kind of like you taking my girlfriend out to dance? All the *studying* you're doing together?"

Seth's rant sent Gidion's eyes hiding in his near-empty cup of frozen yogurt. He didn't realize Seth knew about him and Andrea going dancing after the Zombie Walk this past October. It wasn't like they did anything. They never even so much as brushed against each other the whole time they'd been on the dance floor, and almost everyone from the Zombie Walk had gone to it. He hadn't held her hand, kissed her, or tried anything.

And...

And he knew damn well why he wasn't trying to voice his defense. Shit.

"Jesus, Gid, I think you're seeing her more than I am these days."

"There's nothing like that going on. I promise."

Andrea returned a few beats after that, once again hugging up against Seth. The sight made Gidion want to punch him. Judging by the way she looked questioningly between the two of them, she hadn't heard any of what Seth had said. Thank God.

"You ready to go?" Seth asked her. "I need to get home and finish some homework."

"Sure."

The goodbyes were as brief as a drop of spilled blood. Gidion stayed a little longer watching what was left in his cup melt into a brown puddle. He'd never wished more for a vampire's head to chop off. Hunting bloodsuckers seemed safer than dealing with his friends these days.

CHAPTER FIFTEEN

Gidion spent the next few days and nights in severe isolation. At school, he avoided Andrea and Seth by going off campus every day for lunch and bailing on Andrea for their after-school study sessions. He even limited his contact with Andrea before and after their World History class. At home, he holed up in his room with Page, not that she was much help. Those big, brown dog eyes stared at him as if she knew what an ass he'd made of himself.

By Thursday night, Gidion was hiding in his room from Dad, who was on his last night off for the week. He pulled out his headphones, plugged them into his phone, and played an album by Two Steps From Hell. Seemed appropriate at the moment.

He'd made it through most of the album as he read Lamar Giles' novel *Fake ID* when his phone vibrated. He debated on seeing what the notification would be, worried/hoping it would be Andrea. Maybe it would be his girlfriend. He needed to talk to Tamara, to see her…badly. He'd considered texting her about how life had gone to hell, but the guilt from Seth's accusations had scared him that Tamara might hit him with the same charges. He'd never told her about going dancing with Andrea after the Zombie Walk, and in hindsight, he knew why he hadn't.

It just looked bad.

After a moment's debate, he sat up to look at the notification, but it wasn't a text from Andrea or Tamara. He had an email, or rather, the vampire Bonnie had an email.

After he'd hacked into Bonnie and GQ Drac's email accounts, he'd added them to the email app on his phone to track any messages they received. The subject header, "In case you missed it," looked like spam at first, but the sender used a Gmail account with the username Hunter_of_Hunters.

The email contained no text, only an embedded image of the front window of the Blue Goat in Westhampton. This was the window that had been covered when he and Grandpa had taken Dad to dinner. The vandal had spray-painted a single word on the glass: COWARD. The "O" was done larger than all the other letters and was a smiley face with fangs.

By the time he logged in to Bonnie's email again on Friday night, right after Dad left for work, Hunter_of_Hunters had sent a half dozen more emails with the same subject heading and more pictures. He'd settled into his desk, deciding to pull out Bonnie's laptop and see if he could find anything else useful, anything he might have missed the first time.

One of the new emails included the front of what was once Old World, the club the Richmond Coven had used to meet with their feeders, human servants who were rewarded with a taste of the vampire blood. Another picture was the mailbox in front of the burned house the Richmond Coven's elder had owned. Then there was the garage door to the safehouse where he'd saved his girlfriend. Every location was relevant to Gidion and each one was vandalized with a red smiley face with fangs. Most were done with red paint, but the smiley face on the mailbox in front of the burned house was drawn with a red permanent marker.

The last image made it clear why the sender knew Bonnie wasn't the person receiving these emails. The picture showed another red smiley face painted on the front of an all-too-familiar VW van, which was parked in what looked like a tow lot.

"Just perfect."

At least he knew better than to use Bonnie or GQ's emails, pretending to be them.

As he went through the pictures, another email arrived from Hunter_of_Hunters.

This time, the subject line changed to "Found you."

Unlike the other pictures, this one didn't look familiar. The smiley face with fangs was painted on some kind of beige, vertical slats. A fence, maybe?

There was something about the spray painted smiley face that looked different, too. He was just about to go back to one of the previous emails to compare when a small, white box popped up in the bottom, right corner of the screen. It was an instant message from Hunter_of_Hunters.

'*I see you, hunter.*'

Gidion slammed the laptop shut. He jumped out of his chair and turned off all the lights in his room.

Even before he reached the window to peek outside, he realized he was panicking for no good reason. Page, still lounging on his bed, lifted her head and looked at him as if to ask what his problem was. The last time a vampire had gotten near his house, parked across the street, she'd barked like the Devil had arrived to steal his soul.

He didn't see any unusual cars outside. Gidion would know. He kept track of them. That was one of Grandpa's earliest bits of advice: know your territory.

Then he thought about the webcam on the laptop. Bonnie's had one. He'd confirmed she'd used it to record her "snuff" videos. Could the person on the other end of that IM have hacked into the webcam and seen his face? He didn't know if that was even possible, but the more he considered it, the less likely it seemed. Why would she tip her hand? Hell, why even let him know she could contact him? None of it made sense, but it confirmed one thing.

His assassin was here, and she was getting impatient.

CHAPTER SIXTEEN

A dog barking woke Gidion the next morning.

"Oh, dear lord, Page! Shut up!"

The barking didn't stop, and as he sat up, he saw Page curled up on the floor just outside his bedroom door.

Then it hit him. The barking was his cell phone ringer for Grandpa.

"Shit!" Did he oversleep again? He grabbed the phone and answered it before it could kick over to the voicemail. "Grandpa?"

"Good, you're awake."

"I'm so sorry." He threw off the covers and scrambled around for his clothes. "I didn't mean to oversleep. I can be there in twenty minutes. Promise."

"Calm down, boy." Grandpa didn't shout the command, but it had the same effect. "You haven't overslept, but get your ass down here fast. We got a mess that needs to be cleaned up before anyone else shows up."

Grandpa hung up before Gidion could ask what was going on. Only then did he realize it was just barely daytime outside. He checked the time on his phone, and it was 7:15.

"Good God. Seriously?"

He stumbled his way through getting ready. After having that "panic wake-up," the adrenaline rush was already fading to nil. Didn't help that he was struggling through a melatonin hangover. The byproduct of Dad working overnights was all the various sleeping remedies stashed in the house, and he'd needed the help after the scare he'd gotten from his assassin last night. He'd placed a drop of lavender oil on his pillow and taken a half of a melatonin pill. Dad warned him against taking a whole pill. That stuff worked great, but the after-effects weren't to be trifled with.

He blasted his stereo on the drive to the funeral home to help counter the need for more sleep, not that it did much. Shouting the lyrics sounded like a good idea for all of two lines, at which point he decided even he didn't want to be subjected to the horror of his singing voice. Falling asleep behind the wheel and crashing his car was preferable by comparison. Dad swore Mom sounded beautiful when she sang, but Caelan Keep had kept those musical genes.

No one else had gotten to the funeral home by the time he pulled the Little Hearse into the lot around 7:45. None of the staff was scheduled to be there until 8:30 anyway. He sure hoped Grandpa had some coffee brewed.

Gidion was surprised to find the garage door in the back sitting wide open. Grandpa was sitting on a stool next to one of the long, black hearses and sucking on his pipe. Far as Gidion could tell, nothing looked out of place.

Given that he wasn't making a body deposit from hunting, Gidion pulled into a space in the back of the lot. Before he could walk to the open garage, Grandpa met him halfway.

"No, go back to your car."

"What?" Good God, what was going on? "You told me to—"

"Just shut the garage door with the remote in your car."

"Fine." Lord, he hoped they still only had two escorts scheduled. Gidion was not up for being here all day. He opened the driver side door and reached inside to hit the opener.

The garage door shrieked as it usually did, working its way shut. He turned to see the beige horizontal slats roll down.

"Oh, crap."

The unexplained vampire smiley face from last night appeared on the garage door. Now he understood why this one had looked different from the others. His assassin had painted the smiley face so that it was resting on its side instead of its normal position. She'd taken the picture at an angle, making it look like the paint had somehow smeared to the right instead of dripping down.

"I'm going to have Andy drive the second escort." Grandpa reached past him to reopen the door, which screeched as it rolled back up. "After the first one, you're going to Pleasants Hardware and getting paint. Just a damn lucky thing it ain't raining today. You got a change of clothes in your car?"

Gidion nodded. He always kept a change of clothes in the Little Hearse for when he hunted, and even Grandpa's ban on hunting hadn't changed that habit. "How the hell did she find us?"

"Got a pretty damn good hunch how, but that'll have to keep for now. Just get ready for the first escort and make sure no one tries to close that door."

So much for laying low. Gidion didn't see any point in hiding now that the assassin had tracked down Grandpa's funeral home.

She wouldn't take long to figure out Gidion was her target. The few advantages he had left were almost played out.

CHAPTER SEVENTEEN

The lingering smell of paint fumes did nothing to improve Gidion's mood. People had vandalized the funeral home before, so Grandpa knew the exact paint needed, E5CB60. Grandpa never called it by its name "Quilt Gold," probably because that just sounded too girly.

Gidion spent the entire day puzzling over how this "vampire hunter hunter" had tracked them to the funeral home, and by the time he stored the paint in the garage, he was pretty sure he'd figured it out.

"All done?" Grandpa stuck his head out the door leading from the garage to the main hallway. By now, it was close to two o'clock. They were done for the day, with all the other employees and attendees long gone.

"Yeah, suppose I should be glad she kept the smiley face on the door and didn't decide to go after the bricks." Gidion washed his hands in a sink using an industrial strength soap they kept here for the body removal services people who might get a little dirty delivering the messier corpses. Grandpa tossed him a towel to dry off. "Thanks. By the way, I think I've figured out how she found the funeral home."

"You think so?" Grandpa smirked with a "no shit" expression on his face. "My office. Got something you'll wanna see."

He followed him in there and was surprised to see the computer turned on. Grandpa kept it on a table behind his desk. One of the assistant directors had donated it after upgrading to a laptop. The idea had been to let Grandpa use it to track the funeral home's finances, but all it did was collect dust, until now.

The media player was open and showed an image of the

cremator room with its bright white walls.

"When did you get security cameras?"

Grandpa laughed. "Day after you told me that bitch was coming for you. Want to see what she looks like?"

Gidion had assumed Grandpa had called other vampire hunters. He should have known better. Still, he was impressed. Grandpa came across like some dumb, stubborn hick, but he could be pretty darn clever.

"You knew she'd come looking."

Grandpa nodded as he played the video. "It's what I'd have done if I'd been in her shoes."

That's what Gidion had realized while painting the garage door. She knew he'd killed close to two dozen vampires in a short span of time. That kill rate meant he needed a way to dispose of the bodies without getting caught, and a crematorium made sense. There weren't many in the Richmond area. Wouldn't take long to visit all of them to find the right one.

Grandpa often added some of the leftovers to the ashes given to their customers to help dispose of the evidence. More than one person had scattered the remains of Gidion's kills with their loved one's ashes. He wondered how many people had a handful of dead vampire resting on the mantel of their fireplace.

Just as he was about to suggest they fast forward the video to the good part, a person stepped into the frame. The view was from the corner of the room near the door, so when she entered, all he saw was the top of her head and her back. Even that was obscured by the wide brim of a black hat. He could just make out her straight, black hair, which reached halfway down her back. She stepped up to the conveyor belt and leaned over as if to admire the rolling pins up close.

"She smelled the vampire blood." That's what Gidion had figured.

"Price of success, boy." Grandpa shook his head. "Had the cleaning crew bleach the shit out of that room for days, but just wasn't enough."

The video display included a date and time in the bottom left corner of the screen. "Wednesday night?"

"Slipped in pretending to be here for one of the visitations."

Gidion wasn't surprised. It's what he would have done. She didn't linger after getting her sniff of the place. She slipped out of the room, and the hat hid her face.

"That's not very helpful." Gidion sat on the edge of Grandpa's desk. He crossed his arms as he considered what they'd seen. "At least now we know she's a vampire and not very tall."

He'd stressed over the possibility that the vampires had hired a human. Until now, he'd never fully appreciated the advantage that being able to walk in daylight gave him.

"She's a fucking chink."

Gidion didn't restrain his groan as he rolled his eyes. There were times he wondered how he and his dad could really be related to Grandpa. The old man hadn't met an ethnic slur he didn't like.

"How can you even tell?" Sure the camera was in color, but the quality wasn't that great, and the black dress she wore covered her arms completely. The limited cleavage of her outfit didn't help either. "And for the record, the more appropriate term would be Asian."

"Don't give me that shit." Grandpa's complaint lacked its usual conviction. Navigating the folders on the computer for whatever he was looking for required too much of his attention. "Until you can tell the difference between someone from China and Korea, you can kiss my bony ass. Calling someone 'Asian' don't mean shit. That's like calling a white person European."

"I'm pretty sure Europe has more than white people."

"Just shut up and let me do this." He muttered under his breath, "Liberal bullshit."

Grandpa played another video, but this was a picture of the main entrance. Gidion stood as he looked at the angle. The camera must have been mounted around chest-level just behind where the greeter stood.

"How did you get a camera there without anyone noticing?"

"You're the enlightened expert on everything. Why don't you

go figure it out?"

He did. While Grandpa grumped his way through the video, Gidion went to the entrance. He didn't see a camera, not at first. Sitting on the tall, wooden table next to the hallway entrance, where they usually placed the guest registry, was a new electronic clock. To the right of the large, red numbers was the hint of a circle that could only be the lens of a camera.

"Very sneaky, Grandpa," he said as he walked back into the office.

"Don't you forget it."

He paused the video on a picture of the assassin walking into the funeral home. The wide brim of her black hat left little doubt it was her, that and the time displayed on the video. Grandpa kept the entrance to the funeral home well lit, so the picture turned out clear.

"Didn't bother signing the registry," Grandpa said. "Already gave it to the family anyway."

Gidion noted what he could about her. She'd been turned very young, much younger than most of the vampires he'd encountered. That didn't mean much, but she looked only a little older than he was. Her face was round and attractive with eyes a shade of brown that was colder than ice. They drew you in just long enough to know you should look away.

Even if she hadn't sniffed the cremator room, Gidion would have known she was a vampire just by her walk. Vampires moved with more grace than a normal person and with a predatory demeanor. Height, weight, and build didn't even factor into it. A vampire needed to be a killer, and that's not something easily hidden. They couldn't survive otherwise, but something in the way this assassin took in her surroundings carried an added threat. Her own kind, the wiser ones, would fear her.

"Don't suppose you ordered the super-deluxe security cameras to cover the parking lot, too?"

Grandpa shook his head. "Too wide an area."

"Would've been nice to know what she was driving."

He thought about one of Grandpa's many vampire hunter

wisdoms: once they've seen your face, they've already learned too much. This time, he was the one trying to out the hunter, but having her face didn't feel like it helped much.

"At least I can see her coming."

Grandpa shook his head. "Won't do you a lick of good if she decides to take you out with a long-range rifle."

"Gee, thanks for that cheery thought." Gidion tried to wrap his brain around this, get in her head. "She found this place on Wednesday."

"What's your point?"

Gidion pulled out his cell phone to open up Bonnie's email account. "She didn't start sending the emails to taunt me until Thursday. Why do that? She has an advantage now that she knows this place is where I dispose of the bodies. Giving away that she knows about it negates that advantage completely."

"You ever consider you might be giving this bitch too much credit? Might not be that smart."

"Given how much they're paying her to kill me?" Gidion shook his head. "She's got a plan. Just need to figure out how it works before she plays her hand."

"She's just trying to piss you off into doing something sloppy." Grandpa pointed his finger like he planned to stab Gidion with it. "Don't do it."

"She doesn't realize I know what she looks like. That's an advantage I need to use before it's too late. I can send her an email, talk her into meeting on neutral ground, a public place. She won't realize I can recognize her. She'll think she can ambush me, but I'll be the one setting the ambush."

The tangy scent of tobacco filled the office as Grandpa pulled out his pipe and opened a pouch. "It's a bullshit plan. She won't fall into something that obvious. Besides, knowing what she looks like won't do you a damn bit of good if she hides on a rooftop and takes you out like a sniper."

"Yeah, I believe you covered that with the whole long-range rifle thing," Gidion said. "So what's the play?"

"Stay low, and keep your eyes open. Don't jump at the next picture she sends you either. Minute you get sloppy, she'll make her move."

Grandpa made it clear they needed to leave the funeral home before sunset, too. Just because she'd figured out where the vampire bodies were being disposed of didn't mean she knew who was involved. If she watched the funeral home at night, she'd eventually piece together that the two of them were the ones to target. Even then, it was only a matter of time before she used what she'd learned to figure it out.

Unless Gidion figured out how to find her first, they were as good as dead.

CHAPTER EIGHTEEN

With Dad already at work, the house had an emptiness that emphasized the sound from each of Gidion's movements. The smell of his dog about knocked him down more than her running to greet him with an inquisitive nose to his pants. She was especially curious about the beige spots of paint on his clothes.

"Seriously, dog?" He pushed her aside with a pat on the head. "I don't think there are enough paint fumes for you to get high, but let's not test it."

After wading past the constantly moving furball of curiosity, he made his way into the kitchen. He grabbed a large bottle of orange juice from the fridge. Since Dad wasn't here, he didn't bother with a glass and drank straight from the bottle. Dad had left a note next to the mail on the kitchen table. Even though this was supposed to be his night off, he'd agreed to go in for overtime and work until four in the morning.

"Wasn't like I was planning to hunt tonight anyway."

What he really needed was a brilliant idea to find this assassin and take her out. Every idea he'd had so far just made him an easier target.

Gidion balled up Dad's note and set it aside. The small pile of mail included a plain white envelope with his name on it. He smiled as he saw the return address was Phoenix, Arizona.

He patted Page on the chest as he held up the letter for her nose to inspect. "My girlfriend."

Dropping into a chair, he opened it. He wasn't sure what he'd expected, but a simple hand-written letter that only filled one page wasn't it. They had email, after all.

Then he read it.

'I'm sorry I haven't kept in touch...' Her apology made him feel guilty for avoiding her this past week, but it wasn't until he reached the start of the second paragraph that he realized where this letter was going.

'I've been applying to college, and I've made a decision that I can't go back to Richmond. I can't go out at night alone without being terrified. Getting on with my life has been hard enough here. Even though you'll be there, going back to Richmond will be like walking back into a nightmare for me. You're still hunting, and I don't think you'd stop, even if I asked.'

He slammed his fist on the table. Hunting vampires had brought her into his life, and it was taking her away, too. He wanted to ball up the letter and burn it, but he couldn't stop himself from reading the rest.

'The truth is that there's more to it than that. I've met someone.'

Of course she had. Now he understood why her replies to his texts had been so slow. What had she said that first night he'd gone after GQ Drac? She was "out with some friends." She wasn't just avoiding him, she'd been hiding him from the other guy.

By the time he made it down to her signature, he felt like he'd been cut open with an ice cream scoop.

'P.S. If you're going to keep hunting, please promise to keep the rabbit's foot with you and stay safe.'

He grabbed his phone to text her but stopped himself. What was he going to say that wouldn't sound desperate and stupid? She was right. He wouldn't quit hunting for her. He looked over at Mom's portrait, all the reminder he needed why it wasn't even in doubt.

Page rested her chin on his leg. Her large, brown eyes stared up at him as if she knew what had been in the letter.

His phone had already gone dark. He placed it on the table, resisting the urge to hurl it across the room. He stayed like that with Page until just after sunset.

Then his phone vibrated. He snatched it up, thinking it might be Tamara. The text wasn't from her. It was Andrea. *'You busy?'*

Gidion rubbed his forehead as he debated whether to reply,

even though he couldn't be much less busy. He thought about ignoring the message and climbing into bed. The idea of sleep sounded like the smart choice, except that the idea of sleeping in the dark without Dad here and an assassin hunting for him didn't sound all that pleasant.

'No, I'm not busy,' he said.

He just hoped Andrea and Seth weren't trying to invite him to tag along with them tonight. Little doubt it wouldn't be Seth's idea, not after the other night at Sweet Frog. The last thing he was in the mood for was to watch Andrea cuddle up to her "teddy bear." He certainly didn't want to discuss anything after the other night.

Her reply took longer than usual. He saw that little word balloon with the three dots showing she worked on a reply. Sleep was sounding less stupid by the time she finally replied.

'Want to see Seth at work. Could you give me a ride? My mom is out.'

As long as she'd taken to respond, he'd expected something three paragraphs long, so the short reply was a relief. Even so, he came close to telling her he couldn't do it, only he knew that was a lie. He didn't want to sit here feeling sorry for himself either. He needed to go somewhere and do something, anything to stop thinking.

Page, her head still resting on his leg, shifted her eyes in a way that resembled a human arching an eyebrow.

"Fine. Why not?" He scratched Page's back. After Gidion replied to Andrea, Page strolled into the den and hopped onto Dad's recliner near the door. Apparently, she agreed with his decision.

• • •

Andrea didn't live far from his house, so he made it there in less than ten minutes. The entire house was dark except for the porch light. He pulled into the driveway. As he cut off the engine, that sensation that he'd been hollowed out was replaced with an urge to flee. Now that he was out of the house and faced the prospect of human contact, he didn't trust himself to act like everything was fine.

"Man up." He slammed his fist on the steering wheel and got

out of the Little Hearse.

Andrea walked out the front door before he could even climb the steps. She was bundled in a long, black winter coat. The outfit beneath was also dark and decidedly "un-Andrealike." Her hair was pulled back into a long pony tail. If he hadn't seen her walk out the front door, he might not have recognized her.

"Thanks, Gidion." Her lips quivered in a hard line. "Just sucks not being able to drive, you know."

"Yeah." The single word croaked, and he forced a smile.

Neither said much as they got in the car. Gidion scanned the yard, the neighboring properties, and the road. If his vampire assassin was already following him, she had half a dozen ideal places to hide with a rifle. This neighborhood didn't have any street lamps near Andrea's address, so the only real light came from her front porch.

"You sure this is okay?" she asked as he cranked the car.

He fought down the first barb to enter his thoughts. Was a little late to ask him now, after all. "It's fine." He pulled out of her driveway and made his way to the Midlothian Turnpike.

Andrea stayed blessedly silent for the rest of the drive to the movie theater, an unexpected surprise. Then again, he wasn't making an effort to hide his mood.

Within fifteen minutes, they reached the cinema where Seth worked, just west of Route 288. The parking lot to the theater was packed.

"Can you park on the side?" Andrea pointed to the far left of the movie theater where there was additional parking. Seth had clued him in that this was where the employees were expected to park.

Gidion didn't bother to answer. He pulled into one of the better lighted spaces. An irrational part of him kept looking for his assassin, but she'd need to be a fortune teller to know he'd come here tonight. Several cars had followed him into the lot, but none of them had parked near him.

Andrea looked startled when he got out of the car.

"You okay?" he asked.

Even though she was looking over the top of the car, she wasn't looking at him. He glanced at the cars in the lot and back at her. She seemed just as distracted as he was, but he didn't think she probably had any assassins gunning for her.

"You mind waiting for me?" she asked as they walked towards the entrance.

"Was thinking about seeing something since we're here." Not that he had a clue what he'd want to see, but he had plenty of cash left over from his latest paycheck and the wallets he'd taken from Bonnie and GQ Drac. Unfortunately, the movie posters on the outside of the theater promised little more than a bunch of chick flicks. Great.

They split up once they got inside. Andrea ditched him and ran through the next set of glass doors into the lobby. A hint of fresh popcorn in the air reminded Gidion that he hadn't eaten dinner. He got in the line that snaked all the way to the door and ended up behind a couple holding hands and violating multiple rules regarding PDA. He tried his best to focus his eyes towards the ticket booth and the light board mounted on the wall that listed the movies and start times.

The only film that had cool guys with swords and/or guns in it was one he'd already seen twice. Given the options, he resigned himself to making tonight his third viewing.

He'd only made it halfway through the line and watched the PDA violations of the couple in front of him double when Andrea reappeared.

"Let's go." She didn't give him a chance to respond. Hell, she hadn't even slowed her pace for those two words.

"What the hell?"

She didn't hear him. She'd already stormed out the door and must have been halfway to the car. He decided the movie he'd picked wasn't really worth a third viewing anyway.

Sure she was a space cadet sometimes, but this was pushing it, even for her.

"Andrea! Wait up!"

She didn't wait, and the only reason she hadn't gotten into the car without him was that he'd locked the doors.

"Andrea—"

"Can we just go!" She stomped her foot, and the panic in her voice left little doubt that if she'd been chained to the spot, she'd have gnawed off a limb to get free.

He hit the button on his keyfob to unlock the car. He didn't get in with her right away. He looked back towards the theater. He considered going inside to ask Seth what was going on. Then he noticed what he'd missed when they got here, what should have been obvious.

They'd parked in the same place as the theater staff, and Seth's green Mini Cooper wasn't here.

He pulled out his phone and sent a text to Seth. *'Dude, where are you?'*

The response was prompt. *'Sorry. Can't talk. Out with friends.'*

If Seth had been standing there, Gidion would have slammed his face into the asphalt. That was the same kind of thing Tamara had said in her text the other night. "You goddamned asshole, tell me you didn't do this."

He needed to know, as much for Andrea as himself. *'Are you on a date?'*

Seth's reply didn't come right away. *'Why are U asking?'*

'Because Andrea just figured it out.'

Gidion put his phone away. As he opened his car door, he heard the cat meow sound effect that Andrea used to let her know she had a text. He didn't bother asking her if it was Seth.

Her face was turned away from him as she read the message, but the light from her phone's display made her face visible in the passenger door window. Much as he wished he could, taking her back home wasn't going to be an option, but he knew where to go.

CHAPTER NINETEEN

One of the benefits to Gidion's patrols was that he knew when and where to get a lot of things at night. Instead of driving Andrea home, he took her to Church Hill. They made it to Proper Pie just before it closed.

While they waited in line, Andrea's phone did the "meow" sound effect to alert her to a text message. Gidion worried it might be from Seth, and the thought of that made him want to plant his fist in Seth's face.

"It's my mom checking on me." Andrea showed him the text which asked why she was in Church Hill.

"How did she know where you are?" He and Andrea had the same kind of phone, and it made him worry that if her mom could track her, then maybe his dad could do the same to him.

"What can I say? Big Mother is watching." Andrea muttered the explanation, managing only a small smile to show she was intending it as a joke. "She loaded the app on both of our phones when we got them. As long as she can get online, she can log into the account and plot our phones."

Andrea sent her mom a message to let her know she was okay and out with Gidion. She left out the part about what happened with Seth.

By the time she finished texting with her Mom, it was their turn to order. Gidion got a slice of chocolate chess pie. Andrea went for a lamington, which was this cube of chocolate sponge cake covered in grated coconut, which was the only reason he wouldn't eat it.

"What have you got against coconut?" Andrea asked, as they walked across the street to Patrick Henry Park. As far as parks went, there wasn't much to it, taking up only half a square block. It was trees, tables, and an absurdly short brick walking path.

"It's a texture thing." He couldn't hold back a cringe at the thought of eating coconut.

"I've always loved coconut," she said as they sat on top of a wooden picnic table to enjoy their desserts. The sun was long gone, and the only light came from some of the nearby street lamps.

Gidion kept looking around as he took another bite of his chocolate chess and washed it down with a chug of coffee. This wasn't exactly an ideal place to take Andrea in terms of safety, because the park had lots of shadows with neighborhood rooftops that were all too accessible for a sniper eager to target him. Fortunately, he felt certain they weren't followed here, and since they hadn't run by his house, there wasn't an opportunity for anyone to pick up their trail. In that sense, sitting in the shadows of a park at night was probably the safer option. He'd armed himself before leaving his house, just in case, with his box cutter and sword. Both were concealed beneath his hoodie and jacket.

The picnic table was across from a fire station, and an engine responding to a call whined to life in a blinding display of red lights. The noise eventually faded somewhere up North 24th Street.

They hadn't spoken since sitting down, but for whatever reason, the passing of the fire engine brought Andrea out of her silence.

"It's that girl who started working at the movie theater before the holidays, Laura Hefner." She didn't look up from the black lid of her coffee cup. "She wasn't there tonight either. I asked."

Gidion just nodded, deciding against pointing out he'd already guessed as much.

"Things haven't been so great." She slid a finger along the slit in the lid, trapping and then releasing the steam. "It's not like he's ever made a demand, but I could tell. At first, he'd say it was okay when I'd try to slow things down, but then I noticed him roll his eyes when he'd look away. Lately, he hasn't even really bothered to hide it. You can tell a lot in a kiss, especially when the person kissing you doesn't want to."

Her last few words crumbled before she could form them. When she recovered, she looked at him with a gaze as hard as bullets. "Don't you ever do that to Tamara. You understand me, Gidion Keep?"

"Yeah, I don't think that's gonna be a problem." Gidion retreated into his coffee. When he came up for air, the steam of his coffee breath only partially obscured the look from Andrea that demanded details. "She dumped me. Did it in a letter. Just got it today."

"Ugh, that lousy bitch!" She slammed her foot on the bench of the picnic table. "I never liked her."

Gidion leaned back from the outburst. She sounded angrier about Tamara than she was about Seth. "You were the one who said she was a really nice girl."

Her head shook in a mild seizure as she pulled together her protest. "I said that's what I'd heard. Never said I liked her. So there."

"You are so full of shit," he said as they both laughed.

"Hey, at least my best friend isn't an asshole."

"You're not an asshole."

She slapped him on the shoulder. "I was talking about Seth, you ninny."

He nudged her with his elbow and leaned towards her in his most conspiratorial fashion. "I know what you meant, and I know what I meant."

She hooked her arm in his and scooted closer to place her head on his shoulder. "For a Moody Mike, you're not half bad. You know that?"

"Who are you calling moody?"

She lifted her head from his shoulder to give him that 'you-must-be-an-idiot' look again. "You always walk around in dark hoodies and go out at night doing God knows what. If you acted any more like Batman, you'd get sued for copyright infringement."

"I think Time Warner has better things to do with their lawyers."

Oh, damn. And there was that look again.

"I'm just saying." His plea must have worked, or she simply took pity. She withdrew the "Look" and put her head back on his shoulder.

"Put your arm around me," she said. When he hesitated, she added with a smile in her voice. "Relax, Gid. I'm just cold and out of coffee. It's not a marriage proposal."

He put his arm across her shoulders, pulling her tight. After a moment, she chuckled.

"What?" he asked.

"You're much more handsome when you shut up and do as you're told."

"Don't get used to it."

"Then don't expect me to call you handsome very often."

Even as he laughed, a small twinge of guilt twisted in his heart. Part of him enjoyed this, being alone with her, and he'd missed it since that night at Sweet Frog. Seth had been right about how Gidion felt about Andrea. No matter what Seth had done, that didn't change what Gidion had been doing. At some undefined moment during the past few months he'd stopped hanging out with Andrea because of Seth and had started hanging out with Seth because of Andrea.

He thought about trying to kiss her, but he couldn't work up the nerve to do it. He stroked her hair. This close, he could smell the floral scent of her shampoo. Even if he wasn't bold enough to kiss her lips, he was willing to kiss her on the forehead. She canted her head and smiled, about to say something.

Then a loud electronic tapping sound, like a woodpecker on steroids, made both of them jump and pull apart.

"Sorry, I need to check this." He stood and then stepped off the park table.

He'd chosen that obnoxious alert in case anyone sent an email to Bonnie the vampire's account. Considering there was no way to know what that vampire assassin might send him, he couldn't risk Andrea seeing it. He walked a few steps deeper into the park's shadows.

When he opened the email, he found a picture embedded in it. The latest image had that same red, fanged smiley face, but it wasn't spray-painted this time. This looked like someone had used a brush or their fingers to paint it on a door.

The door.

He recognized it.

That was the front door to Grandpa's house, and it was cracked open.

CHAPTER TWENTY

Grandpa's answering machine picked up on the fourth ring and played the same generic greeting as always. The damn beep took forever.

"Grandpa! Pick up!"

His eyes shifted all over the park as he yelled. He was looking for any hint of movement. The only thing moving was Andrea, coming up beside him. She looked more panicked the longer he yelled into the phone.

The machine hung up on him. He dialed again.

"Gidion." Andrea's fingers wrapped around his bicep.

He shook his head, refusing to answer her unspoken question.

All the details ran together. Grandpa wasn't answering. That meant one of three things: not home, not sober, or not alive. From here, he could make it to Grandpa's in five minutes, but only if he didn't take Andrea back home.

He hung up when the answering machine picked up again.

He tried Grandpa's cell phone. It went straight to voice mail. Probably not even turned on. He tried the office phone at the funeral home.

Andrea turned him to look at her. "Gidion, you're scaring me."

Five minutes to reach Grandpa's, but only if he left Andrea here or took her with him. The other option required taking her home first. That changed five minutes into a half hour or longer.

Grandpa didn't answer the office phone.

Not home or not sober or not alive.

"Do you know anyone who lives around here?"

"What?"

He grabbed her by the hand and pulled for her to follow him. "Anyone around here!"

"No, why?"

"It's my Grandpa." They climbed into the Little Hearse. He shoved the key into the ignition, but then stopped. "Andrea, I don't have time for a lie. How much did you hear when you listened to me and Ms. Aldgate the other day?"

"What?"

"When she kept me after class."

He was rewarded by a look that could only be described by one word: caught.

"All of it?" Gidion asked.

"Was late to English because of that." She crossed her arms. "I was worried about you."

"Fine." He nodded to himself as he reached his decision, then cranked his car. "I hunt and kill vampires. Don't tell anyone."

The Little Hearse launched out of its parking space. Andrea shrieked and grabbed the door handle.

The few minutes of conversation between Church Hill and across the river to Grandpa's house went about the way Gidion expected. Vampires are real. They don't sparkle, and they aren't nice. No, they don't change into bats or anything else. They can live forever, assuming they avoid the sun and a hunter. The catch is that they have to feed on human blood, and there's no animal substitute. No, seriously, they don't sparkle.

Gidion slowed the car as they pulled onto Grandpa's street. Even though it was only a few minutes past nine, the street was deserted. People didn't walk around here at night without a gun or a knife. That worked to his advantage, because if anyone was watching Grandpa's house, then they had to find a pretty inconvenient place to hide.

Grandpa's white, single-story house wasn't competing for a place in *Better Homes & Gardens* magazine. The small front yard was more dirt than grass, but then the Keep family had always been better about putting dead things in the ground.

The beat-up pickup Grandpa drove was parked in the driveway, forcing his internal mantra to reduce from three possibilities to two: not sober or not alive. He'd never prayed so hard for his Grandpa to be drunk.

Even without the front porch light on and his car driving by at twenty-five miles per hour, he could see that the door wasn't closed. The fanged smiley face was impossible to see, though.

He circled the block.

"I'm going to park the car in a moment," Gidion said as Grandpa's house disappeared from view. "When I get out, you're going to switch to the driver's seat. Keep the car locked. If anything happens, you drive like hell for home. Don't wait for me. You got it?"

Andrea hadn't released her death grip on the door handle, even though the car was no longer flying past the sound barrier. "I don't have a driver's license. I don't even have my learner's permit yet."

He didn't need to look her in the eyes to know she wasn't convinced yet. Who would be? Ms. Aldgate had been attacked by a vampire, had its fangs to her throat, and if not for Gidion, she might have convinced herself the guy had just been a mugger.

"I need you to do this. No arguments."

"Gidion—"

"No!" They'd rolled past the house directly behind Grandpa's without a sign of anyone. "You need to do what I'm telling you, or you're going to get yourself killed. It's that simple."

"Why not call the police?"

"Bringing them into this isn't going to help anything. These things have time on their side. It's either kill them now or spend every night after that looking over my shoulder until they come for me."

Of course, there was also the matter of his dad. There was no way to call the cops without Dad finding out. That Grandpa's house was in the city of Richmond and not in Dad's jurisdiction of Henrico County didn't help. This wasn't the kind of thing where he and Grandpa could keep him in the dark.

Gidion parked on the street in front of the neighbor's house.

He left the car running.

"Anything happens, you drive home. No arguments."

"The front door is open. Just call the cops, Gidion."

"I just told you not to argue about this."

"This is stupid. You're getting ready to walk into a house that's possibly been broken into. There could be someone in there with a gun, and I'm pretty sure you aren't wearing a bulletproof vest." She grabbed his arm. "Call the cops, Gid."

"Anyone comes near this car, you drive away." He didn't say anything else, just got out and locked the car.

He told himself she'd drive out of here, if something did happen. He didn't believe it, but he couldn't focus on that.

The night's cold and silence worked in his favor, if someone was hiding out here. They couldn't sneak up on him. That advantage ended at the front door. If anyone was waiting inside, they'd know the instant he stepped on the front porch.

He considered circling the house but decided it wasn't worth it. The main point of doing that was to find any signs of entry, and that was staring him in the face. The front door was half open. As he neared it, the fanged smiley face became visible in the thin moonlight. He forced himself not to focus on it or on the fact that it probably wasn't paint at all.

The inside of the house was draped in night, denying him from seeing anything inside as he approached. He took the first step, and the warped wood groaned as it took on his weight. The box cutter in his hand didn't offer much comfort. The last time he'd been forced to check on Grandpa in the middle of the night, the old man had stumbled out the front door with a rifle pointed at Gidion's head and a full tank of alcohol in his brain. The faint scent of blood in the air drew a silent prayer from him for history to repeat itself, but nothing and no one stirred.

This house, with its aged wood and peeling paint, suffered from the architectural equivalent of arthritis. If anyone was inside and hadn't heard him on the front steps, they certainly would hear the door once he pushed it.

Time to abandon subtle.

He shoved it open and jumped to the side. The metal hinges grated, but that was the only noise. Still no attack. If anyone was here, what were they waiting for?

His eyes needed a moment to adjust after he slipped inside. He wasn't going to be any more vulnerable than at this moment.

As his pupils widened, the lines of the room became more defined. He saw the sofa, the coffee table. Weapons lined the walls. Grandpa kept a small armory in this place, swords and guns mounted and displayed. No matter where you started in this house, Grandpa had placed a weapon within easy reach. This was how an older, retired vampire hunter lived.

The smell of blood grew more pronounced as Gidion pushed deeper into the small house. He listened for any movement, but the only sounds came from him. He gripped his box cutter more tightly.

Then he saw the shape on the hardwood floor, just past the coffee table. He hesitated, fighting against the urge to run to that silhouette that could only belong to a prone body. The shape and size of the body was right for Grandpa, but Gidion wasn't even positive it was a body; he didn't want it to be.

His heart raged against the inside of his chest. Gidion found it difficult to hear anything over his own breathing, which was getting faster. The closer he came to the body, the less he held to his control. The incoherent screams he wanted to release battled within his mind against the reptilian need to survive.

His eyes adjusted enough to finally see the long smear of blood along the floor leading to the body. The body hadn't fallen there. The realization silenced his inner turmoil.

Only one reason explained moving his Grandpa's body.

Ambush.

He glanced around the house, looking for the perfect place for his attacker to hide. That's when he noticed the door to Grandpa's bedroom. It was open. He kept it closed.

He'd already pulled in too close. Whoever was there would realize in a few seconds he'd discovered the trap. He needed to act.

Gidion ran to the wall behind him, towards the fireplace. Something snapped, a sound that didn't belong to him or the house, and was followed by the sharp sound of something burying into the wall. He spotted a narrow dart sticking from the wall beside the fireplace as he dropped his box cutter and grabbed the pump-action shotgun off its mount from above the mantle.

Footsteps warned him he didn't have time to confirm whether the rifle was loaded or if the safety was off. He placed his faith in Grandpa's obsessive paranoia, aimed towards the oncoming shadow and pulled the trigger.

The recoil drove the butt of the rifle into his right shoulder. He'd been unable to get a proper stance, and the pain shooting through his upper chest was the reward. A burning, metallic odor perfumed the air. A single tone droned through his ears even as he heard the scream of his target.

The shadowed figure slowed just enough for Gidion to see her outline and the familiar length of a sword in her hands. Gidion bolted to his right towards the kitchen. The sword hissed through the air where he'd been standing. He parried another swing with the barrel of the shotgun. He grabbed the round fore-end beneath the barrel, which was slick in his sweaty palm. He pumped it, squared his shoulders towards his attacker, and pressed the heel of the stock near the center of his chest.

The second shot shoved him back. Even though he was better prepared for the recoil, the pain in his shoulder made him incapable of maintaining his stance. She shrieked. He hit his target, but he couldn't be sure where. He pumped, then pulled the trigger again, repeating the process three more times as he chased her through the house with gunfire.

The sixth press of the trigger was answered with a click he felt more than heard. The ringing in his ears blocked everything else. The moonlight from the front windows and open door outlined the sleek shape of his attacker. Her left arm hung limply at her side. The gun bought him time. She'd lost her sword, dropped it when his shots hit her. He had to press the advantage while he had it.

He drew the short sword from behind his back and charged her. She parried the swing with a dagger he hadn't seen in her good hand until he was on top of her.

Being a vampire didn't grant a person inhuman speed or strength, but anyone witness to the way she countered his attacks would believe the myth. He held the longer blade in this fight, but he couldn't cut her. Anything she didn't counter with the dagger, she dodged. Even worse, she was doing this essentially one-handed. Up close, he could see the black stain to her purple top, bleeding from her left shoulder to the center of her chest. The longer this took, the better the chance she'd heal enough to bring both arms back to the fight. As soon as that happened, he was dead. He needed a way to shut down this fight before that happened.

He tried to retreat and move closer to another of Grandpa's firearms. A rifle rested in a mount just two steps from the front door. This one was an old single shot, but Grandpa promised it could rip open a hole the size of a grapefruit straight through a man's chest.

His attempt to pull away from the assassin only fueled her attacks. She suspected what he was trying to do. The way she placed herself between him and the wall near the door was proof enough, but then she kicked behind her, knocking the shotgun off its mount. The weapon clattered to the floor.

Even one-handed, she'd taken the offensive. He wasn't going to get his hands on another weapon.

A corner of his mind realized he'd made a mistake in what to expect. Somehow, he'd anticipated some fluid, dancing style of combat, something very *Crouching Tiger, Hidden Dragon*. Even the kick hadn't fit that description. She was fast and brutal, an angry street fighter.

He went low, hoping to catch her in the stomach or the thighs. That pushed her away, but he didn't cut her, not even close. He had the advantage and pressed it. His arms burned from the effort as he forced each swing to move faster than the last. The only reward was that it pushed her back.

They moved into the moonlight, giving him his first good look at her face. Dark brown eyes stared at him. They lacked any emotion. A slim smile curved her lips.

His attacks pushed her into the corner of the room, cutting off any retreat.

The assassin's wounded arm sprang back to life. She snatched one of Grandpa's swords from its mount on the wall in a blur of movement. Moonlight flashed across the blade, giving Gidion his only warning. The blade sliced across the front of his right shoulder. He jumped back with a scream.

She hammered at him with her borrowed sword. The strike of metal on metal sent ripples down into the hilt of his sword, which threatened to rip free of his grasp.

His body shook. Fatigue was setting in, a problem she didn't suffer. An unsettling reality burrowed into him: he was going to lose this fight.

They'd shifted to the center of the den. The front window was behind her. A flash of red and blue light from outside outlined her silhouette. Then he heard the sirens. His ears, still ringing from the gunfire, hadn't recognized the sound of the police racing to the house.

The assassin said something that sounded like, "Ta ma de!" Whatever language she'd just used, he suspected it was a curse.

She bolted for the back of the house. He saw her drop the borrowed sword and snatch up the one she'd lost at the start of this fight.

He took one more look out the front window and saw two more sets of red and blue lights jerk to a stop in front of the house. Even if the cops stopped her, it wouldn't do him any good. That wouldn't kill her.

He sprinted after her, followed her out the back door in the kitchen. The old, bent screen door slammed open and shut with a pair of loud slaps as he leaped out to the ground.

She hopped the side neighbor's chain-link fence. Not an easy task with a sword in one hand. He appreciated that as he performed the same leap. The neighbor's dog snarled and barked as it chased after the inhuman intruder.

A sharp yelp let him know she'd made it past the dog and that he wouldn't need to worry about it.

Muffled shouts chased after both of them. The police had seen them, and it wouldn't take long to cut off any escape. Just going by the cruisers he'd seen, Richmond Police already had three officers here. If the B&E and the gunshots hadn't been enough to draw their attention, the addition of a foot pursuit guaranteed they'd flood this area. The officers already in place would establish a perimeter while they waited for a tracking canine and a plane to arrive. The real challenge for Gidion and the assassin was to get outside of that net before the cops could trap them.

Gidion was already screwed, though. Even as he and the assassin scrambled over fences and through back yards, he knew he'd lost any hope of getting out of this. Andrea was still in his car in front of the house. That was assuming she hadn't done as she was told, but an instinct told him there was little chance of that. The police had honed in on Grandpa's house too fast. She must have called.

A light bobbled ahead of him. The vampire was on her cell phone. They were coming up on the end of the block.

He didn't see any police cars. The only sounds of pursuit came from behind him, save for the distant sirens from all directions that were getting less distant with each second.

Just as the assassin hopped the last fence, a car screeched to a stop in the middle of the road. The black four-door rumbled in place. The side door flung open for the assassin to scramble inside. The interior light came on with the door open. That gave Gidion a brief look at the driver as he neared the fence. White male, thick neck, and...sunglasses?

Gidion's heart hurt, rattling like a wild beast as he struggled for breath and the strength to get over the last fence. He couldn't let her get away, not like this. The image of Grandpa's body hit him, assaulting him with all the details that the ambush had forced him to delay analyzing.

The door slammed shut as his feet landed on the sidewalk. The tires squealed, and the black car rolled away before he could even get a hand on it.

Gidion dropped to his knees on the cement and screamed. His body was finished. He tried to memorize the license plate, but the car disappeared around the corner too fast for him to get all of it.

"Stay on the ground and put down the sword! Now!"

He didn't need to look to know the shout had come from a police officer. Only a cop could yell orders like that. Another officer ran from around the corner of the street, gun out and aimed at Gidion.

"Radio, we've got one at gunpoint, corner of 25th and Hadrian."

Gidion kept his movements slow. He placed the sword on the ground. His hand shook, as much from adrenaline and exhaustion as from rage. The blade clattered against the sidewalk.

She'd gotten away.

A big hand wrapped around his right wrist and jerked it behind him. The metal bracelet of a handcuff dug into his wrist.

The officer in front of him moved closer and lowered the gun once the handcuffs had both his hands hostage. The tall man in his black uniform pressed the transmit button on his shoulder mic and angled it towards his mouth. "Radio, we've got one in custody."

Only one other thought went through Gidion's head after that, the single fact that had driven him to scream as the Mustang had disappeared with the assassin.

He tried to hold onto what details he'd seen about that car, the license plate, and the driver, but all he could see was his grandfather's blood-covered body on the floor in the dark.

Grandpa was dead.

CHAPTER TWENTY-ONE

The hardest part of the next hours was not being able to talk to Andrea. Police shoved him into the back of a police cruiser and questioned him. Then they moved him to the back of an ambulance and questioned him more. After that, they took him to the emergency room, and a detective asked the same questions he'd already answered twice over.

The entire time, he had to take on faith that Andrea didn't tell them anything about what he'd revealed. Her loyalty wasn't so much what he trusted as the fact she'd probably never expect the police to believe her. The only danger was that she'd think he was delusional and needed help.

The last time Gidion had seen the inside of an emergency room had been fifth grade. He'd been playing tag and managed to fracture both of his forearms. The twin casts had been uncomfortable. The simple act of taking a bath was humiliating, because he'd needed his father's help.

He didn't want to think about his father. The hospital provided plenty of distractions. His bare chest and back were cold. They'd cut off his t-shirt when he'd determined he wasn't going to be able to pull his shirt off over his head. The only part of his upper body that was covered was his right shoulder where the assassin had cut him with her sword. The nurse had given him a shot to dull the pain before stitching the wound and covering it with a bandage. Thanks to the painkiller, his shoulder didn't hurt. What he felt was numb with the promise of pain.

A uniformed officer went in and out of the room during the procedure, but by the time the nurse finished stitching him, a detective had arrived. The nurse went to find Gidion a shirt, leaving him alone with the detective.

"Why were you there?" Detective Bristow resembled a quarterback stuffed into a brown suit with a pale green shirt. His paisley tie glowed, reflecting the light from his iPad, which he appeared to use to take notes. His dark skin, combined with the room's dim lighting, made the rest of his body look like a tall and intimidating shadow. The cramped space of the room only added to the effect.

"I tried to call my Grandpa." His voice sounded strange. Even though the ringing from the shotgun blasts had vanished, everything was muffled as if he had cotton stuffed into his ears. "When he didn't answer, I got worried."

The answer had satisfied most of the police up until now, but the detective wore a scowl more visibly than the badge clipped to his belt. He also made a habit of leaving a long silence between the end of Gidion's answers and his next question. Dad used that same technique on Gidion when he was younger, relying on the intimidation of silence to trick him into admitting things. People had a tendency to keep talking, responding to the unspoken suggestion that they hadn't provided enough of an answer yet. It worked on Gidion for a long time. Dad admitted to the trick after he realized Gidion had gotten wise to it. As frightening as this detective was, he didn't hold a candle to Dad.

"Why were you calling him?"

"I was over this way, so I figured I'd see if he wanted me to bring him anything for a late dinner."

Gidion didn't need to ask if the detective believed him, because his scowl deepened. He fixed Gidion with a silent stare. Gidion answered with his own silence.

"You're from Chesterfield. What were you doing over this way?"

"I took my friend to get a bite from Proper Pie."

"You were going to take your date by your grandfather's?"

The word "date" plucked at Gidion's conscience. Why that, of all things, made him feel guilty was absurd. Certainly, he'd committed fatter crimes to keep his Jiminy Cricket hopping mad.

"Andrea isn't my girlfriend."

He couldn't afford to lose focus, because one wrong answer would end with him in a jail cell. The danger was less about being charged in Grandpa's murder, even if that was what this cop was jonesing for an excuse to do. The real risk came from exposing his other activities. Most of what he had to say was delicately bent truth. He'd worked through all of this in his head after they'd cuffed him.

That had been one of Grandpa's lessons. Never lie unless you have to, and when you do lie, make sure to bury it in a lot of truth. You always remember truth; lies you forget.

"What time did you get to your grandfather's house?" The detective stared at his iPad as he took notes with each of Gidion's answers.

"I'm not sure. I think it was close to nine."

"Proper Pie closes at seven."

Gidion didn't register the accusation until he looked up at the detective. Eyes filled with conviction insisted he'd made a mistake.

"I'm sorry. What?"

"I said Proper Pie closes at seven." The detective took a step closer as he looked back at his iPad. "You said you tried to call your grandfather because you thought he'd want some dinner, but Proper Pie had closed almost two hours before you got to his house."

Gidion nodded. This guy was sharp, but he'd considered this already. "I wasn't calling to see if he wanted anything from Proper Pie. He probably wouldn't eat there anyway. He hates that kind of—"

He stumbled as he realized he was still talking about Grandpa in the present tense. His hand shook. Clenching his hand into a fist didn't help him steady his nerves. He kept telling himself not to fall apart, but then he'd see Grandpa's body in his thoughts.

"I figured he'd want something from Siné or City Dogs." He closed his eyes and the words he pushed out sounded like they belonged to another person. "He liked those places better." That one word "liked" stuck in his throat as if it was a sand spur.

"So why were you so worried about your grandfather?" The

detective shrugged with a show of exaggerated confusion. "Nine o'clock? My old man isn't much older. He usually crawls into bed before that, if he hasn't already fallen asleep in his recliner."

"Does your old man drink a lot?" The venom in his reply was a mistake, but this entire night had pitched his emotions on a roller coaster. Even worse, he hadn't hit the lowest point yet.

"That upset you?"

Was this son of a bitch really trying use Grandpa's drinking as a way to dig up a motive? "Yes, it upset me. I worried about his health."

"You always carry a sword and a box cutter to visit your grandfather?" The detective didn't miss a step with his questions. Gidion got the impression he was just pushing his buttons to trick him into saying something inconsistent. Fortunately, the weapons he carried were the safest part of this conversation.

"If I'm going to his house at night, yes. It was his idea. He gave me the sword."

"Why?"

"Because his neighborhood sucks. I'm pretty sure your incident reports will confirm that."

"Who was this woman? How do you know her?"

"I don't know who she is." This part of the conversation made him nervous. He had to be careful not to give up the fact that he'd seen her before tonight. The look in her eyes as she fought him hadn't looked any different than in the security camera recording from the funeral home.

"Really? She didn't look familiar at all?"

The detective's skepticism didn't surprise Gidion. More than once while talking shop over dinner, Dad had pointed out that random victims are the exception, not the rule. Gidion tried everything not to connect too many dots for this detective, because every set of lines led back to him. Grandpa's repeated warnings that he needed to lay low after taking out the local coven were chiseled into his conscience. That made it difficult to lie about his connection to the assassin.

"I have no idea who she is." The truth behind the words hurt. He needed to know more about her. She still held every advantage.

"Describe her for me."

"Asian female, shoulder length hair, brown eyes. Looks a little older than me, but not by much. I didn't see any scars; no tattoos."

"Would you recognize her, if you saw her again?"

His hands gripped the edge of the bed, wishing his fingers were wrapped around her throat. "Without a doubt."

"What about the person driving the car?"

Gidion shook his head. "A white male wearing sunglasses."

The detective held up a hand. "Sunglasses? While he was driving?"

He nodded. "The frames were red, thin. The kind you'd get at the beach."

"Recognize him?"

Gidion shook his head.

"If you saw him again?"

"I don't know. Didn't get a good look. Was more focused on the car."

The detective looked up from his iPad. "Don't suppose you got the tags?"

"Not all of it. They were Georgia plates starting with What The Fuck."

"Excuse me?" The detective's scowl was replaced with something to suggest he was on the verge of getting pissed.

"W-T-F," Gidion said. "That's what the tags started with. Was kind of hard not to remember that."

"You're serious?" He covered his mouth, but Gidion caught the smile.

"There were only three more characters, numbers. Couldn't get those." Lord knows, he'd tried. "I think it was a rental."

"That so?" The detective leaned back against the wall and canted his head. "How could you tell?"

"There was a tiny green square with a white 'e' on the trunk like you see on Enterprise cars."

Gidion didn't mind giving up that information. He needed to give this detective something to suggest he was being helpful. If all his answers had been variations on "I don't know" or "I don't remember," then it wouldn't take long before this interrogation got a lot tougher. Besides, money favored that the vampires would ditch the car somewhere and that they'd rented it using a fake ID and a credit card stolen from someone they'd eaten for dinner. The information wasn't going to help these cops find Grandpa's killer. The bad news was that it probably wouldn't help him either.

A knock at the door interrupted the interrogation. When the door cracked open, the uniformed officer leaned inside and whispered something.

"Thanks." The detective turned off his iPad. "Stay with the kid while I go talk to him."

The officer entered, and the detective left, like relay runners passing a baton. This guy wasn't interested in talking, and Gidion wondered if he was discouraged from doing it. Instead, the cop pulled out his phone and appeared to text someone. Gidion wished he could do the same. They hadn't taken his phone, but they'd made it clear he wasn't to use it. He wanted to send a message to Andrea, to know if she was still with the police or if they'd let her go home.

He knew she was all right, though. The police had called him an ambulance as soon as they realized his arm was cut. While sitting in the back of the ambulance, he'd been able to see Andrea sitting in a police car. She wasn't hurt, just worried. He'd seen it in her eyes. The best he could do was mouth a reassurance that he was okay. She must have understood, because the urgency in her eyes had ebbed.

When the detective returned, he wasn't alone. Dad was here.

Until that moment, he'd held himself together. When Dad wrapped his arms around him, he lost it.

CHAPTER TWENTY-TWO

The detective didn't press Gidion for more information, but the limited exchange between the detective and his dad left an unspoken accusation in the air. They both knew Gidion wasn't telling them everything.

Before they left, the nurse brought Gidion a dark blue, short sleeve shirt, which looked like it was taken from the top half of a set of hospital scrubs. The shirt, a size too big, swallowed him. Gidion wore only his hoodie and jacket. The nurse helped him into it, which wasn't easy to do without lifting his right arm. The hoodie went on more easily since it zipped up the front.

Any doubts Gidion had that Dad suspected what had really happened tonight were confirmed twice. First, by how Dad didn't ask him anything at the hospital about what happened. The effort not to ask wrinkled his father's brow. The second confirmation came after the hospital discharged him at close to two in the morning. The walk to the parking garage was silent, and the night's chill slithered against his arm and chest through the hole the assassin had cut into his shoulder and the thin material of his borrowed top.

Dad watched everything but Gidion as they walked down the sidewalk. His father's eyes focused on their surroundings, searching for signs of an ambush. Gidion would have done the same, but being with Dad somehow made hunting vampires feel like a fiction from a past life. If the assassin had chosen this moment to come after him, he wouldn't have lasted ten seconds.

Only after they'd climbed into Dad's blue Corolla did the silence end.

"We'll get your car later," Dad said as he started the car, "but not until after sunup."

Those last few words hurt more than the cut to Gidion's shoulder, which had exchanged numbness for raging fire. The shot they'd given him was wearing off.

Dad drove to the exit of the garage. He didn't pull out just yet. His attention stayed focused on their surroundings.

"I just need to know one thing before we go any further," Dad said. "Is it safe to go to our house?"

He heard Grandpa's admonition to lay low repeat itself in his mind.

"Gidion?"

"I don't know. They found the funeral home a few days ago."

Dad cursed under his breath. He didn't ask who "they" were. Instead, he drove towards the interstate and got onto I-95 northbound, the opposite direction they would have taken to get home. Gidion didn't ask where they were going. He didn't really care.

He stared out the car window, scared to look at Dad. He remembered something Grandpa once said about this inevitable day, when Dad would figure out what Gidion had been doing. *When he gets done fumin' and bitchin', he'll be like me—damn proud of ya.'* Until tonight, he'd never doubted that. The idea that he'd make Dad proud had pushed him to hunt all the harder. He never dreamed he'd get Grandpa killed, that this was how Dad would find out he'd been lying to him.

Despite the time, Gidion and his father weren't the only car on the road. Dad's vigilance didn't ease a bit. Dad slowed the car, keeping it just a hair below the speed limit, which compared to the rest of the traffic on I-95 was the equivalent of crawling. The way Dad kept checking the review mirror made Gidion realize he was waiting to see if anyone tried to match their speed.

As much as Gidion dreaded the tirade he knew must be coming, he wished Dad would say something to end the silence. Only after they eventually took the ramp from I-95 onto I-64 did Gidion realize where Dad must be going. They didn't travel much longer, getting off on West Broad Street. Gidion was reminded of the night he'd gone hunting for GQ Drac. The bright lights from the businesses still open this late on a Saturday night felt more subdued this time.

"I need some coffee." Dad's words came out in a dull voice. "You probably do, too." Now that Gidion dared to look directly at him, he saw just how wrinkled and drawn Dad looked. When he got like this, Gidion could see some of Grandpa's face in there.

"Food?" Dad asked.

The thought of food made his stomach roll. "No."

Familiar businesses and street signs rolled past them. They were very close to where Dad worked. Their stop ended up being a Wawa, one of those 24-hour convenience stores with a beige brick building decorated in red and yellow.

Dad circled the business. This location had parking in the front and back. Five police cruisers were parked in the back. He'd heard Dad joke about how you could measure just how slow a night was by how many cop cars were parked at the Wawa, because the business let officers have free coffee. Dad didn't park by the police cars. He pulled into a space in front, an area that was well-lit and placed them in full view of anyone inside the store.

He turned off the car. "Come on."

Following Dad into the store was another set of mixed emotions. On the one hand, he feared being near the anger he knew must be buried in his father, but on the other, the thought of just sitting in the car by himself scared the hell out of him. That was funny, in the worst way. Some vampire hunter he'd turned out to be.

Another fear gripped him as they went inside. A few people looked their way, and he'd never wished so badly to go unseen. He felt like he wore his failure, that the slice to his jacket's shoulder was an open-mouthed scream.

Maybe he didn't want coffee that much, after all. He still got it. The Henrico County Police officers in their grey uniforms were clustered next to the island where all the condiments for the coffee were kept. One of the officers, an older one with salt and pepper hair, nodded to Dad and walked up to him. Gidion turned his back to them as he poured his coffee into a large cup.

"We heard about your dad. I'm sorry."

The way Dad's breath caught before he replied hurt like another cut to his shoulder.

Gidion forced himself not to listen to the rest. The conversation between Dad and the officer was brief, though. When they went to leave, the cashier waved for them not to worry about it, said one of the officers had already taken care of it for them.

Everything felt wrong, even the warmth from the coffee cup in his hands. He remembered something Andrea said during a rant at school earlier in the school year. She'd gotten a rare C on an algebra quiz and said she felt like a Renaissance refugee trapped in an abstract painting.

"I need to text Andrea."

Dad's protest made it far enough for him to open his mouth, but his brow furrowed. He nodded. "Keep it short."

He did. The message let her know he was all right and asked if she was. She didn't respond, but considering it was well after two o'clock, that wasn't much of a shock. At least, he hoped that was the reason she wasn't answering. He wanted to go back to that moment in the park before he'd gotten the email. He should have kissed her.

Dad didn't take them far, just a few blocks. The Public Safety Building where Dad worked was very close. This place was more like three buildings in one. Instead of going to the parking lot off of Parham Road where Dad usually parked to go to work, they stopped in the main lot off of Shrader Road. Very few cars were in this lot, which provided access to two parts of PSB, as it was usually called. A tall fence surrounded several dozen police cars not being used at the moment in the far end of the lot, which was pressed up against the tree line.

Before they got out of the car, Dad reached into his jacket and pulled out his blue ID card. "Let's go."

With his coffee in one hand, Gidion reached with his other hand into his jacket's front pocket for his box cutter only to remember it wasn't there. It was probably still on Grandpa's floor or in an evidence locker. He didn't have a single weapon, and somehow, he doubted Dad was carrying anything other than his coffee and ID card. Not seeing any choice, he got out and followed.

Gidion watched for any movement. They were the only ones in the lot, though. The only decent hiding places were so far from them that anyone trying to set an ambush would be hard-pressed to reach them before they could get inside PSB.

The nearest of the three buildings was the training center. Dad had brought him here a few times when he'd been even younger and money was a lot tighter. The training center included a weight room and a small basketball court.

As they made it up to the doors, Dad waved his card in front of a thin, red light. It beeped and the door made an obnoxious metallic sound that resembled a pop. Dad pulled the door open and motioned for Gidion to get inside. The door clattered shut behind them with a second metallic pop as the security lock engaged.

This building didn't open to the public until after sunrise. He didn't think the vampires were crazy enough to break into this building, and to Dad's credit, that probably made this the safest place they could go at the moment.

They went to the basketball court, which was completely dark. Dad turned on just enough lights to dispel most of the shadows. The police and sheriff's office both used this space for a lot of training. One corner had several ropes hanging down from the ceiling, which he'd always wanted to try to climb when he was little, but Dad wouldn't let him. The far wall had several large blue mats rolled up. The rolls were massive, coming up to just below Gidion's waist. Dad sat on one and motioned for Gidion to join him.

They were close to the door to the locker room. Four basketballs were clustered together on the floor near the door.

"Been a long time since I brought you in here, hasn't it?"

"Yeah."

Even though they hadn't said much up until this moment, their words had been covered in a layer of everything they weren't saying. Gidion realized that awkwardness had been there a lot longer than tonight. When Dad spoke again, the lies that had covered their lives pulled back.

"I stopped bringing you here because I hate this place." Dad set his coffee on the floor. "All my worst moments seem to bring me to this room. It's where I go to retreat. Your mom and I even had one of our worst fights in here."

Gidion didn't ask what the fight was about. He supposed it didn't really matter. Dad had never talked about him and Mom having fights.

Dad's jawline tightened, his gaze focused on something in his thoughts. "So, how long has this been going on?"

Gidion placed his coffee on the floor. He hadn't sipped it yet, wondered if he was even going to have the ability to before it turned cold.

"Last summer. I mean, that's when I started hunting."

"Jesus."

"Spring was the first time I saw a vampire. You were out of town, and Grandpa took me downtown a few nights until we managed to find one. Didn't even know that was why he was taking me there until I saw it. Grandpa stopped it from killing this guy. He didn't fight it or anything, but once it knew there was a witness, it ran."

He caught Dad nodding. More dots connecting to Gidion. Grandpa had said he'd told Dad about training him to defend himself, lying that he'd keep Gidion in the dark about vampires. The excuse had been to make sure he could protect himself if any vampires from Dad or Grandpa's pasts came after him for payback. Grandpa even admitted that was why Dad had gotten their dog, Page.

"Made my first kill in August."

Dad sighed. "It was you."

Gidion wasn't sure what he meant, but Dad's next words explained it.

"I know about the coven that got killed in the fire in the East End."

"You knew about that?"

Dad answered with a glare, the first hint of the anger Gidion had dreaded seeing tonight.

"Yes, I knew. I hunted more years than you've been alive. Do you have the vaguest clue how stupid and dangerous it was for you to eliminate that whole coven?"

"I didn't have a choice."

"Bullshit!"

Gidion remembered more of Grandpa's words of wisdom, telling him he couldn't save everyone, but that was exactly what he'd tried to do.

"They were going to kill people."

"People die every damn day." He was about to say something else, but then he paused. Dad leaned back as he stared at him, and Gidion could see Dad making more connections. "Pete. Your friend was involved in that whole mess, wasn't he?"

Gidion didn't have to answer. He supposed his guilt was easy enough for Dad to see.

"You could have gotten yourself killed." Dad reached up into the air as if to choke Pete's ghost. "And he just killed himself anyway!"

The rest of the conversation didn't go much better. Gidion admitted to most everything. His job at the funeral home? Just an excuse to make sure he had a job that wouldn't interfere with his hunting. The night he'd been pulled over by a police officer for speeding when he wasn't supposed to be out? Dad had been working the police radio that night and instantly realized it was Gidion's car that was stopped. He'd been furious enough back then, when he just thought Gidion was out later than he was supposed to be. Now that he realized Gidion had been transporting a decapitated vampire in the trunk at the time, he was sixteen shades of livid.

"Your grandpa was right. You should've backed off after the coven."

"Then what would have been the point!" Gidion was done in so many ways. He was on his feet. He had his rabbit's foot out, the one Tamara had given him. He held it in his left hand in a death grip for all the good it had done him tonight. "Backing off would have just opened the door for another coven to move in."

Dad leaned back against the wall and crossed his arms. "Did

it ever occur to you that maybe these vampires are just part of the natural order?"

"How can you say that?"

"I know these things better than you or your grandfather."

"Really? 'Part of the natural order?' Is that how you justified when you stopped hunting after Mom died?"

Even in the limited light of the gym, Dad went pale. Gidion's body shook. He'd wanted the answer to that question ever since he figured out the vampires must have been responsible for killing his mother. He deserved the truth, but he'd waited until the question was nothing but a cheap shot.

"How much did your grandpa tell you?"

"Nothing. Only that Mom dying was why you stopped hunting."

Dad averted his eyes. He reached down for his coffee, and his hand shook as he lifted the cup. His eyes closed as he took a sip. Gidion got the feeling Dad wished something stronger than caffeine was in that cup.

"I stopped hunting because of you. I didn't want you to go through what I did when I was your age." He shook his head as if to rid himself of whatever memories he'd dredged up from the past. "We can have that conversation later. For now, we need to focus."

Gidion threw the rabbit's foot at the wall. "No!"

"We have to figure out a way to keep you alive. I'm more concerned with that than anything else."

"Did you even avenge her?"

He nodded without looking at him. "Killed every last one, for all the good it did."

There was a strange comfort in that. The truth didn't change anything, didn't make things any better. The truth simply made things a bit more just.

Dad stood and walked over to the basketballs on the floor. He picked one up, put it under his arm, and then got another. "Come here." He canted his head for Gidion to follow him closer to the far end of the gym.

"I'm not really in the mood to shoot hoops, Dad."

"Wasn't planning on it." He placed one of the balls on the floor and turned to face him. "Kick it."

"Why?"

"Because it's better than beating yourself up. Kick it, throw it, whatever it takes." Dad screamed as he threw the other basketball at the wall, a full body motion that resembled a baseball player delivering a pitch, but without any finesse. The ball bounced off the wall, flying past both of them. "Why do you think I come here when things are bad? It sure as heck isn't to meditate."

He walked after the ball, which had settled on the opposite side of the room. With another roar, Dad kicked it into the wall down there.

Gidion looked at the ball Dad had placed on the floor for him. It was a ratty looking thing, bits of thread sticking out in places along its black rib lines, the basketball equivalent of mange. He roared as he charged at the ball and kicked it with every bit of energy he had left. The ball launched into the air, hit the wall, and came right back at him.

"Crap!" He jumped to the right too late. The basketball nailed him on the left shoulder. Thank God he hadn't gone left. He'd probably have ripped open his stitches otherwise.

Dad walked up beside him. He was laughing and smiling at him. "Yeah, you gotta watch out for the rebound. Nearly hit myself in the head one time."

Gidion went after his ball and kicked it a few more times. He tried not to scream on the first few, but yelling helped him more than kicking the ball. Kicking it just gave him an excuse for the noise.

By the time he finished, sweat dripped from his forehead. He hunched over with his hands on his knees for support. The posture made the cut in his shoulder burn, but he welcomed the pain. He'd never wanted to sleep so much in all his life. Everything in him wanted to shut down.

Dad came up beside him and put a hand on his good shoulder. "Feel better?"

"Not much." Coupled with how late it was, brutalizing that

basketball had left him dizzy and tired.

"Well, 'not much' is better than not at all."

Dad pulled out his phone to check the time. "I need a place to rest and think," he said. "This vampire that's after you—after us—knows too much. We need to get Page and find a place other than our house to sleep, somewhere they won't think to look."

"Crap." There was one thing he hadn't admitted to Dad yet, a detail he'd been careful to hide even as everything else about the past year had spilled into the open.

"What is it?" Dad asked.

"I know where we can go, but you've got to promise you won't get mad."

"Son, I'm not sure I could be much more ticked at you."

"No, not with me." Gidion gripped his injured shoulder as he straightened. "I mean someone else."

CHAPTER TWENTY-THREE

Dad directed more than one angry look at Gidion from his driver's seat as they drove to Ms. Aldgate's. Getting back across town didn't take long, given that it was just after sunrise on a Sunday morning.

Gidion told Dad about how Ms. Aldgate had insisted on him confessing to him about the hunting or to stop altogether. "She felt really badly about having any secrets between the two of you. I think she likes you a lot."

"I'm curious," Dad said as they drove down a near-empty Midlothian Turnpike. "What did you tell her?"

"Told her I'd quit hunting."

Dad grunted.

Gidion knew he'd regret asking, but curiosity won. "What?"

"Was just wondering which lie you'd fed her."

For all of two seconds of what must have been certain insanity, he considered pointing out it wasn't a total lie. He did stop hunting, at least temporarily.

"Turn here," Gidion said as they reached the stoplight for Ms. Aldgate's neighborhood off of Midlothian Turnpike.

That earned another angry look from Dad.

"What?" Gidion shrugged. "Oh, yeah. Sorry. Forgot you've been here before."

"I wasn't aware you had."

The way Dad said that, Gidion decided not to offer details. That had been the same night he finished off the Richmond Coven.

Only once they pulled into the driveway on Crater Street did it occur to Gidion he'd never seen Ms. Aldgate's home in the daytime. The last time he'd been here, he'd focused on the possibility of an ambush. He remembered the small statue of an elephant by the front door and little else. Ms. Aldgate loved elephants, even had an elephant-shaped pencil holder on her desk at school.

"So, how many times have you been here?" Gidion asked as Dad turned off the car.

Dad tapped a finger in a slow, steady manner on the steering wheel, adding a whole extra layer of menace to Angry Look #57 of the night.

"I'm guessing that's none of my business."

"Amazing," Dad muttered as he got out of the car. "You can be taught."

Before getting out of the car, Gidion silently repeated Dad's words in an appropriately mocking imitation, but only because he knew Dad couldn't see him at that moment.

He cringed at the baby blue color of the vinyl siding.

"For what it's worth," Gidion said as he followed Dad up to the door, "this will be the first time I've gone inside."

"Good."

"I'm guessing it's probably not yours."

And there was Angry Look #58.

The front door jerked open before Dad could press the doorbell or use the elephant knocker. Under the circumstances, Gidion wished Ms. Aldgate hadn't done that. He was jumpy enough as it was. Even Dad jolted back.

"You got here fast." The words rushed out of her, suggesting she'd been racing to get her house ready. Under the circumstances, she didn't look like they'd just dragged her out of bed early. She was wearing a dark green top and black pants. Her long, brown hair was pulled back into a pony tail without a hint of bed head.

Gidion waved, not that she noticed. He couldn't repress a smirk at the way she smiled at Dad. The cute part was how they each hesitated. Dad gestured like he was going to take her hand as she moved to hug him. They both stopped short, and then the roles reversed.

With a nervous laugh they both looked in his direction. If

his right shoulder wasn't so tender, he'd have crossed his arms for maximum effect as he said, "You might as well kiss. Clearly, you've already made it past first base anyway."

Angry Looks #59 and #1 all at the same time. He should get extra points for managing that. Ms. Aldgate's glare didn't last long as she noticed Gidion's right shoulder.

"What happened?" She tried to look at Dad as she asked, but she couldn't make eye contact. This was a different kind of awkward, and not the cute kind. Gidion felt guilty about that.

"Let's get you two in here." She stepped out of the way and waved them into her den.

The thermostat must have been cranked, because the change in temperature wrapped him up like a blanket. Gidion couldn't say the condition of the house shocked him. Even at school, she kept her classroom in perfect order. If her home was any cleaner, doctors could perform open heart surgery on her hardwood floor. The stack of magazines on her coffee table was fanned out in a deliberate pattern that made Gidion wonder if she'd used a ruler to do it. The only thing that looked out of its usual place, presumably, was a square-shaped throw pillow on the sofa which had fallen on its face, something she promptly corrected. The house even smelled clean, and he'd never realized "clean" had a smell to it.

"Sorry about the mess."

In unison, Gidion and Dad said, "You're kidding, right?"

She smiled at that. A familiar, mechanical snort came from the kitchen. "Do you two want some coffee?"

Gidion shook his head. He hadn't even been able to finish the twenty ounce cup he'd gotten from Wawa. "I think if I had any caffeine right now, I'd barf like a volcano. Been awake close to twenty-four hours." Then it hit him again. Almost twenty-four hours ago when Grandpa had awakened him with a phone call, since he'd driven to the funeral home to see that sideways, fanged smiley face.

The last morning he'd seen Grandpa alive.

Dad's hand on his shoulder brought him out of Grandpa's house and back to Ms. Aldgate's. "He needs sleep more than anything."

"I've got the guest bedroom ready." She led them to it. Her house wasn't very big. She pointed out the bathroom. Her bedroom door was closed. "That actually is a mess," she said.

The guest bedroom lacked anything elephant-like, as if she'd decided that would be imposing her style on a guest. She'd decorated the entire room in blue and gold. The bed maintained the motif with gold sheets and a comforter with a floral pattern of gold leaves on a blue background.

"Give me a few minutes," Ms. Aldgate said to Dad. "I can get my room ready, if you want to get some sleep, too."

"Actually, I think I'll take you up on the coffee, if that's all right."

His answer made her smile. She hugged Gidion before she left the room, and he was struck by how strange that felt. Mom died when he was four, and there'd never been a woman in Dad's life since. Ms. Aldgate was the first. Despite how nervous they'd initially been in front of him just now, they fit well.

"You all right?" Dad asked.

Gidion nodded. "It's just—Dad, I'm sorry."

"It's not your fault."

Guilt and exhaustion made Gidion's stomach turn, and he thought for a moment he might run for the bathroom.

"No." Dad grabbed him by the head, forcing him to look him in the eyes. "Listen to me, and listen good. This isn't your fault. You understand me?"

Gidion nodded, but his heart couldn't shake the blame he felt.

"Get some sleep."

Dad left the door cracked open as he walked out. Gidion heard him talking to Ms. Aldgate in the kitchen. He could make out bits of it as she asked how they were doing.

After some brief internal debate, he decided to sleep in just his underwear and the scrub top. Wasn't much choice given that what he was wearing was all he had.

Sleep scared him. As he fought against its pull, his fingers traced a place in the golden pattern of the comforter that resembled an eight, a lucky number.

Just as he was about to nod off, something he heard Ms. Aldgate say jerked him awake.

"Aric, I hope you can forgive me for not telling you."

The silence that followed worried him. He climbed out of the bed and went to the door to listen. If this ruined Dad's chances with Ms. Aldgate, he really would be the one to blame. He didn't want to live with that.

"I'm not mad." Dad sounded like he meant it, too. "I know I probably should be, but I'm just relieved."

"About what?"

"It's been a long time since I had anyone to talk to about all of this."

Gidion climbed back into bed. He traced two more eights in the pattern of the comforter, one for Dad and the other for Ms. Aldgate, and then fell asleep.

• • •

Light, shaded in orange and red hues, crept through the edges of the curtains. Gidion found his phone where he'd left it, on the bedside table. The time was a quarter to eight. He'd slept more than twelve hours.

He was glad to see Andrea had responded to his text. She was okay, just worried about him.

'I'm sorry about your grandfather. Call me, if you want to. And I lied. I wasn't just cold.'

Maybe he'd get that kiss, after all. He decided against responding just yet, not until he was awake enough to form a complete sentence and less likely to make an idiot out of himself.

He sat up. The same ache and guilt he'd taken to bed lingered in the center of his chest. He'd heard things always looked better after a good night's sleep. Discovering that wasn't always true offered an odd comfort.

He reached for his jeans, but they weren't where he'd left them on the floor. He turned on the lamp, after nearly knocking it over while fumbling for the switch.

A black overnight bag was sitting on the dresser. Dad must have made a trip home. Thank God. He pulled on a fresh pair of blue jeans. He debated on whether to change shirts. He'd sweated in his sleep, and the scrub top clung to him in all the wrong places. Changing out of it and into a fresh t-shirt turned out a lot trickier than expected. The cut to his shoulder burned. Right about now, he really envied that super-fast healing thing vampires had.

After a much-needed stop in the bathroom, he emerged to find the clean smell of the house replaced with the promise of dinner and something more familiar.

Dad and Ms. Aldgate were in the kitchen. Dad shredded a block of cheese while Ms. Aldgate browned some ground beef in a pan.

Sitting between them, in eager anticipation of any piece of food that might fall to the floor, was the source of the more familiar non-clean scent.

"You got Page." Gidion gave the dog a quick pat on the head. She spared him a glance, enough to determine he had no food to offer, and returned to her vigil.

"Morning," Dad said with the appropriate irony, given the actual time. He didn't look like he'd been awake much longer. Steam floated from a mug on the counter in front of Dad.

"Coffee?" Gidion's voice croaked.

Ms. Aldgate pointed to the far end of the counter. The black coffee maker was still turned on with half a pot. "Mugs are in the cabinet above it," she said.

"Thank God." He issued a few more silent praises to the Almighty when he saw the honey on the counter and then a container of half and half in the refrigerator.

He felt more human after chugging his entire mug in one shot.

Gidion found it difficult not to smile when they sat for dinner. Was this what it was like to have two parents? Most of his friends' parents were either divorced or hated each other, so it wasn't like he had any frame of reference. Dad and Ms. Aldgate didn't hold hands, but he didn't miss all the glances and smiles between the two of them while they were putting dinner together. The subtle flirting didn't stop even during dinner. None of them talked much while they ate. Ms. Aldgate and Dad appeared almost as hungry as Gidion.

Only after Dad finished off his last bites did he get to business. "We have a busy day tomorrow. Detective Bristow wants to meet with us after lunch to question you again."

Gidion needed to think through that a moment. This was still Sunday, even though he'd slept through most of the daylight. So, he was meeting the detective on Monday. Even with all the hunting at night he'd done, he wasn't sure how Dad did this midnight shift thing and kept his days straight.

"What about tonight?" He'd assumed they'd make some kind of battle plan to draw out the vampire who killed Grandpa.

Dad stared at him as if he'd lost his mind. Ms. Aldgate stayed silent.

"Seriously? We're just going to hide."

"We need to make sure you're ready for that interrogation. Right now, I'm more worried about that." Dad stood. "I have to make a call." He reached for his plate, but Ms. Aldgate touched the back of his hand to stop him.

"Make your call," she said. "Gidion and I will get this."

Dad stepped out the back door.

Gidion wanted to scream. This was going to end just the same as it had with Mom. Dad planned to run from everything.

"He didn't sleep much today." Ms. Aldgate said that like it explained why he was avoiding their problems. She stood and picked up her plate and Dad's. "We spent most of the morning talking. He told me about when he was about your age, what happened to your grandmother."

Gidion took a moment to realize what she'd just said. "My grandmother?"

She stopped in the middle of loading the dishwasher to glance over her shoulder at him. The way her eyes widened gave the impression she'd just let slip something she shouldn't have, something she hadn't realized was a secret.

"He's never told you?" she asked.

"Told me what?"

Her jaw tensed as she continued to clean off the table. Gidion went through the motions of helping, picking up his plate. He wanted to fling it across the room.

"You and your father need some time to talk. I don't think you realize how much you two are alike."

She didn't say anything else. Cleaning up the kitchen kept her occupied. Gidion didn't bother pressing her for details either. What would be the point? The person with all the answers was on the back porch on the phone.

Who was he talking to anyway?

Gidion made a silent promise as he stared out the window at Dad's profile. He wasn't going to let Dad keep him from hunting. He could spout off about the "natural order" all he liked, but Gidion was going to hunt down that assassin and kill her.

And after he finished with her, he'd go after the ones who hired her, too.

CHAPTER TWENTY-FOUR

The next day turned Gidion into a watched pot. The burner was set on high, but his water never boiled. Dad, the one watching him, wouldn't allow it.

All they did was meet with people. They talked to the assistant director at Milligan's to make funeral arrangements and plans for a visitation later that week, one that most definitely wouldn't take place at night. He didn't miss the subtle discussions about the funeral home's future as the assistant director gauged how safe his job was. By the time Dad and Gidion got in the car to go to their next stop, one thing was clear enough.

"You're gonna sell it." Gidion stared out the passenger side window at a world determined to betray him. "Aren't you?"

"I haven't given it a lot of thought yet." Dad's answer offered a tiny chance he might not, but Gidion knew false hope on a first name basis.

The most dangerous stop for Gidion came after that. They'd arranged to meet with the Richmond Police detective after lunch. Detective Bristow wore a black suit this time with a black tie and a pink shirt. Given how football-fit this man was, the pink shirt didn't make him look any less imposing.

Dad spent last night prepping Gidion for this. They role-played the interview with Dad as the good cop and then as the bad cop. He badgered him, and Gidion suspected some of the practice questions were cloaked accusations. They'd gone over it a dozen times before they went to bed around two in the morning.

Richmond's police station, at least the precinct they went to, didn't resemble the building where Dad worked. PSB was built a few years before Gidion was born and still had a shine to it. This red brick building felt old, the kind of age that hadn't borne time well.

The police still had his sword and box cutter. He wondered what his chances were of getting either back. He tried to play the sentiment card, that Grandpa had given them to him. Detective Bristow wasn't swayed by that.

"Sorry, they're going to be kept in evidence for a while, but you might be able to get back into his house sometime tomorrow. I'll call to let you know when we're done there."

The room they'd taken him and Dad to wasn't what he'd expected. He'd imagined some cramped space with grey brick walls, a plain desk, and equally simplistic metal chairs. Instead, pale blue drywall covered the walls. Berber carpet, a similar beige to the garage doors at the funeral home, covered the floor. Even the chairs felt comfortable. They reminded Gidion of the cheap kind of plush chairs found in dorms. When he tried to shift his chair, which was in a corner, he discovered it was nailed to the floor. An angry perp wasn't going to throw this at anyone.

"Have you had any luck locating the woman who killed my father?" Dad made it clear he'd jump in if he decided Gidion was in danger of tipping his hand. Apparently, Dad wasn't pleased he'd asked about getting back his weapons.

"No, but we found the rental car last night." The detective pointed at Gidion with his iPad. "You were right about it being an Enterprise rental. The company figured out which car and used a GPS tracker to locate it. Most of the newer rentals are equipped with those."

"Where was it?" Gidion asked.

"They ditched it in a parking garage in the Arboretum." Detective Bristow let that fact hang on its own, and Gidion realized it was Dad tipping their hand. Dad's face went taut with panic, barely held in check.

"That's very close to where we live."

"Yes." The detective wasn't volunteering anything else. He didn't need to.

The Arboretum was a large business park located within walking distance of their house. Gidion had even ridden his bike down there a few times when was younger. He'd hoped the location where the vampires ditched the car might tell them something useful, and it had. The vampires were sending them a message that they knew where Gidion lived.

The detective tapped a finger on the edge of his iPad as he stared at Dad. "Are you sure you don't have any idea who might have wanted your father dead?"

Gidion realized in that moment that they'd made a huge mistake. They'd spent so much time preparing for the questions this detective would ask him that it never occurred to them they might suspect Dad knew more than he was telling.

"I have no idea who killed him." Dad looked lost for a moment, in his own thoughts, then looked back up at the detective. "Who rented the car? Surely you got a name?"

"We did, but I was hoping one of you might tell me who it was." Nothing subtle about that.

"Detective, I don't know anyone from Georgia. I don't even know why anyone would want my father dead. He ran a fair business. Lots of people feel like they get taken advantage of by funeral homes, but my father did his best to make sure no one walked away angry."

The detective turned his attention back to Gidion. The detective's stare sent a shiver through Gidion. "You work there. Anyone leave there unhappy lately? Any unusual people come by recently?"

"No."

"Then why'd he install the hidden cameras last week?"

The security cameras...Gidion struggled to keep his composure as he thought back to the video of the assassin in the cremator room. It was only a matter of time before they found that, assuming they hadn't already. What would the police make of it? Did they even have the recordings?

"I didn't realize he'd done that." Gidion was only partially lying when he said that. Yes, he knew now, but until Grandpa had played the video for him on Saturday, he'd had no idea about the security upgrade. "I normally only work on the weekends."

There was a knock on the door. Gidion assumed the lady who leaned inside was another detective since she was wearing a dark green business suit instead of a uniform. "Eli, you got a moment?"

Detective Bristow nodded to them and walked out into the hallway.

That didn't leave Gidion and Dad alone. One thing that conformed to the interrogation room cliché was the long window with a one-way mirror in it on one of the longer walls. There was also a video camera mounted up in the opposite corner from where Gidion was sitting.

"You didn't know about Grandpa installing that security equipment?" Dad kept his voice low. He knew Gidion was aware of the cameras. They'd discussed the video recording of the assassin in the funeral home when Gidion spilled his guts in the PSB gym. Dad was acting for the unseen audience.

Gidion followed his lead. "He didn't tell me about it."

"Any idea why he got them?"

Gidion shook his head. Beneath his own acting, Gidion was impressed with Dad's ability to bluff. The way he pretended to be puzzled, staring intently ahead as if working through some list of details, was damn convincing.

The detective returned a moment later. Dad warned Gidion they would probably do this kind of thing, while the two of them waited. Make them sit here long enough, and they'd get tired, perhaps let something slip. That was also why Dad had insisted on coming when they did. They'd eaten lunch before coming here, just enough to keep hunger from making them sloppy and not too much to make them sleepy.

"You never said who rented the car." Dad crossed his arms and fixed his gaze on the detective. Dad didn't look the least bit intimidated, and considering he worked with police all the time and had been a police officer, he supposed it wasn't that surprising.

"Like I said, I was hoping you might tell me."

"Detective Bristow, let's get something straight. My son and I are pretty scared right now. Someone killed my father and almost killed my son. Now, you're telling us they ditched their car within a mile of where we live." Dad leaned towards the detective. "I know you have to eliminate us as suspects. You're not doing your job otherwise, but I think you've learned enough to know that we aren't involved with the people who killed my father. Considering all that and the fact you still haven't caught the woman who killed him, I want some damn answers. Either you start being a bit more forthcoming or we're done."

The detective sucked in his left cheek, as if chewing on the inside of his mouth as he considered his reply. "Justin Wetherington." After the detective said the name, he waited for a reaction. All he got was a pair of shrugs. "Went missing from Columbus, Georgia, seven years ago. He's presumed dead."

After he said that, the detective waited for a reaction that neither Gidion nor Dad could deliver. The name meant nothing to either of them, but Gidion was glad for the information. The detective had given him something he'd never have gotten on his own, and he meant to put that information to good use.

CHAPTER TWENTY-FIVE

Gidion and his dad left the police station a little past four o'clock. They'd gotten through the interview with Detective Bristow without giving away anything that might incriminate them.

Dad waited until they were in the car and pulling onto the Downtown Expressway before he said anything.

"You did well."

Gidion didn't respond. He'd pulled out his phone and opened his web browser.

"What did he say that last name was?" Gidion asked.

"What last name?"

"Wetherington, right?" He wanted to do a quick search for this guy online.

Dad glanced at what Gidion was doing as they went through the tolls. "Oh, yes. That was it, but he never said how it was spelled."

"Doesn't matter, Google figured it out. There's a lot on this guy."

That put it lightly. His search hit on more than a hundred news articles, blog posts, and videos on Justin Wetherington. By the time they went over the James River, which was only a few miles later, Gidion knew plenty about their assassin's driver.

"No wonder there's so much on this guy." Gidion scrolled through a news article from the *Ledger-Enquirer*, a newspaper in Columbus, Georgia. "His family's rich. Horse farmers."

"Horse farmer, huh?" Dad's voice had an edge to it, as if that detail bothered him, but before Gidion could ask, he found what he really wanted. The article included several pictures of Wetherington taken shortly before he disappeared. "That's him."

Gidion held up his phone with the picture, but Dad pushed it away. "Not now, I'm driving." Traffic on the Powhite Parkway got heavy this time of day, leading up to rush hour.

"This is the guy." Gidion stared at the picture of Wetherington standing next to a horse. He wore a pair of red-rimmed sunglasses. "He was driving the rental car, the one the assassin got into. I'm sure of it."

"I thought you didn't get a good look at him."

Wetherington was twenty-four years old when he went missing. He had a wild mane of hair in the picture, even though the driver's hair was cut short. The face of the driver, what was visible to Gidion the other night, hadn't changed much. Someone must have turned him shortly after he disappeared, but it wasn't the face that made him sure this was the guy.

"It's the sunglasses. That's the exact pair he wore."

"He must be a shade."

Gidion put the phone away. He'd read up on Wetherington later. "And just what is a shade?"

"A vampire whose eyes are extra-sensitive to light," he said. "They wear sunglasses to compensate for it, even in the dark."

"Grandpa never mentioned those." Referring to Grandpa in the past tense was already getting more natural. He wondered how long it would take to stop feeling like each time he used the past tense that he was somehow turning his back on him.

"I'm not sure how much your grandpa knew about shades. In the old days, I don't think they lasted very long. Elders who made them often killed them. Shades happen for several reasons. The vampire turning them might botch it somehow. Mainly happens if the one doing the deed isn't a true elder yet or if they rush it."

"Having the option of sunglasses makes a difference, part of where their nickname comes from." Dad got that distant look again. "I've seen it happen."

Gidion couldn't help but smile. The whole moment had a very Batman and Robin vibe to it. Ever since he'd learned Dad was a big bad vampire hunter, he'd wondered what it would be like to hunt with him.

"I'd definitely be Tim Drake, though. Wouldn't want to be Damian."

Dad glanced at him as if he'd started speaking in tongues.

"Batman and Robin?" Gidion shrugged assuming it would have been obvious.

Dad scowled. "Yes, I know who Tim Drake and Damian Wayne are, thank you very much. I might not buy comic books anymore, but I do keep up with my childhood heroes on Wikipedia and Comic Vine."

"Just checking."

"Yes, but we were talking about shades."

"Sorry, Batman." Gidion grinned.

The hint of a smile ruined Dad's scowl. "So, we were talking about shades."

"Yeah, botched conversions and sunglasses," Gidion said. "Means if I get the glasses off, he'll be at a disadvantage."

Dad got this rumble in his throat, suggesting he didn't agree with that. "That depends on the setting. In a pitch black room, the shade has the advantage. Never forget that. If this guy from Georgia has lasted for seven years despite being a shade, then he's a survivor."

"I don't suppose we have any kind of game plan for tonight?"

Dad's silence was all the answer Gidion needed. They weren't going hunting or doing anything productive tonight.

"You know, we could pick up my car?"

The sidelong glance from Dad said plenty. He knew damn well why Gidion wanted his car back.

"Maybe tomorrow," Dad said, then added, "if we get back into Grandpa's house."

Gidion wanted to scream. He'd never recognized just how much freedom he'd enjoyed during the past year. Heck, Dad didn't watch his movements this much even when he was in elementary school.

He needed to hunt. Sitting and waiting wasn't going to make this mess go away, but Dad refused to talk about it. He just wanted to wait until he'd spoken with his "contact" tomorrow night.

• • •

Aside from dinner, Gidion hid in the guest bedroom the entire time. He didn't even bother saying "goodnight" when he decided to go to bed. Unless he had to speak to Dad, he didn't plan to. That all changed at two in the morning.

His cell phone vibrated and started playing the James Bond theme, his phone's default ringtone. He didn't recognize the number, which had an 866 area code, but given the time, he decided to take a gamble and answered.

The man calling talked with a practiced, professional manner. "This is Southeast Security calling for Gidion Keep."

Gidion rubbed the sleepies from his eyes. This guy on the phone was far too chipper for two in the morning.

"This is he."

"Sorry to wake you, sir. I'm calling in regards to the alarm system at 8520 Staples Mill Road, Milligan's Funeral Home. We've received an activation from the hallway motion and the garage door. Would you like us to dispatch at this time?"

Gidion needed a few seconds to register what the security guy had said. The instant he did, he jerked straight up and out of the bed. Ever since Gidion started hunting, Grandpa had placed him on the keyholder list with the alarm company. They'd probably already tried Grandpa's home number.

"How long ago?" Gidion snatched up some jeans and dug around in the suitcase on the floor for one of his t-shirts with the red bat on it.

"We received both activations just three minutes ago. We attempted to call the premises, but there was no answer. Would you like us to dispatch police?"

"No!" Gidion stopped what he was doing and took a deep breath. "No, that won't be necessary. Thank you."

"And the cancellation code?"

Gidion blanked for a split second. Holy crap! What was the damn code word?

"I'm sorry, what was that?" he asked, trying to stall long enough to remember the code word. The last thing they needed was police going on this.

"I just need the cancellation code, sir."

He snapped his fingers. "Templar."

"Thank you. Is there anything else I can do to assist you this evening?"

A cup of coffee would have been great, but he decided not to be a smart ass given what he did ask. "Yes, please call me before anyone else if you receive any additional activations between now and sunrise, I mean—uh, make it until eight a.m."

"Including the premises?" If the guy on the phone thought that was an odd request, he didn't let on. He typed at his keyboard, hopefully adding in the request.

"Yes, please."

As soon as he hung up, Gidion dressed and went into the hallway. He almost tripped on Page, who was curled up on the floor outside the door to the guest room. He cursed, and then hoped Dad hadn't heard him. He needed a second to orient himself, still not used to the layout of Ms. Aldgate's house.

He went straight to the den. Dad had opted to sleep on the couch while they stayed here. Gidion heard him doing his best "Darth Vader" imitation. There was a reason Gidion slept with his door closed when Dad was home.

"Dad," Gidion whispered, not wanting to wake Ms. Aldgate while he did this. Of course, if he'd had his car, he wouldn't have bothered waking Dad. He'd have just hopped in the Little Hearse and gone to the funeral home alone.

Waking Dad required nudging him on the shoulder. Gidion feared Dad might panic given how dark it was, jerk awake, and attack him. Instead, Dad stopped snoring and opened one of his eyes, which slowly turned to fix on the fool crazy enough to wake him.

"Gidion Antony Keep, there had better be a horde of vampires outside this house."

"No, but there might be some in the funeral home."

That got Dad's attention. More importantly, it got him upright for Gidion to tell him about the call from the alarm company.

"You should have gotten me while they were still on the phone." Dad's protest didn't have much teeth to it, because he was already slipping on his pants. "No fire alarm, right? Just the intrusion sensors?"

Gidion nodded. "Yeah. Why?"

"Because if I was the vampires," Dad said as he pulled on his tennis shoes, "I'd burn that funeral home to the ground to take the cremator out of the equation."

Gidion had to admit that would be a smart move. "To be fair, vampires aren't exactly fond of fire. You know? That whole being extra-flammable thing and all that." He added in a nice little poof effect with his hands.

They both jumped as they heard Ms. Aldgate curse from the hallway. "Seriously, dog?"

Page ran from the hallway into the den, leaving little doubt she'd tripped their hostess.

Ms. Aldgate followed a few steps behind the dog. She was wearing a thick, dark grey robe that looked like it was made out of the same material used for towels.

Page ran to the far side of the coffee table to hide.

"Sorry," Dad said, "she does that. She is a protection dog."

"Really?" Ms. Aldgate targeted Page with an "evil eye." "I'm not clear how she's supposed to protect me from a vampire when she can't even figure out to move before my feet hit her."

Dad and Gidion exchanged a look. Apparently, neither of them had a good reply to that. Simply agreeing with her seemed wiser. For Gidion's part, he'd never seen Ms. Aldgate with her hair tousled in that many directions. A powerful urge to live until dawn told him not to voice his observation about the hair.

"So, just why am I tripping over your dog at two in the morning?" she asked.

Dad answered as he slipped on his bright green Henrico Police sweatshirt. "Alarm company just called about a possible break-in at the funeral home."

"And you're going?"

Gidion took a step away from Dad, because he knew that look. Kids getting that expression from her ended up with an F.

"If it's the vampire who came after my father, there's no telling what she's doing. It wouldn't be difficult for her to plant something she's hoping police will find."

Ms. Aldgate didn't voice her objection, but she didn't need to.

"Did you ever get the box cutter I'd suggested back in the fall?" Gidion asked her.

"What do you think you're doing?" Dad put a hand out to stop him from going anywhere.

"Making sure we go in there armed." He tossed in an exaggerated shrug for good measure. "You planning to just take them out with a karate chop or the Vulcan nerve pinch?"

"You are not going."

Gidion launched into his protest with Dad's counter-protest overlapping him.

"Hey!" Ms. Aldgate's shout sent both of them into silence. Benefits of being a teacher, no doubt. "Aric, how many vampires have you killed in the past—oh, say—five years?"

"I hunted for more years—"

"A number." Oh, daaaaaaamn! Ms. Aldgate was taking Dad to school.

"None, but—"

"Gidion?" she asked without taking her eyes off of Dad.

He took an extra step away from Dad as he answered. "More than twenty."

She crossed her arms.

• • •

Five minutes later, Dad started his car as Gidion buckled himself into the passenger seat.

"Don't. Gloat."

Gidion grinned. He was going vampire hunting with Dad.

CHAPTER TWENTY-SIX

Dad might have caved in front of Ms. Aldgate, but he made it clear that this was going to be his show and that Gidion was just along for the ride.

Gidion pulled out his iPhone to plug it in. "Can I pick the music?"

"Not a chance in Hell." Once they came to a stop at a traffic light just before the 288 interchange, Dad plugged in his phone. "I've got a playlist for this."

Gidion leaned over for a look at Dad's phone as he pulled up the playlist with the innocuous title of "Gone Fishing."

Just as the light changed, the first song started.

"George Michael? Really, Dad?"

"I thought you liked this one," he said as they took the ramp onto Route 288, which they had all to themselves at this hour.

"Yeah, but we're getting ready to kick some vampire ass. If you're gonna play George Michael, at least make it something fast like 'Freedom'. You don't play 'Older.'"

Dad grunted. "Well, I like the irony of the title, so get over it."

To Dad's credit, at least the next song on the list was Queen's "Another One Bites the Dust." Around the time they were taking the ramp from I-64 onto Parham Road, Dad decided to set some ground rules while Michael Hutchence and Jimmy Barnes were belting out "Good Times."

"You stay behind me the whole way in there."

"Really?" Gidion pulled out the box cutter he'd borrowed from Ms. Aldgate. She'd followed his advice from when the vampires were trying to kill her and bought a nice silver one with a blue grip.

"I'm the one who's armed here."

"I call your puny blade and raise you a katana." Dad pointed with his thumb towards the back of the car. "I've always kept a bag of weapons in the trunk. I retired from the hunt; doesn't mean I'm not prepared."

Gidion looked forward to seeing what kind of vampire extermination equipment Dad was packing. He was also curious to see where he was keeping it. This wouldn't be the first time he'd seen the inside of Dad's trunk, and he'd never noticed a bag in there big enough to carry a sword.

Once they reached Staples Mill Road, a few blocks from the funeral home, Dad pulled into the rear lot of a pharmacy.

"Let's be quick about this." Dad popped the trunk. Where he'd parked placed them close to a light in the rear lot, but not directly in its beam.

Gidion got out of the car with him. Except for a bottle of oil, jumper cables, and a tire pump, the trunk was empty. Dad reached inside for the back of the trunk. He pulled down the panel that went up against where the back seats were. Only, the panel wasn't right up against the back seats. Instead, it hid a thin compartment containing a long, black bag.

"Had a friend in a woodworking class back in high school who showed me how to build that. Of course, he used this trick to hide drugs." He paused as he unzipped the bag to fix Gidion with a stern look. "Not that I ever did."

Gidion held up his hands as if to surrender. "I wasn't gonna say a thing."

"That'd be a first."

Dad smiled as he pulled out his katana. The wooden scabbard wore a lot of scratches, but the blade that he removed from it was sharp and unmarred. The wrap on its hilt was blue and white.

"See anything you want to use?" Dad asked.

He also pulled out what looked like a pair of brass knuckles, but they had knife-sharp points sticking out the front. A lot of the items in his bag had to be custom-made, kind of like the hidden compartment. Gidion wondered how much this gear had cost Dad. He supposed the longer he hunted, the more he'd put his money towards refining his weaponry.

Gidion picked up a bag of black zip ties but put them back. "I'll stick with the box cutter for the moment."

"All right. Once we're inside, no talking unless absolutely necessary. They'll know we're there. Their hearing is too sharp not to hear us, but that doesn't mean we have to make it easy for them."

"Yeah, I know."

"Don't get an attitude with me." He slid his katana back into its scabbard and tossed it into the back seat.

"It's not attitude!"

"You rolled your eyes." He shut the trunk and pointed for Gidion to get back in the car.

"Well, it's not like this is my first day at the rodeo."

"I know." Dad climbed into the driver's seat and shut the door, the overhead lamp going back out. "This is your first time working with me, though. That changes things a bit, for both of us."

"Sure thing, Batman."

"Shut it." Dad didn't smile at being called "Batman" this time. "I'm going to drive around the funeral home. You know it better than I do these days, so if you see anything suspicious or out of place, point it out."

They pulled onto Staples Mill and went the few blocks down to the funeral home. The street lights helped, but not much. All the lights in the parking lot were off, which was normal after hours.

Pulling into the lot, Dad drove counter-clockwise around the building. The front looked as it should, with the door shut and no windows broken. Bushes, neatly trimmed, ran along the walls on the front and the right side. None of the plants were bent or otherwise disturbed.

"Not seeing anything?" Dad asked as they crept around the building.

"Nope." The lack of cars parked in the front or side lots worried Gidion. He wondered if they might have parked in the back, but the lot was empty.

"Damn," Dad muttered as the garage came into view. Light spilled out the open door.

As they pulled in front of the garage door, Dad slowed the car even more. Gidion leaned forward to look past Dad. He didn't see anyone in there. Nothing looked disturbed either, not that he could tell from here. Part of him wondered about the garage door, if the assassin had placed another fanged smiley face over his paint job.

"Which sensors did the alarm company tell you were tripped?" Dad asked.

"The door from the garage to the hallway and the hallway motion detector."

More than a half hour had passed since that call. He couldn't imagine the assassin would have already given up waiting on them, not if this was a trap, but there was no car. Of course, he still hadn't figured out what she could possibly want to get from the funeral home that she wouldn't already know. Just going by where the rental had been abandoned so close to their home, she must have figured out where they lived.

They continued around the building. Gidion didn't spot anything else out of the ordinary. The other side of the building was a covered area where they parked the hearses to load the caskets and mourners after the ceremonies. The double-doors were closed and didn't look damaged in any way.

"Which sensor did they say tripped first?" Dad asked.

"They never really said, but they mentioned the motion detector in the hallway first." Gidion had a bad feeling he knew where Dad was going with this. If the motion detector tripped before the door, then that meant the assassin had gotten inside without tripping the alarm, which begged the question of why she set off the sensors on the way out.

Dad pulled the car back around the building until he reached the garage door again. This time, he stopped and killed the headlights.

"Don't like it." He turned the car off and stared into the garage, which was now the only source of light. "She hasn't sent you any more emails, I trust? No smiley faces?"

"Nope. The one on Grandpa's door was the last." The sudden silence from the assassin felt wrong, but Gidion couldn't say why. The emails and the IM were all about taunting him, but during the fight at Grandpa's, she didn't toss out a single verbal jab.

"They didn't say that the alarm reset, did they?" Dad asked.

Gidion shook his head. "Might not have. Grandpa wanted the alarm silent. He scared the bejeezus out of me the other night, because I didn't realize I'd set it off either."

Dad still hadn't moved to get out of the car. "Let's give this a few more minutes."

"What are we waiting for?"

"To see if this is a trap." He pointed past Gidion towards the back fence. "Keep your eyes open for any movement along the fence, signs we're being watched. I'll keep my eyes on the garage."

Dad made them wait in silence for ten minutes, which wasn't easy to do, given that both of them had been in a heavy sleep less than an hour ago.

"If they were going to make their move, I think they'd have done it." Dad paused and leaned in front of Gidion for his own look along the fence. "If this is a trap, then either we're not seeing them, which I doubt, or they've set up a booby trap in there."

Dad took the lead, as planned. They went inside the funeral home through the garage. Gidion stayed just a few steps behind, enough to stay out of reach of the katana, if Dad needed to use it.

The plan was simple, with Dad keeping his eyes forward for anyone hiding inside and for any tripwires. Gidion's job was to watch their back and make sure no one came in after them. Just having the option for a division of duties felt strange, no matter how much he was enjoying the idea of playing Robin to his dad's Batman.

The smell of Grandpa's tobacco pipe lingered in the garage. The tangy odor made it easy to forget Grandpa was dead and not waiting in his office. Gidion wished Grandpa was here. He wanted to say he was sorry for not backing down and laying low.

He glanced inside the two hearses, making sure no one was

hiding in or under them. Everything looked as it should. Other than the cars, the garage didn't offer any places to stay out of sight.

"Close the garage door." Dad canted his head towards the control panel next to the door to go inside. "No point in letting them get in behind us that easily."

Gidion wished the door leading into the hallway had a window on it, so they could see what was waiting on the other side. He pressed the buttons to lower the garage door, which creaked and groaned its way down. Even though he knew the point was to lock out the bad guys, Gidion felt like they were locking themselves in.

He pointed past Dad towards the unopened door. "There's a light switch for the hallway just inside the door on the right. Control pad for the alarm is just above the switch."

Once the garage door lowered to the ground, Dad gripped the door handle. He nodded to Gidion and then jerked it open. The hallway lights flashed to life as Dad hit the switch, but they only brightened the hallway a little. The sconces lining the walls used bulbs shaped like candle flames. They provided enough light to see that no one was waiting here.

Much brighter light came from the cremator room, just down on the right. Gidion thought about Dad's idea, how the vampires might burn down the funeral home. Hell, maybe they'd rigged the cremator to blow up and kill them. He doubted it, though. The vampires had no guarantee they'd get him with the blast.

The alarm system beeped. Gidion punched in the code to disable the system and then rearmed it so that only the perimeter sensors were active. That would let them move through the funeral home, but if someone entered the building, they'd set off the alarm. Of course, that didn't help them if someone was already hiding inside.

Grandpa's office was the first door to the right. Dad tried the door, but it was locked. Gidion mimed that he could open the door. Grandpa had given him a master key when he started hunting. The message got across, but Dad shook his head, apparently not thinking it likely the vampires were in there. Dad ran his finger over the keyhole, and judging from the way he shook his head again, nothing suggested the lock had been picked. That didn't mean the assassin hadn't gotten Grandpa's keys when she killed him.

Dad led them to the door of the cremator room. He adjusted his grip on his katana and then leaned to his left for a quick look through the open door. The curse he whispered made it clear something bad was in there, but his stance relaxed suggesting whatever it was in there wasn't an immediate threat.

Gidion got a glance in the room once Dad stepped aside. The vampire was resting on the conveyer belt. One look eliminated any doubt whether he was a threat, because whoever put him there had decapitated him. The head was propped up to face the door, looking at them through a familiar pair of red-rimmed sunglasses.

· · ·

They finished searching every room in the funeral home, including Grandpa's office. Dad sent a text to Ms. Aldgate to let her know they were all right but that they were going to be a while longer.

Gidion focused on finishing what the assassin had started. With his cell phone opened up to the checklist he'd put together from watching Grandpa, Gidion prepped the cremator for the lost-and-found Justin Wetherington.

"You're sure you know what you're doing?" Dad went through the decapitated vampire's pockets. This vampire didn't have anything of value to offer them, though. Their assassin, if she was the one to blame for this special delivery, had already taken anything useful with her.

"I started taking notes anytime I watched Grandpa work the cremator," Gidion said as he checked the temperature gauges. "Wanted to be sure I knew how to do this, if he wasn't here to help."

"Yeah, but are you sure your checklist is complete?" The way Dad talked, he sounded like Gidion was trying to defuse a bomb. "How do you know you're getting this right?"

He remembered the night Grandpa caught him in here with Bonnie and GQ Drac's bodies. That moment when Grandpa came over to the console to check the settings and realized they were all right had hurt him more than anything Gidion had said. Telling the old man he didn't need him would have been kinder. Gidion wanted that moment back, just to say something to make the sting less for Grandpa and for himself.

"Don't worry, Dad." He cleared his throat and wiped his eyes while they were still hidden from his father. "I'm sure I've got it right."

He turned and realized Dad hadn't been looking at him anyway. Dad was studying the body left for them. The assassin had hogtied her driver and placed him here on his side. The rope had also wrapped around his throat before getting his head lopped off. Even though a vampire couldn't die from suffocation, it did need air to function. They could choke to the point of passing out.

"You notice all the cuts." Dad pointed to a cluster of them along the vampire's arms and even down his throat, the part not cut off with his head. For this many wounds to be visible, she must have drained him past the point of his ability to heal. The pool of blood on the floor attested to that.

"She was interrogating him." He'd used a similar technique on a vampire with the local coven to get information out of him, not that he managed to get a lot. "Had him here a while, too, but I don't understand why. They were working together."

"She left our horse farmer here to send you a message." Dad shrugged. "Just not sure what the message is."

"Beats the hell out of me." Gidion pulled the sunglasses off of the vampire to study them. He considered keeping them as a souvenir, but when he saw Dad's look of disgust, he put them back on the body.

Cleaning up their assassin's mess kept them in the funeral home until 5:30. Gidion took time to check the security camera recordings on the computer in Grandpa's office, but apparently Grandpa had never turned the cameras back on after they'd caught the original recording of the assassin in the cremator room last week. He considered deleting all of the recordings, including the one of the assassin, but the police already knew about the cameras. They might have already copied the files for themselves. Deleting them now would just look suspicious.

"Let's get back to Lillian's and get some sleep." Dad groaned as he stretched his body, reaching up as if to crack his back. "Wish we could just go straight there, but we need to stop somewhere safe along the way and make sure no one put a tracking device on my car while we were in here."

The entire ride home, Gidion kept thinking about what Dad had said, that the assassin was sending him a message. What the hell was she trying to tell him? Why not just email him the way she had been?

CHAPTER TWENTY-SEVEN

After staying up late for cleanup duty at the funeral home, both Gidion and Dad slept until just after noon. Gidion never even heard Ms. Aldgate leave for school. They might not have awakened until dinner, but a call from Detective Bristow changed that. Richmond's forensic techs had finished with Grandpa's house.

Dad wanted to get a few things, including some of Grandpa's weapons. Gidion just wanted his car.

They pulled onto Grandpa's street a little after four, and a rush of relief made it easier for Gidion to breathe once he saw his car still there and with all its tires.

Dad parked right behind the Little Hearse. He took a deep breath as he looked at the front of Grandpa's house. "You don't have to go in with me if you don't want to."

"I'll be fine." He wanted to see if his assassin might have left something inside that the police overlooked. Odds didn't favor that, but after her special delivery at the funeral home, nothing guaranteed she hadn't left something for them here after the fact.

"Still nothing from her?" Dad asked as they approached the house.

"No more emails since that night."

He'd considered sending her an email to see if he could prod her to make contact. In his more heated moments, he wanted to dare her to meet one-on-one. He'd started the email but never finished it. No matter how many times that he tried to think of a place that gave him an advantage, he remembered how she had handed him his ass. His right shoulder still hurt where it was cut, and the vampires made it clear they were willing to create a spectacle to stop him. Even a public place might not deter them.

Dad stopped at the front door. The crime scene tape, shaped like an "X," only partially hid the fanged smiley face. This one was drawn in Grandpa's blood. In the daylight, he could see the telltale signs of smeared fingerprints. The assassin had painted this one with her hand. Dad's hand shook as he reached up and then pulled down the two strands of yellow and black tape. He pushed forward without any further hesitation. The door creaked open.

At first glance, the den looked as it always had. Age had warped the hardwood floors, but a dark red smear started a few feet from the door and ran along the floor to beyond the coffee table where Gidion had found Grandpa's body. He also saw several bloody shoeprints, no doubt from the swordfight with the assassin.

The police hadn't done anything to clean the house. When the detective gave them the green light to go inside, he suggested a cleaning service that specialized in this sort of thing. The thought of washing away Grandpa's blood filled him with mixed emotions. Wiping away this blood also erased the last sign that Grandpa had lived here.

Gidion avoided looking down. He turned his attention to the walls. They were half-bare, with all of Grandpa's firearms missing and only his swords, knives, and axes left behind. The police had taken the guns to test which one, if any of them, had been used to kill him.

For the first time since that night, Gidion realized that seemed strange, that a vampire would shoot Grandpa instead of feeding on him. The detective said they received a call from someone who heard a gunshot in the area around the time they estimated he'd died. No one had seen anything, though, including the officer who responded on that initial call.

Dad stopped by Grandpa's bedroom door and the dried remains of a large, dark red puddle of blood. "See if Grandpa has any bolt cutters in his toolbox and bring them to me." He went inside the bedroom before Gidion could ask why.

The toolbox lived in Grandpa's utility room. The room looked skeletal, without any drywall to hide the wooden studs and the wiring to and from the circuit breaker and the washer and dryer. The whole house would give one of those TV house renovators a heart attack.

Grandpa kept his toolbox on an old metal assemble-it-yourself shelving unit. Gidion helped him put it together when he was seven. He still remembered Grandpa complaining about the lack of any written instructions, just pictures and diagrams for how everything went together.

He laughed as he remembered Grandpa's exact words. "What kind of illiterate fucks are they making these things for? And don't you go repeating to your dad what I just said."

Grandpa kept a big set of bolt cutters on the top shelf. Each handle was almost two feet long.

"Got it," Gidion said as he walked in on Dad in the bedroom. The room itself was a mess, and not in the Grandpa way. Every drawer had been upended and all their contents dumped on the bed. Dad was digging through the pile of clothes. "Did you do this?"

"No, and it's a safe bet the police didn't." Dad looked under the bed. "Dammit."

Gidion knelt to see what the problem was. A piece of floorboard just under the far side of the bed was removed.

"Get me a flashlight."

Gidion pulled out his phone and crawled under the bed from the other side.

Dad scowled at him. "The display screen isn't bright enough. I need—"

Gidion turned on the light on his phone, which blinded Dad for a second. "Behold. I bring fire to the caveman."

"Your phone has a flashlight on it?"

"Yeah," he said, drawing out the word. "It's just the flash for the camera. Your phone does it, too."

"You'll have to show me how to do that later." Dad pointed at the hole. "See if there's a small box in there."

Gidion had to shift around a few times to adjust his angle, but he was pretty sure the only thing in the hole was dirt and probably spiders and bugs. Thankfully, nothing bit him.

"Sorry, nada."

Dad pulled out from beneath the bed to sit on the floor. He leaned against the wall by the window.

Gidion shifted back out from under the bed like a submissive dog in retreat. He was relieved when he managed to get free without banging the back of his head on the edge of the bed.

"What are we looking for?" Gidion asked.

"Not positive." Dad looked at a black-and-white picture of Grandpa with Grandma on the bedside table. The picture was one of those posed, studio portrait jobs with the fake forest background. They must have been a little younger in that picture than Dad was now, and the resemblance between him and Grandma was uncanny. They shared the same nose and eyes, but Dad had inherited Grandpa's ears, unfortunately. "Your Grandpa never let me see everything that was in that box, but the only time I saw him pull it out was when he told me a little about your Grandma. He'd been drinking enough to loosen up and talk about how they met. He showed me a picture of the two of them when they were in Paris before they married. Was a very touristy picture, the two of them in front of the Eiffel Tower.

"I always got the impression there might be more in that box, maybe even something about other hunters, how your Grandpa became one in the first place." Dad looked around the room. "I just really would have liked to have seen that picture of them again. The box was nothing fancy, just dull steel with a small Templar cross engraved on the top."

Gidion thought back to the other night, when the assassin got in here. "She didn't have it when she ran out."

"Might have already handed it off to her driver."

Gidion tried to think through that theory. Something didn't feel right about it, the idea of her searching through this room while waiting to spring her trap.

"She didn't search the rest of the house," Gidion said.

Dad stirred from whatever thoughts had distracted him. "What do you mean?"

"Why did she only search this room?" Gidion stood and pulled open the door to the closet. "Going by what the detective said, she must have been in here for an hour, but she only searched this room. That means she either knew what she was looking for and found it, or I got here before she could finish searching the rest of the house. An hour seems like plenty of time to search the whole place. Why stop with this room?"

Dad stood and glanced out into the den. Gidion already knew that room wasn't searched. The only sign of a mess came from his fight with the assassin.

"The most dangerous vampire is the one that gets away." Although Dad said it, Gidion recognized the wisdom from Grandpa's vampire hunter catechism. "We've been assuming this vampire came here for you. Maybe she came here for your grandpa."

Grandpa never talked about any of the vampires that got away from him, but he warned Gidion about the dangers. Hell, his house was a testament to what it meant to be an aging vampire hunter. The front and back doors both had a steel bar that could drop into place like a door bolt on steroids. The old man had placed an arsenal in this place so he could reach a weapon within two steps in any direction. That preparation saved Gidion's life the other night.

"I don't suppose that means she's done with us." Gidion wished that were true. Lord, he wanted this business done. He'd convinced himself Grandpa's death was all his fault. The idea that it might not be sounded inviting, but it didn't make him feel any better, probably because he didn't believe it.

Going by the look on Dad's face, he didn't buy into that theory either. "They abandoned the rental within a mile of our house. They aren't finished with us, not yet." He picked up the picture of Grandpa and Grandma on the bedside table. "I really would have liked to have gotten that picture of them in Paris."

Gidion thought about what Ms. Aldgate said, that there was something about Grandma that Dad hadn't shared. He decided to go for it.

"Why didn't you and Grandpa ever talk about Grandma?"

Dad glanced out the window and the fading light that promised sunset in an hour or less.

"We should go."

Even though Dad started to leave the room, Gidion crossed his arms and stood his ground by the closet. "Dad, what happened to Grandma?"

The look in Dad's eyes pled for Gidion to let this one go, but he wasn't going to.

"She killed herself." Dad's body shivered. He grabbed the frame to the bedroom door to steady himself. His voice caught as he struggled to say more. "Before I was born, even before they married, a coven abducted your Grandma. They held her captive for more than a week and kept feeding her vampire blood. They weren't trying to turn her. They wanted to get her addicted to their blood like one of their feeders. I don't know why they chose her. Your Grandpa never said, but he rescued her. Damage was done, though." Dad leaned his head against the door frame and closed his eyes. "She never really got past the withdrawals. She would cut herself and drink some of her own blood to take the edge off."

Dad kicked the door. It slammed against the wall and then shuddered to a halt on the rebound. "I was only twelve, had just walked home from school. Found her on the floor of the bathroom. Blood was everywhere. I don't know if she did it on purpose or if it was an accident—maybe cut herself too deeply while trying to get a taste of her blood."

Gidion had often seen Dad distracted, staring off at things he couldn't guess. The older Gidion got and the more he learned about his dad's days as a hunter, the more he wondered where Dad went in those moments. Looking at the picture of Grandma and Grandpa in his dad's hand, Gidion could reconstruct Dad's memory of her body in the bathroom. He'd taken enough heads and shed enough blood to know how it spilled, spread, and stained.

The house had been dark for Gidion when he found Grandpa. He never got a good look, and his imagination kept trying to fill in the blanks. Watching Dad stare through three decades into that blood-covered bathroom, he realized he'd always be trying to decipher every line of light and shadow of Grandpa's body for what had been there.

Dad slid the picture of Grandpa and Grandma into his jacket's inner pocket as he walked back into the den. Gidion found him walking the perimeter. He paused in front of one of Grandpa's katanas and lifted it from the cradle. He blew the thin layer of dust off the wooden saya. He gripped the hilt, wrapped in a dark green silk binding, and pulled the blade from its scabbard. The way he held the blade so close to his face, Dad looked like he was trying to catch the scent of the metal. Then he angled it to stare down its length at the wave of the fuller.

"That was Grandpa's favorite," Gidion said. He'd only gotten to hold it once, when Grandpa started his training. He made it clear that Gidion wouldn't get to use this one. Never mind that it was too long to conceal, but he said it came with a history.

"He ever tell you its name?" Dad asked as he twisted the blade to get a better look at its edge.

"Grandpa said naming a sword was a sissy thing to do."

Dad laughed before sliding the sword back into its scabbard. "In his defense, he didn't name it. This one came with a name, *Shi no Yoru*. Means 'Night of Death.'"

"Any of these others have names?"

Dad smiled. "No, naming swords is for sissies." There was no missing the hint of Grandpa's rough voice in the way Dad said that, and it was tough to tell if it was on purpose or just genetics rearing its head.

Gidion went straight towards the front door. Grandpa kept a katana with a blue wrapping on the handle and a matching, smaller wakizashi in a stand on a small table. The smaller sword was similar to the one the police had confiscated. He took both.

"We all set?" Gidion asked.

"You're not going with me tonight."

"That's stupid."

Dad shook his head. "I'm meeting someone for information. I don't plan to hunt."

The way Dad didn't meet his eyes to say that last part left Gidion unconvinced.

"If the person you're meeting isn't a threat, then what's the big deal?"

"I never said they weren't a threat."

"All the more reason to—"

"Gidion!" Dad pulled the front door open. "That's enough. Have you got your car keys?"

He could list a dozen reasons why Dad shouldn't go alone. Half of them made an argument for Gidion even going without him. When had he last hunted? Grandpa once admitted through gritted teeth that Dad was a better hunter in his prime than he ever was. That didn't mean much when Dad had let his skills collect dust for more than a decade.

Gidion held up his keys and jangled them. "Yes, I've got them."

"Good." Dad placed Night of Death in his car and then walked with Gidion to the Little Hearse.

They looked it over, inside and out, for any sign of a tracking device. "I don't think it's likely," Dad said as he crouched for a better look at the undercarriage, "but the price on your head could afford an assassin a lot of toys. Better to play it safe."

After searching the Little Hearse for fifteen minutes, they decided they were as certain as they could get.

"We go straight to Lillian's," Dad said.

"Actually, I promised Andrea I'd stop by her place."

Dad looked close to launching a protest, but then smiled. "All right. Go see her, but get to Lillian's right after that. Are we clear?"

Gidion nodded.

"And tell her I said, 'Thanks.'"

"For what?"

Dad looked at him like he was an idiot. "For saving your ass the other night."

Gidion didn't say anything, just nodded. The reminder that he'd nearly gotten himself killed by the assassin still stung.

He sent a text to Andrea to let her know he was on the way. He stayed behind Dad most of the way. No matter what Dad said, Gidion knew that him going alone tonight was a mistake. Unfortunately, there was no way to follow him without Dad spotting him. He needed to fix that, or Dad might not make it back home.

CHAPTER TWENTY-EIGHT

The first time Gidion visited Andrea's house, the single-story rancher and the front yard had been decorated for Halloween. Ever since then, the faded brick house looked obscenely plain by comparison.

He knocked on the door, using the rather generic brass knocker. No sooner had he let go of the knocker than the door flung open and Andrea jumped out to grab him in a hug.

Her words tumbled out too fast for him to even say a simple "Hi."

"Oh my God I'm so glad to see you I've been worried sick are you okay is your dad okay I'm so sorry about your grandpa is there anything I can do sorry I haven't texted more but I didn't want to drive you crazy or pester you I know this has got to be awful."

In spite of himself, Gidion laughed.

That earned him a stern look and a slap on the shoulder, thankfully the left.

"Ouch! What was that for?"

"You're laughing at me, Gidion Keep." She stomped back a step with her hands on her hips.

Andrea's mother walked up behind her. "I suspect he's just not used to dealing with people who speak in run-on sentences."

Andrea fixed a melodramatic glare on her mother. It was nice to see that his dad wasn't the only parent who took a perverse pleasure in dishing out snark to their child in front of others.

"How are you and your father holding up?" Ms. Templeton asked as she waved him into the house and closed the door behind him.

"We're okay."

The awkward silence that followed made it clear she'd interpreted his answer for the opposite of what he'd said. She was right.

"Thanks for asking," he said, more to end the awkwardness. He glanced at the inside of the house. He'd only been inside here a few times since he and Andrea had started studying together. The condition of the place often varied. Even though it was just Andrea and her mom living here, the place sometimes turned into a mess. Her mom worked as an accountant and did a lot of costume work for the community theaters. Sometimes they kept the den pristine. Other times, Andrea's mom buried it in all manner of clothing supplies or tax documents. Paperwork had conquered the den this evening.

"Have the police found out anything?" Ms. Templeton asked.

"Not really. We still don't know who the lady was."

"Well, I'm glad you didn't get hurt."

Gidion might have grown up without a mom, but he didn't miss the undertone to Ms. Templeton's words. Her entire posture was different from normal with her arms crossed and positioned so that she was almost between Gidion and Andrea. A step to her left and she would have blocked Andrea from his view. She didn't know how much to trust him, and truth be told, the lady was smart to think that way. Andrea might have been killed, and he put her in that situation.

None of them moved. Gidion couldn't think of what to say to get out of this position.

"Can Gidion stay for dinner?" Andrea asked.

Whether the idea terrified him or her mother more was a tough call.

"I can't." Gidion saw the tension melt from Ms. Templeton's shoulders when he said that. "My dad wants me home as soon as possible. I probably shouldn't stay more than a half hour."

Given that it was almost sunset, he expected Dad to have one of his "father fits" by the time he reached Ms. Aldgate's house.

"In that case," Andrea reached around her mom to take Gidion by the hand and pulled him to the hallway and dragged him to her room.

Andrea's mom called after them. "The door stays open."

"Yes, Mother." Andrea rolled her eyes. She didn't close her door, but that didn't stop her from pushing it to within an inch of the door frame.

She smiled at him, but now that they were alone and in her room, Andrea's eagerness vanished into a nervous wobble. He glanced around the room, because staring at her felt dangerous. The walls were painted lavender, at least the parts of the wall that weren't hidden by furniture or movie posters, which included *Hunger Games* and *Ladyhawke*.

He canted his head in the direction of the den. "I take it you didn't tell her about..."

"Oh, yeah, sure." She slapped him on the shoulder, lighter this time as she kept her voice to a whisper. "You see, Mom, I'm dumping my loser boyfriend for that cute guy, the one who hunts vampires."

It took him a moment to realize what she'd just said. He fumbled for a reply, and what came out probably wasn't his best choice. "So how have you been getting to school? I mean, I'm assuming you aren't riding with Seth now."

No missing that mistake, not with laser beams shooting out of her eyes.

"No, I've not been riding with He Who Shall Not Be Named." She turned and then sat on the end of her bed. "I've been riding with my mom."

"Ah, yeah." He looked for a place to sit. She had a desk, but the chair was occupied by a stack of books. He looked back at her, positioned in the center of the bed. That didn't leave enough room for him. The look on her face held a challenge to it, but he wasn't sure if that meant he needed to ask if he could sit or if she wanted him to suffer on his feet.

"Well?" Her smirk put him even more off balance. She was toying with him. No question there.

"Should I ask if it's okay to sit?"

Oh, great. She was peeved again, arms crossed and her face

giving him the full-on Medusa glare.

"What you should be doing is explaining what the heck happened the other night," she said and then added, "without me needing to ask."

Gidion pointed to the edge of the bed. She scooted over for him. "I'll answer what I can," he said as he took his assigned seat, "but I can't stay too long. The vampire who killed my Grandpa is also after me."

Andrea didn't let him get away with a Cliff's Notes version of his vampire hunting career. He checked the time on his phone a few times. As he told her how he'd finished off the Richmond Coven months ago by burning the house down with them inside, she moved another inch away from him.

"Are you believing any of this?"

"I'm not sure I want to." She touched his shoulder, the one where he'd been cut by the assassin. The way she gingerly touched it made it clear she was thinking about that. He smiled at her, relieved she was willing to touch him.

"My Grandpa had to show me." She never saw the assassin that night. He'd chased her out the back of the house.

"Explains a lot, though. You really are like Batman."

Gidion laughed. "Wish I had his bank account and half of his gadgets."

"Well, you've at least got me."

"Actually, that's another reason I came here. I need your help."

She pulled back again as he said that. Ouch. He deserved it, too. The main reason he'd come here was because of this, and she probably sensed it. "I need to borrow your phone."

That part of the conversation didn't go smoothly, not at all. As he explained why he needed it and what he planned to do, he worried she'd refuse to help him. She pulled her phone out and stared at it.

"When I heard those gunshots from your grandfather's house, I wanted to drive away like you'd told me to."

"You should have." He smiled as he said that, thinking about

Dad's request to thank her for calling the police.

"If I had, I'd never have forgiven myself." She reached for his hand and gripped it. "I was scared I'd be leaving you to get killed. I don't think that's something I could live with."

Gidion thought about when they'd been sitting on the park table that night. That same desire to kiss her was back. He didn't ignore it this time.

This wasn't his first kiss or hers, but he felt his body shake as he tilted her face to look him in the eyes. She looked just as scared, like a wild animal that knows it's crawled into a trap. Their lips met, timid at first, but as their kiss lingered, they grew more confident. They fit together just right, and if her mom hadn't been there, he wondered how much longer they might have stayed that way.

He smiled at her as he stroked the back of her hand with his thumb. "You do realize you saved me that night, right?"

"What are you talking about?"

"Calling the police," he said. "My dad even told me to thank you for him, because if they hadn't shown, that assassin would have killed me."

She leaned back, and her stare left little doubt she was still confused. "I didn't call the police. I was close to doing it, but then I heard the sirens and saw them pull up."

"But they came straight to the house." That made no sense. Thanks to his dad, he knew enough about how police responded on those kinds of things to know there was no way they'd have been going lights and sirens for someone just saying they'd heard gunshots in the area. They needed to know someone was being targeted by the gunshots. "Did you tell them which house to go into when they got there?"

She shook her head. "I didn't say anything until a cop came up to the car and asked me why I was there."

Gidion's phone vibrated with a text from his dad. "I need to go."

She placed her phone in his hand. "I better get this back."

A few minutes later, she walked him out to his car as a light rain started. Gidion fought the urge to kiss her the way they had in her room. He kept this kiss short, despite the hunger he could feel from her lips.

"Sorry." He looked up and down the street—the few parked cars all looked unoccupied, but that didn't mean much. "It's just not safe for us to linger outside. I'll email you later, okay?"

"You better. Don't get hurt tonight."

He kissed her again, another quick one.

His windshield wipers squeaked as he drove for Ms. Aldgate's house. Half of his ride there, he thought about that kiss in Andrea's bedroom, but the rest of the time, he kept asking himself the same question.

If Andrea wasn't the one who called the police, then who did and why?

CHAPTER TWENTY-NINE

The light rain turned into something much heavier and unpleasant by the time Gidion pulled onto Ms. Aldgate's street. He was relieved to find Dad's car still there. He parked behind the blue Corolla.

He didn't go inside right away, and when he eventually approached the front door, he spotted Page's head sticking through the curtains to watch him.

He knocked five times, the first two knocks slow and the last three close together. Dad had insisted on that as a pass code of sorts. Four fast knocks by themselves would have indicated he was in trouble.

Dad pulled the door open and looked past Gidion. He'd already pulled out his sword. If he didn't have a hand on the hilt and the other on the door, Dad probably would have pulled him inside.

"I did the knock right."

Dad didn't look at him, focused on the front yard and the street. Gidion already knew all too well that the only thing moving was rainwater flowing into the gutters.

"You were out there a long time," Dad said as he locked the door.

Before Gidion answered, he caught the scent of what could only be dinner.

"Chili?"

Ms. Aldgate had camped out on her couch with her large purple school bag sitting at her feet. A stack of papers were piled onto the coffee table. She held a red "Pen of Doom" in her hand as she graded quizzes. Gidion couldn't say he was sorry to have missed that part of school today.

"Yes," she said, "making your father cook seemed kinder than charging rent." She didn't look up as she said that, but he could hear the smirk in her voice.

"Good choice. Dad's not a great cook with most things, but his chili—"

Before he could finish his sentence, Dad barked his protest as he went back into the kitchen. "I heard that!"

"Hey, I was going to add that your chili is one thing you cook better than anyone else."

"One thing?" Dad sounded ready to pick his sword back up and go a round with Gidion.

"I didn't say it was the only thing." Seeing Dad was busy checking on the pot of spicy good stuff on the stove, Gidion turned to Ms. Aldgate as she looked up at him. He mouthed to her, "It really is the only thing."

Even though she turned her attention back to the quiz in front of her, she said, "I trust Andrea was pleased to see you?" She had this very knowing tone, too.

"You could say that." Gidion couldn't stop himself from smiling.

"I hear she broke up with Seth Parson."

"She's officially calling him 'He Who Shall Not Be Named.'"

She made a mean looking "X" on the sheet she was grading. "Is she doing all right?"

Gidion cleared his throat. "Oh, she's doing fine." Oh so very, very fine, he thought to himself.

"Good, then I suppose you two can finally start dating."

"Hey!" Even to him, the attempt at indignation sounded pretty weak.

"Oh, please, if you two get any worse about mooning over each other in my class, I'll be moving you both to opposite sides of the room."

Dad leaned into the den. "Trust me, just move them now. I've heard nothing but 'Andrea this,' and 'Andrea that,' out of his mouth ever since the start of the school year."

"Really, Dad? I couldn't stand her when the school year started."

That was true, too. She annoyed the ever-loving hell out of him.

They responded in unison with Dad going, "Bingo," and Ms. Aldgate saying, "Exactly."

He realized he wasn't going to win this one and headed into the kitchen. "Anyway, we have a small problem."

That got Dad's attention. He stopped stirring the chili and leaned against the counter. Talk about a sign of how bad things were. Dad was actually taking him seriously.

"I thanked Andrea for you," he said, then added, "for calling the police."

"And that would be a problem because?"

"She didn't make the call."

Dad stared into space as he processed that detail in a way that reminded Gidion of a computer. "When the police showed up, were they going code three?"

"Lights and sirens." Gidion nodded. "Came straight for Grandpa's house, too. Someone called and gave them all the right details to get the police there as fast as possible."

"Any idea who it might have been?"

Gidion shook his head.

"And you're sure Andrea wasn't lying?"

"When I thanked her for calling 911, she was completely confused. Besides, why would she lie?"

Dad took off his glasses and rubbed the bridge of his nose. "We have a third player."

"Are you sure that's a bad thing?" Ms. Aldgate asked. She'd gotten up and was standing in the doorway to the kitchen. "That call saved Gidion's life. That suggests this third party is on your side."

"I wouldn't be too quick to assume that." Dad didn't look up from his thoughts as he said that. "If they're really interested in helping us, then why haven't they contacted us? Plenty of ways they could have done that, even without us being at our house."

"Back before Grandpa installed the security system at the funeral home, he said he was going to make some phone calls." Gidion hadn't given that any thought until now. "Calling a security company is one call. What if he called in some extra help?"

"I don't think he had contact with any other hunters. In all the years since I first started hunting, he never gave me an indication he knew any. I never ran into anyone either."

"Doesn't mean they aren't out there." The idea of extra hunters, especially now, was the kind of encouragement Gidion could use.

Dad turned his back to them, taking the lid back off the chili to stir it. "I don't think it was another hunter. Doesn't make sense."

"Because they called the police instead of going in after the vampire themselves?" Ms. Aldgate asked.

"Exactly." Dad didn't look up from stirring the chili. "Might be another vampire, someone with a grudge against this assassin."

"Is it really so unlikely that it was just a neighbor?" Ms. Aldgate asked. "Maybe they saw Gidion and this vampire fighting through the window."

Dad looked back at Gidion. "Well?"

"I doubt it." He'd be lying if he didn't admit that part of him didn't want that to be true. The idea of more hunters offered some hope. Why should the vampires be the only ones with some kind of underground network?

He didn't realize they'd all gone silent until a phone vibrated. Gidion reached for his pocket to pull out his phone and check. "Not me."

"No, it's me." Dad pulled out his phone and made a visible effort to hide whatever message he'd just received from both Gidion and Ms. Aldgate. "It's the person I'm meeting tonight." He put the phone away without responding to the message.

"And?" Gidion asked.

"And you don't need to worry about it. This is something I need to do alone, and it won't take that long."

Ms. Aldgate had kept silent, but one look made it clear this was a silent protest. Maybe Gidion could draw her in to back him up on this.

"Look, you finally agreed it was better to have a backup when it came to the funeral home," Gidion said. "I don't see what the difference is."

"That was because we knew we were probably dealing with a vampire." Dad turned his back to them as he pulled some bowls from the cabinets. "This is an informant. I won't be in any danger, and they might not show if I bring someone they don't know."

Dad had called this person an informant more than once, but the way Dad said it left Gidion convinced it was code for "friendly vampire." As far as he was concerned, there was no such thing. He didn't care what Dad said.

"You should go wash up, son." Gidion recognized that was more code speak, this time for Gidion to get out of the room so Dad could have a moment with Ms. Aldgate.

"Sure." Maybe she'd talk some sense into him, not that Gidion had much faith in that happening.

Gidion needed to test something before Dad left anyway, and the sooner he got a moment alone to test it, the better.

• • •

The one-on-one between Dad and Ms. Aldgate didn't go well. The silence over dinner proved that. If he'd served her a bowl of nails instead of chili, she'd have chewed through it just as easily.

Gidion waited to make his last argument until well after dinner. Dad was standing by the front door, getting ready to leave.

"This is stupid. You let me go with you to the funeral home, and I've been dealing with vampires more than you this past year."

"You aren't needed for this." Dad glared at him over the edge of his sword, giving the blade one last check. Gidion had asked if he was going to take *Shi no Yoru*, but Dad insisted that Night of Death would always be Grandpa's sword. "I'm just meeting someone for a conversation, not to hunt."

"You've checked that sword a lot of times for someone just going to have a conversation." To Gidion's surprise, that observation came from Ms. Aldgate.

"Lil, I need you to trust me on this. I won't be long." He slid the sword back into its wooden scabbard. "Three hours, at the most."

"I could just drive," Gidion said, "and wait in the car."

"Enough, Gidion." He didn't shout, but Dad never needed to. As deep as his voice could go, just the barest hint of anger turned the simplest warning into the equivalent of a steel beam to the head. Ms. Aldgate must not have seen that side of Dad much, if at all, because she was watching both of them with this wide-eyed surprise.

Gidion offered his best glare to Dad, for what that was worth.

"Look, I'll be back soon." He placed a hand on Gidion's shoulder. "I promise. Just trust me. There's a good chance we can end all of this tonight."

He kissed Ms. Aldgate next. "I'd say don't wait up," he said, "but I suspect there's no point."

"You would be right." They kissed again, and despite how irritated he was with Dad, Gidion couldn't hold back a grin. He'd never seen Dad kiss a woman. The past decade, he might as well have been a monk for all the lack of dating. If not for Gidion, the man would have been a hermit.

Ms. Aldgate's head nestled into Dad's shoulder. "Please be careful," she whispered.

"Always am." Dad pointed at Gidion with the butt of his sword's hilt. "Hold down the fort." The gesture revealed he was wearing the *Gatchaman* wristband Gidion gave him on his birthday. Gidion hoped it would bring him enough luck to keep him safe, but he kept the thought to himself.

Dad pulled open the door and walked out.

Gidion stood next to Ms. Aldgate in the doorway. They stayed there until Dad made a u-turn in his car and disappeared down the street. Gidion was the first to walk away from the door. He headed for the guest room, but Ms. Aldgate's voice stopped him.

"You do know my window in that room is painted shut, right?"

Shit. "Not sure what you mean, Ms. Aldgate."

"You are twice as stubborn as your father, and I've listened to you argue yourself blue in the face in my class even when it was obvious you were wrong."

"Hey, the pyramids could absolutely have been built by aliens. You can't prove they weren't."

"You're only proving my point." Ms. Aldgate closed her front door and locked it. "That was the lamest attempt at a protest I have ever heard out of your mouth. It barely qualified as a token effort. The only reason I think your father didn't realize it is because he has a bad habit of seeing what he wants to see."

Gidion didn't have an argument for that. "Your point?"

"My point is that the window in my guest room is painted shut, and if you break that window to sneak out, I will kick your ass from here to the East End."

"I wasn't going to break your window." Gidion sighed. She'd pretty much read him right the whole way except for that. "I was going to use the rain as an excuse to take Page out with an umbrella to use the bathroom."

She got a far-off look as she considered that. "That probably would have worked, too. So how are you planning to track your father? You must have something figured out."

"Yeah, I'm tracking Dad's car."

"How did you—Oh, never mind." She rolled her eyes and sat on the sofa. Her school work was still piled in neat stacks on the sofa cushions, coffee table and floor. "Your plan was stupid."

"Stupid! You just said it would have worked."

She pointed at him with the Red Pen of Doom as if to give him an F for his effort at subterfuge. "To get out of my house, yes, but you can't really believe that barking machine would have kept quiet in your car and not given you away."

Page curled up on the floor in front of the television. She licked her lips, her big brown eyes going between the two humans in the room as if she realized she was the focus of their discussion.

"Okay, yeah." Gidion shrugged. "That was a bit of a risk, depending on where Dad goes."

"Well, fortunately for you, I agree that your father is being an idiot. Leave the dog, and get after him."

Gidion ran for the guest room and quickly changed. He layered up about the same as he had the night he'd run into GQ Drac outside of the Blue Goat. The only difference this time was that he put his black t-shirt with the red bat on over the turtleneck. He wasn't going to risk burying his luck tonight.

He geared up. Even though the police had the box cutter he'd dropped in Grandpa's house, he still had Ms. Aldgate's. He also brought the katana and wakizashi he'd taken from Grandpa's earlier today.

Last but not least, he grabbed his phone. He'd left it charging, and a quick check showed the battery was at a hundred percent.

Ms. Aldgate stopped him just short of the front door. Lord, what now?

"Not so fast."

She hugged him, the hilts of the swords trapped between them. The gesture caught him off guard. The emotions of the past few days, Grandpa's death and all the secrets that had spilled into the open from him and Dad, choked him.

"Are you sure this isn't a mistake?" She reached into his hood and brushed a stray hair into place.

"Yeah."

"Then I'll be in the bathroom."

"Huh?"

She disappeared around the corner into the hallway. "That's how you're getting out without me seeing you."

Gidion admired that. She could be pretty damn sneaky. This way, she wouldn't be lying when Dad pitched a fit later. Nice.

He covered the swords with his jacket before he ran out the door. The rain hit his face like ice pellets, sending a shiver through his body. He placed the swords on the floorboard of the backseat before diving into his car.

He plugged in his phone to play some appropriate hunting music, going for some Imagine Dragons. As Dan Reynolds pounded out the lyrics to "Friction," Gidion opened the web browser on his phone. The website for the GPS tracking account Andrea's mom used had stayed logged in. This was the same GPS app her mom used the other night to figure out when she'd been in Church Hill with him. Andrea helped him set it up before he left her house. A map displayed and showed the location of Andrea's phone. Before going into Ms. Aldgate's house earlier, he'd hidden Andrea's phone in the trunk of Dad's car.

According to the app, Dad was traveling eastbound on Midlothian Turnpike, not far from here.

"Andrea, I owe you big time."

He'd tried to get his hands on Dad's phone to load something like this, but anything he could afford lacked the level of stealth required. Besides, that meant finding a way to hack into his phone. Most any app he'd found that he could afford, would send a notification to Dad's phone. He'd be busted. Besides, he had no guarantee Dad wouldn't turn off the phone once he got wherever he was going.

The request to plot Andrea's phone would also send a notification to her phone, displaying on her phone's screen as it had the other night in Church Hill, but with the phone hidden beneath the mat in the trunk of the car, Dad wouldn't know it.

Gidion was forced to do a bit of stop and go. Especially with the roads slick from the rain, he couldn't check the GPS tracker and drive at the same time. He drove just short of each plot, pulled over into a nearby parking lot, and repeated the process. Gidion didn't go very far before he realized Dad had already stopped.

His car plotted along Woolridge Road, a little ways off the Midlothian Turnpike, not far from the Urban Farmhouse where Gidion studied with Andrea. Most of that area was residential, though. Surely he wasn't meeting with someone in a house or townhome. If the person had one of those there, then why would Dad have waited until tonight to meet with them? That's when it occurred to Gidion that he wasn't technically tracking Dad's car. He was tracking Andrea's phone. What if Dad had found it and ditched it?

Gidion stopped in the lot of a large fitness center to make the latest plot. He zoomed in on the map to check Dad's exact location.

If it plotted right, then Dad wasn't meeting at someone's house. Dad stopped at the entrance for the Midlothian Mines Park. Gidion had never actually gone there, just driven past it.

He ran a quick Google search on the park, not that it helped him much. Changing the map view to display a satellite picture of the area showed a bunch of trees with several neighborhoods bordering it on opposite sides. There were two places to park, with one of the lots located across Woolridge next to Loch Lothian. That part he recognized from driving by it many times in the past. A wooden structure that reminded him of a stubby, short skeletal tower was positioned next to the loch. Dad plotted on the other side of Woolridge where most of the park was located. That assumed the plot was good and that Dad hadn't tossed Andrea's phone.

Dad had left the house at about a quarter to ten. He and Dad both tended to time things so they arrived almost right as the event started. Going by that, Gidion figured the meet must be set for ten o'clock. The clock on his dashboard already showed it was a minute past that.

So the next question was where they were meeting: in the park or did they just plan to rendezvous at the park and then go somewhere else? If they were meeting there, then they'd either stayed with their cars or gone into the park.

Then he realized...if they met in the lot and planned to go somewhere else, Dad might leave his car and ride with the contact.

Gidion zipped out of the lot onto Woolridge and floored it. If his dad left in another car, he didn't have a way to track him.

He slowed his car as he neared the park. Trees hid the parking area on the left where Andrea's phone plotted. He also glanced at the parking area on the right. He didn't see any cars, just a tall, wooden structure that the park website had called a headstock, a type of mining machine.

Gidion kept going down Woolridge until he reached the shopping center with the Urban Farmhouse and the library. He turned around and went back towards the park. From this direction, thanks in part to the way the road curved, he saw his dad's blue

Toyota in the parking lot. Another car was parked on the other side of Dad's.

Gidion parked on the opposite side of the road in front of the wooden headstock. A sign warned against parking here after dark. The same held true for the lot across the road. That suggested Dad wasn't going anywhere else. He ran the risk of the car getting towed if he left it there too long.

The parking lot Gidion chose turned out to be bigger than he expected. The lot sloped enough to hide his car from the road.

The rain ensured Dad couldn't know he was here. This stretch of road was especially dark, too. Gidion considered waiting in his nice warm, dry car. He couldn't see the road well, and if Dad left, he'd never know it. Even worse, if the assassin attacked Dad in the park, Gidion wouldn't know until it was too late.

He pulled up his hood and climbed out of the car. The rain came down harder than when he left Ms. Aldgate's. That might help him go unnoticed, but it also made it more difficult to see if Dad was in his car once he got across the street.

Gidion grabbed the swords from the backseat. The katana went through his belt on his left hip. He wore the new wakizashi he'd taken from Grandpa's on his back, using the same strap that kept his regular sword in place.

Something told him that if he needed a sword tonight, having two might not be a bad idea. The park also stayed secluded enough to make the katana less of an issue. Now that he considered it, Dad's decision to take his longer sword with him made a meet in the park a lot more plausible.

Gidion squinted against the raindrops getting in his eyes as he checked both ways on Woolridge. After he decided the four-lane road was clear, he sprinted for the other side.

Would be just his luck if a cop decided to come down this road now. Sure, the park would be secluded enough for the katana, but he had to get in it first.

Once on the other side, he crept up to the trees that blocked his view of the small lot. Dad parked near the back next to a black

Mustang, not the typical vampire car given the limited trunk space. Dad might not be meeting a bloodsucker, after all. That begged the question of who or what he was meeting?

Gidion pushed his way into the trees for a better look. He hoped he wasn't giving himself away, but the weather wouldn't make it easy for Dad to notice him. The leaves and branches above him funneled the rain into a miniature waterfall. His clothes had soaked in so much rain, he felt like he wore more water than fabric.

Deciding Dad's car was empty, Gidion moved down the treeline to get a better look at the Mustang. The sports car came from South Carolina, going by its license plate. The rental the assassin used came from Georgia, also on the southeastern coast. He wondered if that was a coincidence, or if he was just searching for non-existent connections.

So with the cars empty, that meant they'd either gone into the park or left in a third car. Gidion assumed Dad planned to meet with one person, but he'd refused to share any details.

After a short internal debate that amounted to little more than going "eeny, meeny, miney, moe," Gidion decided to search the park. He found the path to the right of the parking lot's entrance. A small sign mounted on a pole warned against trespassing after dark. Gidion kissed his fingertips and then pressed the kiss to his chest where the red bat was on his t-shirt.

The asphalt path lacked any artificial light. It curved to the left and led him under more tree cover. The thick foliage above blocked what little natural light the clouds might have permitted. Sadly, the trees didn't stop the rain from pelting him.

He decided to risk the flashlight on his phone, which did little more than brighten his surroundings to a lighter shade of pitch. He kept the light pointed straight down and adjusted the brightness, reducing it to a weak glow. The light improved the chances of a vampire spotting him, but Gidion couldn't risk stepping off the path into a ditch.

A short way into the park, the path split, giving him a choice to push straight ahead or turn right onto a narrow bridge. He assumed that would take him back towards Woolridge Road, so he stayed straight.

He slowed as he neared what looked like a bench on his right. No one was using it. The rain increased its belligerence as the trees cleared to his right. A flash of his light in that direction revealed a small stream running parallel to the path. That made him a bit more cautious as he continued, not wanting to misstep and fall into that water.

For all his focus on navigating in the dark, he kept puzzling over who Dad was meeting. He also thought about Andrea and how good it felt to kiss her. He really wished he was doing more of that right now and not freezing his ass off.

He reached a short, wooden bridge where the creek turned to intersect the path. Gidion worried that walking on the wooden bridge would be noisy, but his footsteps on the bridge didn't make a sound. The path beyond the bridge turned out to be much worse. Dirt and gravel replaced the pavement he'd walked on up to this point. Each step crunched and filled him with panic. He slowed his pace, but it lessened the noise very little. He hoped the loud patter of the rain would conceal his steps.

Everything about the park placed him at a disadvantage: the darkness, the noisy gravel, and all the potential hiding places. The terrain changed, replacing the ditch on his right with a tall hill. That provided far too many hiding places for a potential ambush. He stopped every few steps to flash his light across the edge of the hill, searching for any movement. The area to his left became more inconsistent, sometimes a steep ditch and then other times a hill.

The path turned into an incline. The rain ebbed. He stopped as he heard a voice from somewhere over the hill. He couldn't discern anything being said, but he realized there were two voices. One was Dad. The other belonged to a woman.

He stopped and turned off his phone's light, putting it away. The voices continued, apparently oblivious to his presence. He still couldn't tell what was being said, but he picked up the tone of the voices. Little wonder he hadn't drawn their attention. They sounded too busy arguing.

He needed to get closer, but that risked being heard or seen.

After giving his eyes a chance to adjust to the dark, Gidion crept up the path. He placed each step with care. Just because he'd managed to avoid detection this far didn't mean his luck would last and made him long for the rabbit's foot he'd tossed aside in anger.

He put his phone away and gripped the hilt of the katana. The way he'd positioned the sword on his left hip, the butt of the hilt was almost right in front of his belt buckle. A documentary he'd watched during a History Channel binge had talked about how samurai would quick-draw their swords like gunfighters, waiting until the moment they needed to strike. He didn't hold much faith in his ability to do that, even if he was wearing the weapon properly, so he drew the sword to have it ready.

After he reached the top of the hill, he saw down into a clearing. He moved to the right edge of the path to crouch in the shadows of trees.

Dad and the woman stood near the far end of the clearing, just past some ruins on the right side of the path. What little moonlight made it through the trees illuminated the crumbling structure. God only knew what the building might have been back when the mines were active, although the layout of the bricks and wooden beams that were visible from his position reminded him of a small church. A chain-link fence with barbed wires along the top kept anyone from getting close to the ruined building.

Dad's military-grade flashlight, a holdover from his police officer days, provided the only means to see him and the woman arguing with him. Unlike Gidion, he wasn't trying to hide. Unfortunately, Dad had the light pointed at the ground, which kept any details of the woman hidden.

Every step Gidion took sounded as loud as thunder to him, so even with the rain in his favor, he stayed put. Much as he wanted to hear what Dad and the lady informant said, he didn't come for that. All he wanted was to make sure Dad got home safely. He could do that from here.

The woman yelled louder, letting Gidion pick up bits of words, even if he didn't catch whole sentences. She sounded desperate. Dad lowered his voice and reached for her neck, but not to grab her. He caressed her throat. The flashlight shifted enough to see a flash of the woman's long, red hair and a pair of sunglasses.

Holy shit. Dad was meeting with a shade. The informant was a vampire.

She spoke, her voice firm enough for Gidion to understand exactly what she said.

"I'll do whatever it takes." Her next two words came out loud and firm. "I promise."

Then she kissed him, and it wasn't the hesitant embrace of a stranger. Dad answered in kind. His arms slid around her, the flashlight pressed against her back.

Anger burned in Gidion's chest. If Dad had been within arm's reach, he'd have hit him. This was a betrayal in every way—to Grandpa, to Mom, to Ms. Aldgate, and sure as hell to him.

Dad wanted to come without him because of this. How long had this been going on? Back in the gym at Dad's work, he talked about a fight with Mom. Had this been why? Had she found out about Dad and this shade?

Was this what got Mom killed?

He stood. To hell with stealth. He deserved answers, and he was going down there to get them.

Before he could take the first step, someone else moved. Down the path, just ten yards in front of him, a shadow the shape of a man emerged from the trees.

More shadows shifted on the path, just beyond Dad and the shade. The beam from the flashlight shifted against the woman's back and ran over the man rushing from his hiding place along the path behind her.

Gidion saw two things in that split second. The man was a vampire, and he had a gun pointed at Dad.

CHAPTER THIRTY

Vampires pride themselves on their ability to hide in plain sight. Grandpa taught Gidion that when he started his training. That rule came with a caveat: some vampires don't understand the true meaning of stealth and some are too stupid to give a shit.

Ever since Gidion started hunting, he'd never run into a vampire with a gun. Tonight, he'd stumbled onto an entire gang of them, and if he didn't play this smart, he'd get himself and his dad killed.

Without a word or the war cry he desperately wanted to unleash, he charged up behind the vampire closest to him.

He issued a silent prayer to God, and a list of need tumbled through his mind in that split second. Don't let this vampire hear me. Make my aim true. Let this sword's blade make the kill. Don't let me get shot. Don't let me trip. Give me some damn answers. Make me faster. Keep me alive. Give me a chance to do more than just kiss Andrea. Don't let me get Dad killed. Let those vampires be here for the shade and kill her instead.

Running up behind the vampire, he lost sight of Dad and the shade. The vampire's blond buzz cut made the back of his pale neck a clear target. A step too late to stop Gidion's swing, the vampire heard him and turned. A stray line of moonlight revealed the black handgun in the vampire's right hand. He never got to aim it.

The katana's blade buried into his throat. The swing fell short of completely shaving off the vampire's head, but the blade made it deep enough. According to Grandpa, the older ones could survive most anything. He claimed one duct taped his throat until his healing ability fixed things. This vampire dropped his gun as he reached for his throat, not that it helped. His body collapsed with the sword still stuck in his neck. Clearly, a younger vampire.

Gidion almost lost his grip on the hilt as the vampire dropped, but he jerked the sword free in time. He wasn't interested in taking any heads, though. Not yet. He snatched the fallen gun off the ground.

He was too late to warn Dad. The vampires had already gotten the drop on Dad but not before he drew his sword. Gidion couldn't make out the details of the fight, but at least the vampires hadn't shot him.

Gidion gripped the fallen vampire's gun and aimed it at the ground. Much as he wanted to shoot the vampires, he needed to get a lot closer to be sure he hit them instead of Dad. Grandpa had given him enough practice with guns to know how hard it was to aim a gun, even from a short distance. He held his arm as straight and rigid as possible as he braced for the recoil and pulled the trigger. The handgun pushed back, but after shooting Grandpa's rifle the other night, the recoil was negligible in comparison.

The noise, however, was not. He wondered if he'd make it through this week without permanent damage to his hearing, assuming he lived that long. He fired the gun three times to make sure it would get the attention of the people living in the neighborhoods around the park. One of the casings bounced off his arm after it ejected from the chamber. The gunshots wouldn't bring the cops with their lights and sirens, but they should send a lot of people reaching for their phones to call 911. The people in the nearby homes were why he'd also aimed for the ground and not into the air, which would be a fine way to accidentally get someone shot when the bullet fell back to earth.

He looked back in Dad's direction. He counted at least four vampires around his dad, not counting the shade. The unexpected gunfire had stalled the fight.

"Gidion, run!"

The vampires aimed in his direction. He ran for the edge of the path and hoped the trees might shield him. Through the ringing in his ears, he heard the gunfire and the whistle of the bullets as they whizzed past him.

"No!" That shout didn't come from Dad. The shade grabbed one of the vampires by the arm.

Dad moved faster than Gidion would have ever expected. He charged the closest vampire and slammed the blade of his sword into its throat. He grabbed the shade by her arm, pulling her back to use himself as a shield to protect her from the other vampires.

Before Dad could attack the other three, the shade pulled out a gun of her own and slammed the butt of the grip into the back of his head.

"Dad!"

He crumpled to the ground. The unexpected attack didn't take all the fight out of him, but one of the remaining vampires pinned him. Dad roared as he struggled.

Gidion ran down the hill towards them, but then the vampire raised his gun to shoot. The anticipated gunfire forced him off the path and into the woods, running along the edge of the fence wrapped around the ruins. To Gidion's surprise, the gunshots never followed. He heard the shade yell something again, but couldn't make it out this time. The only thing he felt certain of was that she was the one giving the orders.

Not knowing what else to do, Gidion ran around the ruins, along the outside of the fence. From what he'd seen, that would bring him out on the far side of the ruins and just a few feet from where Dad was. He might make it close enough to catch them by surprise and kill the remaining vamps. His plan also risked that the vampires might surround him. If he ran fast enough, he might turn that against them, split them up and make the kills.

The rain-soaked mud sucked at his shoes as he ran. He still had the gun in his right hand, but as long as he held it, then the sword in his left was of little use and the gun wouldn't kill a vampire. That was another of Grandpa's warnings. Guns only wounded a vampire. You needed a powerful shot to do any damage that lasted more than a few seconds. Unless you hit them in the eye, the jugular or the heart, you might as well throw pebbles.

Gidion ran behind the ruins. From here he saw the rectangular glow of the nearby homes' windows. He couldn't decide if he was better off with the people in those houses calling the police. So far, the only kill belonged to him, so odds favored he'd be the one to go to jail, if he got caught.

Nearby lightning blinded him for a split second. Thunder shook the ground. For the first time, he wondered if anyone had actually heard the gunfire through this storm.

Then he rounded the next turn along the fence, which placed him on the far side of the ruins. That gave him his first warning. He should have run into one of the vampires by now, if they'd tried to surround him. They could see in the dark far better than he could and would have moved much faster. When he made it all the way to the path, another flash of lightning struck, giving him a clear view of the area. No sign of Dad, the shade, or the other vampires. He didn't even see the one Dad had sent to the ground.

"Dad!" He hoped Dad might be alert enough to respond, but he didn't answer. Instead, Gidion found himself trying to guess which way the vampires went. Only now did he realize he'd surrendered the path to them. Running into the woods had given them a clear shot at reaching the parking lot without a fight, but he didn't expect them to move this fast.

He had a choice: push deeper into the park or run for the parking lot. The latter made more sense to him, so he headed back the way he'd come. He tossed the gun into the woods. At this point, it wasn't helping him. The vampires must be carrying his dad, so he couldn't risk a shot anyway.

He ran over the hill, the path curving. The wind picked up, and the rain dropped in buckets. He raised his hand to block the water from his eyes, his drenched hood rendered almost worthless for protection. More lightning offered him a clear view down the empty path. He reached the bridge. His footfalls were loud slaps against the wood and then the welcome asphalt once he made it to the other side.

He stopped when he reached the turn with the first bridge

going towards Woolridge that he'd seen earlier. For what little good it did him, he used the flashlight on his phone to look down the path towards the parking lot and then the bridge to his left. His light reflected off something down the bridge.

Running onto the bridge, he realized it was Dad's sword. Gidion slid his sword into its scabbard. Had Dad caused them to drop it, a breadcrumb for Gidion? They might have decided stopping to retrieve it was too risky, but just as likely was that they'd tossed it here to lead him down the wrong path. Worst of all, it might be a distraction to make him stay still long enough to shoot him.

The last possibility forced him to crouch and do a quick 360, looking for any signs of attack. He didn't see anyone, though. Gidion slid his sword into the scabbard. He couldn't behead a vampire with a one-handed swing, so he decided to stick with Dad's katana for now.

Gidion stayed with the bridge. He ran as carefully as possible to avoid tumbling over the side into God only knew what muck. The light of a house appeared to the left as he reached the end of the bridge. His fear of being spotted by anyone not involved in this mess forced him to slow. He rounded a curve in the path and reached a fork. One led up and to the left going past a large house into the neighborhood. The other direction went down a tunnel, running underneath Woolridge Road and connecting it to the other side of the park where he'd left his car.

Even though he could see through to the other side, most of the tunnel was a maw of shadows. He raised his hand trying to look into it, but that accomplished nothing.

He pulled out his phone for the light. The phone only required one hand, but the sword in his right was meant for two. That left him unprepared for the vampire that lunged out of the tunnel.

The taller and much bigger vampire grabbed Gidion by the front of his jacket and flung him into the tunnel. Gidion lost his phone. The faint glow of the display gave him just enough light to see the vampire rush at him. Gidion swung his sword as the phone went dark and missed. The vampire grabbed him by the right arm, preventing him from a second attempt.

A fist smashed into the right side of Gidion's face, catching him on the temple.

The world blinked. One second he was on his feet with his sword in hand, and the next he found himself on his knees and the sword lost. The assault changed his position enough to let him see the silhouette of his attacker against the near end of the tunnel, illuminated by the light from the nearby house.

The vampire's leg came at him, the toe end of his boot aimed at Gidion's chest. Gidion twisted his upper body just enough to avoid the full brunt of the kick and grabbed onto the leg. The vampire hadn't expected that. The moment's confusion gave Gidion the opening he needed. He grabbed the bastard by the balls and squeezed hard. He grinned as he heard Grandpa's voice in his head. No such thing as fighting dirty. Either fight to win or don't bother walking out the damn door at night.

The crotch grab gave Gidion just enough advantage to knock the vampire to the floor of the tunnel. The vampire scrambled to his feet, but that gave Gidion the time he needed to arm himself. He pulled his box cutter from his pocket instead of going for his swords. He held it so that his body hid the weapon from his opponent. He retreated from the vampire, who swung at him. Frustrated by his misses, the vampire lunged. Gidion expected that, letting the vampire take him down to the floor of the tunnel. He held onto his box cutter, determined not to lose it in the fall. Pain shot through the entire left back side of his body, but he avoided cracking his head against the concrete. The vampire looked ready to fix that. He pinned Gidion to the ground between his legs.

The vampire pulled back to punch him out cold. Gidion struck faster. He sliced across the vampire's throat with the box cutter. He knew he'd hit the mark, too. Blood spilled from the cut onto Gidion's chest. The vampire gasped and gagged as he fell back and grabbed at his throat. Gidion drew the wakizashi from his back and slit open the vampire's stomach.

That sent the vampire stumbling into retreat. His hands shook in confusion, the need to defend himself conflicting with the fear of losing all his blood. Gidion never gave him a chance to decide which need mattered most. He sliced off the vampire's head, which required three separate swings of the wakizashi, partly from his exhaustion and from the thickness of the vampire's neck.

He scrambled across the floor of the tunnel, finding his phone and then using the light from it to recover Dad's sword, which had slid over to the edge of the tunnel floor. Doing that took far too long. His entire body worked against him, shaking from adrenaline and fear. He didn't know how long he had before someone might find him. What if the police were already in the area? His dark clothing would mask the stains from the vampire's blood but not the stench of it.

His brain raced through every detail of what had happened in the park, struggling against panic to piece together how utterly screwed he was and what options remained.

The tunnel had been a trap.

The vampires wanted him to come this way. That meant they'd probably gone to the lot where Dad parked. The delay gave them all the time they needed to get away, too.

Gidion searched through the headless vampire's pockets, lifting his wallet and a cheap flip phone. Apparently, the thick-necked bastard's cell phone plan hadn't made it into the current decade.

The far side of the tunnel brought him out on the side of Woolridge where he'd parked. Each raindrop landing on the right side of his swollen face stung. What had started as a numb sensation bloomed into the endless, throbbing pain of a thousand tiny daggers. He didn't bother touching his face to confirm whether blood ran down his cheek and along the edge of his jaw.

He stumbled along the path at a half-run and then climbed the hill to his right. The wooden structure he'd seen when he parked his car came into view. The relief that he'd correctly guessed where he was gave him the strength to break into a full run to his car. As soon as he was past the wooden headstock, he spotted the Little Hearse. He tossed the swords onto the floor of the back seat, then climbed into the front and locked the doors.

Still no police. If the cops had gone to the other lot, he would see their headlights, even if they didn't turn on their mounted blue and red light bars.

He drove straight across Woolridge to the entrance of the other parking lot. His headlights gave him more than enough light to see the bad news. No Mustang. Only Dad's empty car remained. Gidion scrambled out of the car to retrieve Andrea's phone from the trunk.

Dammit! He'd hoped they might take Dad's car, too, but they must have had a driver nearby in another car waiting to pick them up.

He left Dad's car there. No other choice. He'd come back later with Ms. Aldgate to pick it up. For now, he was done. He rocked forward and back in his seat as he drove away from the park. He decided against going directly to Ms. Aldgate's house. He didn't want to risk being followed, and he needed to pull himself together. The pain from the right side of his face didn't compare with the ice in his chest.

Grandpa dead.

Dad captured.

And Gidion didn't have the first damn clue how to find him.

CHAPTER THIRTY-ONE

Going back to Ms. Aldgate's house was the smart play. Gidion knew that. He drove a circuitous route with that original intent, but after an hour of going in ever-smaller circles, he drove past Andrea's house several times. Stopping to see her wasn't an option, no matter how much he wanted to. He glanced at her cell phone resting in his passenger seat. Not being able to text her hurt more than the right side of his face. He'd promised to return it to her in the morning and give her a ride to school.

He knew why he wanted to avoid Ms. Aldgate's house: he'd failed. He thought about Pete. Even though Gidion had killed the vampire coven that had recruited his friend as a servant, he couldn't keep Pete from killing himself. Even without knowing the circumstances of Pete's death, Dad had warned him that you can't save everyone. He couldn't let himself accept that lesson, not when his dad was the one at risk.

The vampires kidnapped Dad. He kept telling himself that, replaying what he'd seen, trying to make sense of why.

Realizing he was already near his house, Gidion went there. Going home was the dumbest thing he could do. He knew that. The risk that the vampires were watching the house was huge, but after several days with it abandoned, he hoped they would have given up any hope of finding him or Dad here. He drove past his house at least five times before he stopped. He didn't spot any unfamiliar cars. No one tried to follow him, and part of him wished they would. At least that would give him a chance to confront and question one of these vampires or track them to where Dad was being held.

Their house sat on a corner lot, so Gidion parked on the side street instead of in the driveway. He figured that would improve his chances of going undetected here. He also went in by the back door and into the kitchen.

They'd kept all the lights off. He felt, more than saw Mom's wedding portrait to his right. He didn't look, avoiding her smile out of guilt from failing to save Dad and from what he'd seen. Dad had kissed the shade, another redhead. Gidion choked on the irony and his anger.

Keeping the house dark, he relied on his phone's flashlight to navigate. This house had never felt so empty. Knowing Page wasn't here to warn him with her insane barking the instant a vampire approached the house added another layer of insecurity. That constant paranoia tingled through the back of his neck and forced him to search every shadowed nook and cranny of their tri-level with his wakizashi in hand. Even after he'd finished his search, he spent the next half hour sitting in the den and held onto his sword the entire time. Every few minutes, he caught the foreign scent of the vampire blood covering his clothes. The stench made him nauseous until he went "nose blind" again.

He pulled out a change of clothes before he peeled off his rain and blood-soaked outfit. The dirty clothes went straight into the washer. Once inside the bathroom, he closed the door and turned on the light, giving him his first real look at himself since the park.

The right side of his face had turned purple. A trail of dark red crust ran down from a cut near his temple, but at least he'd stopped bleeding. Grandpa had planned for this kind of problem. He knew a retired doctor, but until now, Gidion hadn't needed the old doc's help. He didn't know who the doctor was or how to reach him. His ignorance reminded him of a snide remark Grandpa once made about operating the cremator, that it was a one-step process: just call Grandpa. Calling the doctor was supposed to be a "one-step process," too. The same anger from that moment burned fresh in his chest, but the memory of Grandpa's body on the floor of his house, his eyes open and empty, flipped the switch to guilt and fear.

"Dammit, Grandpa." He slammed a fist on the countertop of

the sink. "I don't know what to do."

Grandpa's voice answered him, chastising him to get cleaned up and then put the brain God gave him to use.

He turned the shower on as hot as he could stand it. The spray stung his cold flesh. More pain flared within his temple as he leaned into the water. Once that subsided, he savored the rediscovered joy of warmth. The rushing water drowned out everything except his own movements. He imagined little creaks and groans from the house every few seconds. He feared he'd open his eyes, blinking away a water-blurred view of the world, to find the assassin there. The weight of her threat forced him out of the shower too soon to melt away all of the ice in his bones.

Now that he was something closer to room temperature, he found it easier to focus. A glance in the mirror after he dried off let him know he still looked like crap. He'd considered calling the police to report Dad missing, but he'd need to explain his bruises. Maybe a day or two would reduce the swelling enough to avoid suspicion from the police, but that might not be time Dad could afford.

He turned the light off in the bathroom and let his eyes adjust to the dark. Even then, he stumbled across the hall to his bedroom.

He went for comfort, slipping on black sweatpants and a bright blue Henrico County Police hoodie, the white outline of the police patch over his heart. Every so often, the 911 dispatchers placed an order for these, and Dad bought a matching sweatshirt in the same batch a few winters back. Gidion drowned in the medium when Dad first bought them—the sleeves drooped over his hands and forced him to push them up out of the way every time he needed to handle something. Dad told him he'd grow into the sweatshirt, and those same sleeves now hugged his biceps and shoulders.

That line of thought almost overwhelmed him, so he pushed it aside. He pulled out his phone and opened the notepad app to enter what facts he had to work with. One detail gave him a small bit of hope: they'd taken Dad alive. If the vampires just wanted to kill him, they'd have done it in the park. They didn't take him for a meal either. Gidion felt certain of that. That meant they needed something from him.

"Grandpa's box." The assassin had searched for that box. Maybe. Dad seemed convinced she'd looked for it. The past few days had left him too raw to think straight, but as he sat in the shadows and jotted down the details in his mind, he realized something else that should have been obvious.

The assassin had shot Grandpa, but when it came time to kill Gidion, she'd taken a different approach. Hell, she tried to get him with a dart gun, and when that failed, she'd gone for a sword. What explained that? Murder by multiple personality disorder? He doubted it.

Then there was the phone call to 911 that hadn't come from Andrea and had saved his life.

He also didn't see the assassin among the vampires in the park.

The woman he fought might not have killed Grandpa. For all he knew, she might have found Grandpa dead and was searching the house when Gidion walked in on her. How many players was he really dealing with? Grandpa's killer could have been the one to call 911, or that might be yet another player in this mess. That might even explain the red, fanged smiley faces which seemed to tip the assassin's hand when she had already found the funeral home.

Then there was Dad's contact, the shade in the park from earlier tonight. What if she'd been in Richmond all this time? She might have killed Grandpa, or maybe she'd been the one to call 911 to save Gidion's ass. Only, why she would have helped him and then turned on Dad made no sense.

The blow to his temple gave him a raging headache, making it harder to think.

Then there was Dad's theory, the one that suggested this might have more to do with Grandpa than with Gidion. Hell, this could be a perfect storm of all their past hunting fuck-ups drawing together at the same time.

Then his phone vibrated as a message popped onto the screen.

It was a text from Dad.

CHAPTER THIRTY-TWO

The text message appeared on the screen of Gidion's phone with news that was far too good to be true.

'*I'm all right. Managed to get away.*'

A second text from Dad's phone followed before he could respond.

'*Where are you? Are you okay?*'

Gidion stared at the messages, not sure how to respond. He wanted to believe it was Dad, but every instinct in him had jumped to DEFCON 1. The way the messages were typed out, with full words instead of abbreviated characters, definitely seemed like him. Except for Andrea, he didn't know many people who worried about spelling out all the words in their texts.

He growled, hoping to push back the headache that made thinking a hell of a challenge. How to respond to this message? Did he really believe this was Dad? No, but if it was, then Dad needed his help.

He considered playing along, pretending he believed it was Dad, but he decided the vampires might not buy that.

'*How do I know this is you?*'

That question seemed a win-win. If it was Dad, then he could respond with something to prove it. Of course, if it was one of the vampires, then maybe Gidion could pretend to be fooled and trick them into meeting in a public place. Then he could follow them back to where they were holding Dad.

After a moment of silence, the answer arrived. It wasn't what he expected.

'*Your first NFL jersey was the Carolina Panthers.*'

For the first moment, he believed this might be Dad. He stood and headed for the kitchen to get his keys when a thought stopped him halfway down the stairs. Dad believed in double-verification. His laptop even required two passwords. What if Dad fed the vampires the first detail, a real one and then planned to give him something false on the second as a warning? That would be very Dad. Besides, why would Dad text when he could just as easily use a cell phone to call?

Gidion knew the perfect question to send next. *'Which player and number?'*

The reply arrived before he went down the stairs.

'Number 13, Keep.'

"Holy crap."

No way the vamps could have guessed that. Dad bought him that personalized jersey for Christmas back when he was in elementary school. Gidion had pestered him for months.

Dad sent another text, knowing he'd proven himself.

'Where are you? Are you safe?'

'I'm safe. Are you?' Gidion didn't say where he was. If Dad got caught again, then the vampires might see the message. That and Dad would flip if he knew Gidion had risked coming to their house.

'Safe for now. Got out, but can't risk talking on the phone if the vampires try to track me.'

Gidion smiled, imagining his dad going all Jason Bourne on the vampires to get free from the vamps. He wished he could have seen it. The need to stay quiet made sense, too. While a lot of the myths ventured way off from reality, all vampires possessed heightened senses, including exceptional hearing.

Gidion sent his reply. *'I'll head your way. Where are you?'*

'Somewhere along the James River in the West End. Meet me on Cherokee Road, underneath the Willey Bridge.'

Gidion still couldn't fully shake his doubts. Dad kept asking where he was, which seemed a lot less important than Gidion getting there to help him. This felt too convenient, but maybe his luck was finally getting back on track.

He turned into the kitchen when he reached the bottom of the stairs. He planned to leave by the back door, same as he'd arrived. Moonlight cut through the window.

Just before he opened the door, he spotted an unopened, white envelope in the center of the table. He'd overlooked it when he came into the house, focused on making sure no one was hiding in here to ambush him.

Someone wrote on the back of the envelope in a black marker. Dad didn't leave this here. The messenger drew each letter and number like fine art.

The note contained a phone number, an arrow, and three words that split his life in two.

'Who is she?'

CHAPTER THIRTY-THREE

Gidion stared at those three words. 'Who is she?'

The arrow above the words pointed towards the far wall and the wedding portrait of his mother. The train of her long, white dress spilled out behind her to form a circle on the floor. She'd been in her early twenties at the time the picture was taken, less than a decade older than he was now, but her young face wore an air of an earlier time. He often wondered what she would have looked like if she was still alive. He wondered how she died, all the things Grandpa and Dad hadn't told him.

For her wedding, Mom pulled her long red hair up into an elaborate style, wearing it like a crown. This picture was how he remembered his mother, what she looked like, but she'd never worn it in that fashion when she'd been alive for the first four years of his life.

'Who is she?'

He wondered who left the note. One of the vampires from the park? The assassin? He couldn't understand why they'd find anything about his mother's portrait interesting, why they'd even give away that they'd been in his house.

His eyes went to the message and then back to his mother's face and that crown of red hair.

Then he saw it.

He saw her, and every lie he'd ever been told by his father and grandfather, even the ones he'd never known about until this moment, made sense. The truth buried into his heart, a dagger more painful than steel. His chest ached. He stumbled back, unable to look away from his mother's face. The image of what she'd look like in a pair of sunglasses slid into place, and he didn't need to imagine how she might look today.

He knew.

He'd seen her in the park tonight.

Mom was the shade.

CHAPTER THIRTY-FOUR

Gidion no longer felt the cold. Everything went numb, a defense mechanism to make him think and act. He always believed he got that from Dad, but now he wondered how much of his detachment and guile came from the woman in the portrait.

He pulled out his phone and looked at the messages he'd exchanged with Dad—no, the exchange he'd had with someone holding Dad's phone. The confirmation he'd gotten came from something in his childhood, the kind of thing he didn't doubt Dad would have shared with Mom.

He glanced at the phone number on the envelope. Who left that there?

Only one thing was certain. Dad needed his help, either held captive or on the run.

Gidion needed to know which problem he faced.

He needed something from the past few days, something even Mom wouldn't know, that Dad wouldn't have bothered to tell anyone.

'Where did we get our coffee the night Grandpa died? Who gave it to us?'

Typing the text took longer than usual. His hands shook so much that he didn't feel the vibration of his phone as the reply appeared on the screen.

'Gidion, I need you to hurry. I'm near the bridge.'

He considered his options. Press for the answer or go for the bridge and try to turn the tables on what was looking more like a group of vampires planning an ambush? Could he wait them out at their own trap and then track them to where they kept Dad?

The ache of his swollen face warned him his odds of taking

down any vampires weren't good, especially with all of them using handguns. Short of knowing how to get to the Willey Bridge, he knew nothing about the location where the vampires wanted to meet him. If they chose that place, then they already knew it better than he did. They'd get there first, before he could scope out the scene. Odds favored they were already there from the first text.

Gidion copied and resent his questions. He smiled as he remembered Dad telling him how dispatchers used that technique to control uncooperative 911 callers: repeat a question with the same wording and tone.

'Gidion, come get me. Hurry!'

He sat at the kitchen table as he resent the questions for a third time. The last answer had already confirmed what he needed to know. He pressed for the answers to taunt them. The display on his phone went dark and stayed that way for several minutes. He glanced back at the clock display on the oven, the green letters glowed that it was almost one o'clock in the morning.

The display on his phone lit up and the phone vibrated. Someone was calling him from Dad's phone.

He stared at the phone, debating on whether to answer. This wasn't what he'd expected, but something in him had hoped for it. Just before it could ring for the fourth time and kick over to his voicemail, he answered.

He let the line stay open, not even offering so much as a simple "hello." His silence wasn't some clever play. He just didn't know what to say.

"Gidion?"

The voice—the sound of her voice—filled him with déjà vu. Hearing her say his name dusted off lost memories: the smell of lavender, warm tea, a halo of sunlight around Mom in her robe on a Saturday morning as she stood in front of the window cooking breakfast, even the way she would sneak up on him and give him a loud zerbert. The memories had once made him smile, but hearing her voice in this moment left his heart raw.

"Are you there?" she asked.

"Put Dad on the phone."

She sighed, as if the request was an inconvenience. "Your father is resting, but he's fine. I promise."

"Resting from getting hit on the back of the head by your gun?"

"Gidion, I need you to listen." Her voice sounded so desperate and human. As he stared at her portrait, he imagined her face and the way her lips moved as she spoke. "There are things you don't understand, and I'm sorry. It's as much my fault as your father's."

He balled his hand into a fist. "Save it, Mom."

There was a slight pause, but he heard the way she smiled as she said, "You recognized me."

"Yeah."

He picked up the envelope from the table. She hadn't left this message here. Who did?

"I didn't come here to hurt you or your father. I love you, more than you can imagine."

He turned away from the picture. Facing the past version of her made it difficult to hold onto his anger, and he needed it.

"What are you doing here?" Keeping his voice from shaking took all of his will power, but he still tasted the unsteadiness coating each word.

"I'm putting our family back together," she said.

"Really?" He thought about Ms. Aldgate and what he'd seen and heard at the park. "Somehow I don't think Dad was on board with that plan."

"Well, here's a news flash. Your father isn't always right." The sudden shift to sarcasm didn't hide the edge of anger in her voice. "How do you think I ended up like this?"

The venom in her question reminded him of what Grandpa said at the funeral home when he caught Gidion there with GQ Drac and Bonnie's bodies. Grandpa had said he thought he was "done with this bullshit" when Dad quit hunting.

"Dad got too aggressive hunting." He couldn't hold back a slight laugh at the irony, history repeating itself. "They came after him, but they got you. Why'd they turn you instead of killing you?"

"Fools thought they could use me." The way she said that was a knife wrapped in silk. "They turned me, then starved me. Thought the hunger would twist and blind me enough that I'd lose control and kill your father when he tried to rescue me. They underestimated how much I love him, so I got the last laugh."

"Really? Ask me, Mom," he didn't spare on snark as he called her that, "they're getting their chuckles more than a decade late."

"Don't you dare talk to me like this! You have no idea—no fucking, goddamned clue—what I gave up for you and your father!"

Gidion didn't say anything. She shouldn't be able to intimidate him more than any other stranger, but it wasn't that simple. How many times had he talked to Dad or Grandpa about this woman, imagined what life would have been like if she hadn't died when he was four? She'd been more of an imaginary friend than a parent.

"Gidion?" Her tone shifted, total one-eighty. A sob clung to the way she said his name. "I'm sorry. You don't deserve that. We left you in the dark for so long, didn't think you'd be able to understand what happened to me when you were little, that letting you believe I was dead was simpler and that we could eventually come clean."

Her last word choked out of her.

"Come clean?"

"We thought it would be easier once you were older, but then you got older." She sighed. Her breath blew the dust off the past dozen years. The regret touched him on an instinctive level. If she'd been there, he might have reached out to hug her, to feel just how real she was. "We couldn't figure out how to tell you in a way that wouldn't make you feel deceived, and then there was your grandfather. He never supported our decision."

That one word, "grandfather," killed the brief bit of sympathy she'd built. The buried rage in the way she spoke of Grandpa told him everything he needed to know. Every piece that puzzled him about the night Grandpa died clicked into place.

"No," Gidion paused to wipe a lone tear from his face, "he wouldn't have." Now he understood why there was a 911 call to save him but not for Grandpa. "He was stubborn like that. Didn't mean you had to kill him."

There was a pause, and then she said, "That wasn't me. I swear."

She said the right words, but they came too slowly. The time between his accusation and her denial held all the confession he needed. Dad told him more than once that truth doesn't require time to think.

"Put Dad on the phone."

"I told you. He's resting, and I think it would be better to have this conversation in person."

"I agree, so let him go."

Another pause. She didn't have an answer for that.

"Tell me something," Gidion said as he considered his earlier questions about why the vampires had taken Dad instead of killing him in the park. "You plan to turn Dad against his will, the same way the vampires turned you?"

"I'm not a monster. Your father understood that. It's why he didn't kill me, the reason he stopped hunting. Your grandfather? He wanted to turn you into a murderer with a crusade."

Gidion hesitated. He didn't know how to play this, and he wasn't sure what answers he could get out of her at this point. All he knew was that he was running out of time to save Dad.

"Keep the phone close," he said. "I've got some things to take care of first."

He hung up before she could answer. Part of him expected her to call back, but she didn't. Didn't even send a text. Maybe she realized he was serious. He might have been better off with her just thinking of him as a child and underestimating him. Of course, it might simply mean she didn't care enough to try, and even though his anger should be enough to prevent that possibility from wounding him, he couldn't stop the ache in the center of his chest.

He looked at the note, written in that skilled penmanship.

"So, now the question is, 'Who are you?'" He wasn't sure if he wanted to thank or kill that person for having ripped his life apart and ending a beautiful lie.

CHAPTER THIRTY-FIVE

Gidion took a moment to rebuild his nerves and then dialed the number. After just two rings, he had his answer.

"Who is she?"

With just a few words, Gidion recognized the assassin. Her Asian accent was thick. Her tongue struggled with English.

"Why should I tell you? You came here to kill me."

Instinct told him that her agenda might have changed, but even if she was focused on his mother for some reason, that didn't guarantee she wouldn't turn back to the task of killing him at the next chance. He still had a price on his head.

"The woman in the painting," she said. "Is she your mother?"

"She was." He emphasized that last word, but he couldn't decide if he was trying to convince the assassin or himself. "Aren't you working with her?"

"She was my guide, not the one who hired me."

"So you still have a contract to kill me. Why should I even talk to you?

"She wants your father." The way she struggled with English made it difficult to gauge if anything she said was a lie. She paused in places that weren't natural, and since she needed more time to form even simple answers, there was no way to distinguish a pause to convert her thought to English versus a moment to craft a lie.

Gidion sighed, the ache beneath his skull flaring with his frustration. She didn't know everything that had happened, didn't yet realize the warning about his father came too late.

"She already has him," he said. "Do you know where she took him?"

"No. Do you?"

"No." This conversation felt like it was going nowhere, and the longer it went in circles, the more paranoid he became that she was tricking him. He stood and walked over to the window by the stove to glance out at the backyard for any sign of movement or any cars going down the side street. All he saw were shadows, street lights, and stillness. "Just tell me why you left the note. I don't see why you want to help me."

"I am helping myself. Your mother means to kill me."

"Why?"

"Money."

Gidion laughed. "Seriously? The assassin has a price on her head, too?"

"We have common problems, hunter."

"We should start a support group." She didn't respond to that, much less laugh. He decided for the sake of his ego to just assume it was one of those cultural divide things. "You aren't tied to this place, not like I am. Why are you still here? Why not just leave?"

"My contract has changed. They now want her dead, too."

"Like mother, like son. Fantastic."

She answered with more silence. Okay...Either she didn't get the joke, or she didn't find him all that funny.

"What's your name?" he asked.

"I do not give my name. Names have power."

Seriously? "Fine, then I'll just call you Blood. You know, like the anime." More silence. "Never mind. Let's just stick to business. What changed to make my mother a target?"

"Unless you know where she is, I see no reason for us to continue to talk."

Gidion laughed as he moved to the front of the house and checked for anyone out there. "Let's get something straight, Blood. I don't need you to find my mother and take her down. I've killed entire covens." Well, one coven, but she didn't need to know that.

She laughed, the snort-like sound carrying twice its weight in condescension. "How many guns did your coven have? Your mother's does not follow the rules. This is why others desire her death. She makes much noise. Has ten others, all armed. Face them alone, you will die."

"Like you'd fare any better? I don't think you're going to stop them from chopping off your head once they've shot you into the vampire equivalent of Swiss cheese."

She didn't laugh at that. This time, he didn't mind the initial silence. Just as he started to wonder if she'd hung up, she said, "You are right."

He savored the small victory for all of a breath, and then he realized the way she'd said it. She knew the odds were stacked against her from the start.

"You already knew she was my mother when you left this note." He balled up the paper in his fist. "Didn't you?"

"I assumed."

"Then why leave this for me? What is it you really want?" He already suspected the answer, but part of him couldn't believe it.

"We act alone," she paused. "Swiss cheese. Both of us."

"What? You think we could actually work together?" Gidion went back up to his room and grabbed an old book bag to fill it with some of the things Dad hadn't known about to get, most of the cell phones, wallets, and the two laptops he'd taken from the vampires he'd killed in the van. "You tried to kill me, lady. Heck, you still have a contract to kill me. The minute my mom and her guys are dead, you'll just go for my throat."

"If I agree to void my contract?"

"What? I'm supposed to take your word on that?"

"You do not trust my word?"

He pulled the phone away from his face and stared at it as if she could see the disbelief on his face. "You might not have killed my grandfather, but let's not pretend you weren't planning to." He zipped up the backpack and slid it on before he continued talking to Blood. "You're a vampire. Your word isn't worth crap."

"Your word is no better. You are a vampire hunter. How do I know you will not turn on me first?"

Much as he didn't want to, he had to admit she was right. Neither of them could trust the other.

"I still don't see why you can't just walk away from this?" He went back downstairs and took another look out the front windows. "All you have to do is leave Richmond, and my mom and her goons aren't an issue for you."

She sighed, and the way she did it left little doubt she thought him dense as brick. "They are short term problem. Price on me? It follows me, followed me here. I need to know who wants me dead. I learn that, then I kill them. No one left to pay, and the price for my death goes away."

He considered that as he watched a car crawl past his house down the street. Her logic tracked. "So you don't need my mother dead as much as you need to know who wants you dead."

"Doi."

He took that as a yes.

Before he responded, he noted what details he could about the passing car: a dark-colored four-door compact. The car disappeared from his sight. A car going that slowly through his neighborhood wasn't that odd at night, but it made the back of his neck tingle. Time to go.

"Yeah, well that leaves you a lot better off than I'll be," he said. "Even if we do kill my mother's coven, the price on my head is still there."

Blood grunted, and for once, she didn't sound like she'd considered that.

"Help me," she said, "and in return, I tell them you are dead."

She made that sound way too simple. "They'll want proof, won't they?"

"They will need a body, picture of one. That part? Easy. But you will have to stop hunting. Can you?"

What was that supposed to mean? Did she think he killed for fun like some kind of death junkie? He glanced at mom's picture. He'd hunted to honor her memory. He could stop hunting if that kept Dad from becoming a memory, as well. "Yeah, I think I can manage not lopping off more vampire heads after this is done. Not that difficult."

"So you say."

Little surprise a vampire would find the idea of not killing a difficult thing to do.

"We need a plan." He went back into the kitchen for a look out the back window. "This whole 'mutual back scratching' arrangement doesn't mean a thing unless we find them in time."

"You have an idea." Even through her accent, he could tell she wasn't asking. She realized he already had something in mind.

"I do." He went out the back door, locking it behind him. Part of him expected to get attacked, but nothing happened. He almost dropped the phone as he ran to the car while still talking. "If we're going to do this, then we meet in person and we do it now."

"Why in person?"

He got in his car. "Consider this a test run to see how much we're willing to trust each other." There was also the risk she wasn't the assassin he'd met, that she was one of Mom's vampires delivering an award-worthy performance. He'd be handing over all his strategy to them.

She didn't bother repressing a sigh. "Very well."

He told her where to go and to be there in thirty minutes. If she kept him waiting even five minutes longer than that, then it was game over for their proposed partnership.

CHAPTER THIRTY-SIX

The most important part of a negotiation process between two hostile parties is almost always a third, neutral party. Doesn't mean that third party needs to mediate matters, just to make both conflicting parties behave long enough to work together without killing each other. The location Gidion chose to meet Blood provided exactly that.

He pulled into the lot of the Wawa on West Broad Street with a little more than five minutes to spare. He circled the building, and was pleased to see a few police cars parked in the rear lot. He'd counted on the cold rain to drive everyone inside and into bed, keeping things quiet enough for these officers to stick their noses into cups of free, hot coffee.

The gas gauge's needle hovered just below three-quarters of a tank. He decided against topping it off for now.

The bright yellow and red signs hurt his eyes as he parked in front of the store. Since he was early, he took the extra time to back the Little Hearse into the space. If he needed to leave here in a hurry, then those few seconds might save his ass.

He knew he was taking a huge gamble meeting this vampire. If she pulled a fast one on him and was working with his mother, then he'd just gift-wrapped himself. The cops might deter things a bit, but they wouldn't stay here all night. Besides, if he stayed too long, someone would get suspicious about why he was here. Public places didn't always provide perfect protection, just enough to get things done.

Déjà vu slapped him for the second time this night as he entered the store, making him wish Dad was here. He tried to recall any decent storylines in the comic books where Batman got caught and Tim Drake had to save the day. Nothing came to mind, not that he really had time to think on it. Much as he didn't want to, he pulled his hood down once he was inside. Walking into a convenience store with a hood up and a bunch of cops around seemed like a bad idea. He did his best to hide from the officers the half of his face that was a swollen shade of smacked-down purple.

Three cops clustered around the coffee island in the back right of the building, so he went to the other side of the store, hanging out near the candy. He saw a peanut butter Twix and realized he was hungry again. The convenience store also made sub sandwiches, so he really hoped this meeting didn't go south, because he needed a sandwich.

"You smell terrible."

The voice to his left startled him. She'd made it inside the store and within two steps of him without any other sound to give it away.

"I just took a shower." He resisted the urge to sniff himself for confirmation.

She picked up a dark chocolate candy bar and studied it instead of looking at him as she spoke. "You wear the dead on your jacket."

Gidion realized she meant the blood of the vampire he'd killed. The guy who let it slip to Gidion that vampire blood has a distinct smell never said whether it was a good or bad scent.

"I'll be sure to dress differently next time."

She turned over the candy bar in her hand several times with a look of confused disappointment drawing her thin eyebrows together.

He'd not gotten a good look at her inside Grandpa's house. Never mind how dark things had been, but a sword fight doesn't offer many chances to admire a person's fashion sense. She had straight, black hair down to the middle of her back and wore a short, black trench coat over a green top with a pair of black jeans. She'd accessorized, wearing a beaded necklace with a dark steel representation of a dragonfly hanging between her breasts. Her face looked smooth and soft. She was almost pretty, except for her brown eyes. They stared with a hard detachment that threatened death or worse for anyone foolish enough to test her patience.

"So how old are you?" he asked. "You know, for real old?" He wondered because she looked about his age, maybe a year or two older, and the vibe coming off her didn't make her seem much older than that.

"Straight to age." She set the candy bar back down and shook her head. "Must be a real ladies' man."

"You get a new driver, or are you driving yourself these days?"

She smiled, not bothering to hide her fangs. "You recognized the pretty boy I left in your cremator."

"Why kill the guy working for you?"

"Worked for your mother." She waggled her finger. "Not me."

Gidion hadn't tried to connect those dots, but they fit. The article he'd read said the family of the guy from Georgia owned a big horse farm. According to Dad, Mom loved horses, used to ride them. He wondered if a vampire could ride a horse, because dogs like Page sure didn't care for them.

She picked up and examined a different candy bar, a Whatchamacallit. "Your plan?"

"Thursday." He hesitated. Technically, since the time was after midnight, this was Wednesday morning. Did she think of Thursday as tomorrow? He never appreciated how little he knew about how vampires thought and lived. "There's a visitation planned for my grandfather. My dad scheduled it for during the day to make sure we would avoid any fanged party crashers. I'm going to change the times to make sure it doesn't end until well after sunset."

"You are certain they will come for you?"

"Wouldn't you?"

She shook her head. "Too public for ambush."

"But a great opportunity to pick up my trail."

She nodded. "You cannot follow them if they follow you."

"No, but I can lead them into an ambush of my own." He smiled as he added, "Of our own."

She shrugged as she swapped out her Whatchamacallit for a

Snickers. "Or, let them capture you."

"Why would I do that?"

"I have tracking devices. You wear one; I follow."

Gidion studied the look on her face. It hadn't changed. She was serious.

"What? I'm supposed to let them take me and then just trust you'll come to my rescue?"

"Faster than interrogation. More reliable." The fact that she was here attested to that. The "pretty boy" hadn't given up the information when she'd interrogated him in the cremator, or she wouldn't be working with Gidion to figure it out.

"Your plan means I won't have a weapon and can't help you get in there. Neither one of us can do this alone."

"Given enough time, one person can plan a successful attack against many."

"Time isn't something my dad has." He stepped towards her and was surprised to realize he was taller. "Let's get something straight. I'm not a pawn for you to sacrifice, and neither is my dad."

Not only did she stand her ground, Blood pushed a step into him. They were close enough to kiss. "Understand, hunter, I am no pawn either. Do not think me a cursed soul for you to free in kindness." Her lips twisted into a snarl as she said that last word. "I breathe. I live. I defy death far more, for I have journeyed closer to the threshold than you."

Gidion flinched first. He stepped back and walked around her to stand on her left as if to peruse the other candy. "Point made."

They made their plans for the visitation, not that they took long.

"And tomorrow night?" she said. "We wait?"

"No, I've got another idea about that. They were going to ambush me somewhere tonight, and I think it might be close to where they're staying."

"How will that help?" She didn't look like she doubted the idea, just how he planned to execute it. "You cannot search every house near there."

"No, but she's planned this for a while now, probably since I killed the coven last year. Until I killed the local elder, she couldn't technically get away with establishing a foothold on this city, right?"

"Dui." Her nod suggested he was right, even if he wasn't sure what she'd just said, but she didn't look convinced.

"If she bought a place sometime between then and now, then I can look up the listings for the homes that have sold in the Richmond area since then and see if any are near the place they wanted to meet me."

She smiled and then walked around him, making him feel as if they were playing leapfrog. She was now at the end of the candy display and stared into a glass display case of beer.

"Then you plan to put this list together, for us to hunt tomorrow night?"

"Unless you have a better idea."

He hoped she might, but she didn't. Instead, they made their plans for when and where to meet next. By this point, they'd reached the corner of the store by the sodas and juices.

"Then we are ready," she said, turning to leave.

"One question." This had bugged him for days now and more so since going by Grandpa's house. "It's about the emails you sent me."

The confused look on her face when she turned around answered the question. She hadn't sent them, but he'd already suspected that.

"It was my mom." He opened the cooler and pulled out a bottle of Mountain Dew. "She didn't know I was the one getting the emails. She wanted to make sure you and I met, that one of us would take out the other."

Mom just didn't realize he was the hunter, so when he showed up, that's when she called 911 to save him.

Blood left then. Her silver Nissan looked like it had a decent amount of trunk space. He considered her comment about having tracking devices and realized he'd need to search his car before he left. He wouldn't put it past her to place a tracker on his car before she came into the store.

He ordered his sandwich, a BLT, and left without drawing the officers' attention. They left before he did.

To his surprise, Blood didn't place any tracking device on his car. He spent about twenty minutes going over every inch to be sure.

Only once he pulled out onto West Broad Street did he let his mind wander to the place he'd avoided for a while now. There was a contradiction to what he was doing. He refused to believe he could trust his mother because she was a vampire, that her soul needed to be freed. In order to kill her, he was placing his trust in another vampire. If he could trust Blood, why couldn't he trust Mom? If Mom wasn't a monster, then what did that make him?

His mother's words from earlier tonight answered him: a murderer with a crusade.

CHAPTER THIRTY-SEVEN

Gidion pulled up in front of Ms. Aldgate's home close to three o'clock. Roughly five hours had passed since Dad was taken at the park and about two-and-a-half since he'd learned all the lies he'd lived with. He couldn't stop himself from doing the math any more than he could stop his brain from latching onto random memories that held new meaning.

Anytime he'd gotten school pictures, Dad insisted on getting at least two that were five-by-seven. He'd put one in a frame in his bedroom. Gidion could never find the extra and even asked about it. Dad said he took it to work to put in his locker, but a few years ago, Gidion saw the inside of the locker. The pictures Dad taped on the locker were all wallet size.

His eighth birthday, someone sent him a green stuffed dragon in the mail. The cute, grumpy-looking toy that Gidion named Windsor contained a hand-written note explaining it came from England and wished him happy birthday. The note was left unsigned. Dad insisted he didn't know who sent it. He looked mad, but he still insisted on getting a picture of Gidion with Windsor.

The worst rewrite to his memory belonged to March 23rd, Mom and Dad's anniversary. Every year, Dad took time off from work and left Gidion with Grandpa. Sometimes, it lasted one night. Others lasted as long as a week. Dad said he needed time to himself. Grandpa always grumbled, as if he was mad about being stuck with Gidion. Last year was the first time Grandpa didn't complain. That was when he took Gidion out and showed him that vampires were real.

Gidion slammed his hand against the steering wheel and

screamed. He was furious with Dad, but Grandpa's lies cut a little deeper. He'd been preparing Gidion for his mother—to kill her. Hell, Gidion could have potentially killed her and never realized who she was. Would knowing who she was really stop him from taking her head like any other vampire? Dad should have done it, but he hadn't. All the rationalizations Dad tossed out in the gym the other night made sense now, but that didn't make them right.

He looked towards Ms. Aldgate's house. The front porch light was still on, but the windows were all dark. He should have texted her, but each time he tried to type a text, nothing worked. What could he send that wouldn't leave her demanding answers to a dozen different questions?

She hadn't tried to send him a text. Dad and he weren't supposed to be this long. Had she really managed to keep her head on straight long enough not to call or text either of them? That's when it hit him that Mom had Dad's phone. She didn't know about Ms. Aldgate—not yet.

Or maybe Mom did know. Maybe Ms. Aldgate had sent a text to Dad, and that was the reason the house was dark.

Gidion gripped the box cutter in his jacket pocket. He breathed deeply and tried to push aside the ache that throbbed beneath the right side of his face.

He looked up and down the street. All the cars he saw looked like they belonged to the neighborhood. He hadn't gone as far as to note the license plates, but he'd gotten to know the makes and models that lived here.

The front of Ms. Aldgate's house looked as it should. The only thing that didn't feel right was that she'd turned off all of the inside lights.

The house to the left of Ms. Aldgate's had a bright lamp post placed in the middle of the front yard. Fortunately, the neighbor to the right didn't have any lights on, so he approached from that side.

The rain had stopped, but enough had fallen during the night to turn the lawn into little more than mud and puddles. Water soaked through his sneakers and into his socks. The slosh and splash from each step forced him to move slower to keep quiet. The back yard to Ms. Aldgate's house didn't have a fence. The neighbor did, and as Gidion neared the back corner of the house, a dog barked and flung itself against the chain link fence. He jumped back and pressed against the side of Ms. Aldgate's house.

Then he heard another dog barking from inside Ms. Aldgate's house. At least Page was still in there and cross with the neighbor's dog for making so much racket in her new domain. He hoped that was a good sign.

He watched for any hint of movement in the back, but nothing moved beyond the treetops in the wind. He leaned around the corner of the house for a look at the back. Door closed, no windows busted. Everything looked about right. The dogs hadn't started barking until he got here, and that offered another confirmation that there weren't any vampires nearby.

Something moved against his hip and sent him jumping back with his box cutter in hand and the blade extended. Before his phone could vibrate a second time in his front pocket, he realized what he was defending himself against: an incoming call. He put the box cutter away and pulled out his phone. The display showed "Ms. Aldgate."

She spoke as soon as he answered.

"Gidion Keep, please tell me that's you skulking around outside my house."

"Yeah, that would be me." He leaned against the side of her house, resting his head against the vinyl siding. His heart slowed some now that he knew he wasn't being attacked by some hip-hugging vampire. With the sudden rush of adrenaline finished, exhaustion settled into every part of his body. "Just didn't want to take any chances. Wasn't expecting to find the house dark."

"Get in here." She hung up before he could respond.

He didn't move right away. What he wanted more than anything was to sleep, but what he needed to do next wouldn't allow for that anytime soon.

The next hour was spent in the kitchen over mugs of hot tea as he reassured Ms. Aldgate that he looked a lot worse than he felt—a lie—and explained what happened at the park. He didn't tell her everything, though. When he got to the part about the vampire contact being Mom and that Dad had kissed her, he just couldn't bring himself to say it. He hid his face from her, sipping his tea and gently blowing some of the steam up into his face. The scents of orange and spice warmed his nose. He was thankful that she hadn't made Earl Grey. Mom used to enjoy that on the rare occasions she wasn't feeling in the mood for coffee.

By the time he'd finished explaining that Dad was caught and that they'd tried to lure Gidion into a trap, texting from Dad's phone, Ms. Aldgate had made up her mind.

"It's time to bring the police into this."

Gidion answered with a laugh as empty as he felt. "Are you kidding? We need to get Dad's car before the police find the bodies at the park." He'd almost forgotten about the damn car. Lord, he just wanted to crawl into bed.

"You are in over your head. These people are armed with guns, something you don't have."

He'd considered going to Grandpa's and arming himself with a shotguns, if the police left any in the house. Didn't take long for him to rule out that option. Even though Grandpa had taught him how to shoot, he wasn't good enough to win a gunfight against a half dozen vampires. The simple act of shooting that handgun in the park had reinforced how lousy his aim was. The only chance he and Blood had was to pick them off one at a time, do as much damage as possible to even the odds before any of them realized what was happening.

"What I have are two vampire bodies with their heads cut off in that park. If I'm lucky, then maybe the vampires cleaned up the mess for me. They don't want to draw the attention of the police any more than I do." It wasn't until shortly after his meet with Blood that he realized he hadn't seen the body of the first vampire he'd beheaded at the park. Given how dark it was and all the rain, there was a good chance he just overlooked the body trying to catch up to the vampires with Dad, but he hoped he was wrong. If they got the one body, then perhaps they got the second, too.

"I'd also need to explain to the police why I look like I got hit with a wall." He pointed at the bruised side of his face.

"We could say that the bruising is from what happened at your grandfather's house."

"Won't take Chesterfield County Police long to compare notes with Richmond and realize that's bull."

She looked out her kitchen window. When he started telling her what happened to Dad, he'd worried she might fall apart. She didn't shed a tear. She focused. Hell, the reason she'd had all the lights off when he got here was so she could see outside and spot anyone approaching the house and make it more difficult for anyone out there to see her. That was also why she'd called him instead of Dad. She spotted his car.

No, Ms. Aldgate was determined to find an answer, one that wouldn't involve him hunting and would get Dad back as soon as possible.

The entire time she was thinking through the problem, she slid the tip of her index finger along the rim of her mug. She stopped as soon as she found her next idea. "Is there a way to contact the phone company and have them track your dad's phone?"

"Already tried it. They've turned off the phone, and the last coordinates placed it exactly where they planned to ambush me at the Willey Bridge." He'd contacted the cell phone company on his way to meet with Blood. Mom was playing it smart. He suspected the next time she turned on the phone, she'd place herself somewhere just as unhelpful.

"There has to be something we can do, some way I can do more than just sit here." She picked up her teapot and poured the last drops into her mug. Her hands shook, the only sign he'd seen that she was close to cracking.

"First, we need to get Dad's car. Have you slept any?"

She avoided looking at him as she answered. "Yes, not sure how long. I'd been sitting in the dark waiting for you and your father. Didn't intend to sleep. Your dog woke me when you started prowling around outside."

"You plan to work today?" he asked.

He recognized the look she was giving him. She'd leveled Ralph Whaley, the dumbest jerk in his World History class, with that same dumbfounded stare when he'd desperately guessed that Rome was invaded by Japan. Idiot got booted out of the class before the first quarter ended.

"No," she said, drawing out that word, "I am most definitely calling out sick. God gave us substitute teachers for reason."

"Good, then I've got a research project for you."

As badly as he needed to sleep, part of him considered staying up to search online for the recent housing sales, the idea he'd pitched to Blood to find Mom. He didn't see how he was going to ever sleep and do that in time to find Dad without losing an entire night. If Mom was serious about turning Dad, then she'd probably started the process. That gave him two more nights, at best. After that, he'd be forced to put both of them down.

CHAPTER THIRTY-EIGHT

Gidion regretted his promise to give Andrea a ride to school, even if that was the best way to return her cell phone. The last of the rain clouds cleared as he reached her house.

The driveway was empty, meaning Andrea's mom must have already left for work, so he parked the Little Hearse in her mom's spot. Andrea ran out the front door as soon as he stopped. She wore a dark red velvet coat that came down just past her knees.

Even though she only kept the rear passenger door open for all of three seconds, she managed to toss her pale blue purse and worn leather backpack onto the back seat and shout "Morning!" before the door shut. By the time his fogged brain registered all that, she was diving into the passenger seat up front.

Her arrival sucked the hot air from his car and the incoming cold smacked him half awake. She was leaning in to plant a kiss on his cheek but then screamed.

"Great Glorianna, Gid! What happened to you?" She winced as she studied the bruised half of his face.

"You should see the other guy."

Her scowl could have stripped varnish from furniture. "Considering what I suspect you did to him, I'll pass. Does it hurt?"

He shrugged, but the gentle stroke of her fingers turned his cool reply of "Nah" into a sharp bark.

"Yes, clearly not hurting you a bit." Her snark surrendered to her concern, though. "Seriously, what happened? If the right half of your face was bruised any more, you could cosplay as Harvey Dent without any makeup. And have you slept at all?"

He shook his head. "Been a long night. I'll give you the Cliff's

Notes version on the way to school."

"I'm half-tempted to drag your happy assets inside and plant you in my bed." Her head bobbed back and forth as she considered that. "Which actually might be fun, come to think of it."

"If I can manage not to get killed in the next twenty-four hours," he said as he looked out the rear window to back his car out of the driveway, "I might take you up on that."

He turned back around once he was on the road. He was about to put the car in drive, but Andrea's silent stare stopped him.

"What?"

"Why the next twenty-four hours?" Snark time was so very done.

She listened to him sum up most of what he'd rehashed with Ms. Aldgate. He thanked her for the loan of her phone, which had worked, and he used the reminder to lift the cell from his cup holder and put it in her twitchy, tech-addicted fingers. The rest of the story came out easily enough: Dad abducted by vampires with guns and no clue where they'd taken him. He left out the part about his mom again. He wasn't sure why that was so hard to admit to her. Hiding it from Ms. Aldgate had been one thing, but for some reason, he was ashamed of the lie his parents had forced onto him. He didn't leave out the part about Blood, working with the very assassin who'd tried to kill him just a few nights ago. He'd expected the idea of him having some form of backup would comfort her.

"That's a mistake." Andrea had held her tongue for most of the drive, staring straight ahead with her jaw set. She crossed her arms and shook her head. She cut him off before he could reassure her. "No, save it. She's the scorpion, and you're the frog."

"I'm sorry," Gidion chuckled. "You're calling me a frog?"

"You know? The fable about the scorpion and the frog?"

Before he turned into the school's parking lot, he saw the look of disbelief on her face. He was about to merge into the line of cars of people dropping off other students when Andrea snapped at him.

"Don't you dare pull up to that curb. You park this car right now and hear me out."

"Yes, your highness."

He avoided her glare as he found a space in the student parking section not too far from the English building where she had her first class of the day.

"There's this scorpion," she said. "It wants to get across this pond, so it asks a frog to give it a ride. Swears it won't sting the frog, explaining how doing that would only drown them both. The frog agrees to take him, but halfway across the pond, the scorpion stings him anyway. Just before the frog dies, it asks the scorpion why it did it, knowing they would both die. It tells him, 'Because it's my nature.'"

"Fine." He held up his hands in a show of surrender. "I won't be a frog."

She touched his chin on the less bruised side of his face and pulled him close. "Promise me." She kissed him, and her lips were warmer than he expected. More than the burst of cold air and her scream from earlier, that kiss woke him enough to wish she'd made good on her threat to drag him from the car and into her house.

Their eyes met as the kiss ended and they pulled apart. The way she looked at him caught him off guard. This girl had the same kind of steel to her eyes as Blood, but where the assassin's gaze came from a vacancy of emotion, Andrea's fears and desires filled a deep well. She was still that crazy, random girl who had invaded his circle of friends back in September, but somewhere along the way, a curtain she kept in place with everyone else had lifted just for him.

He nodded his promise, and she answered with a sad smile.

Her red velvet coat clung to her as she dashed from his car to the Science building. The crowd of students, all running around with less than five minutes before the school bell, obscured her long before she made it inside.

As much as he'd enjoyed that kiss, and could still feel the warmth of her lips on his, he couldn't bring himself to smile. He'd lied to her, an omission hidden in his promise. The truth he'd withheld cut into his conscience as he drove back to Ms. Aldgate's.

Andrea was so worried about him being the frog that it never occurred to her that the real danger was him being the scorpion.

CHAPTER THIRTY-NINE

Gidion was growing accustomed to waking up to life as bad as he left it. Ms. Aldgate might need a shaman to rid her guest bedroom of all the bad vibes he'd brought into it during the past week. He set his alarm for 4:00, not wanting to sleep past sunset. He'd worried for nothing, because he woke on his own. The time on his phone when he got out of bed and threw his clothes on was 2:13.

The local news websites didn't mention any homicides in Chesterfield County. Gidion assumed Mom and her vampires had cleaned up after him. That also suggested the police hadn't searched the park overnight. He'd assumed his gunshots lit up the 911 lines, but the thunderstorm might have negated that. Dad once told him that most firearm violations, meaning gunshots heard in the area without any other confirmation of someone being shot at, rarely resulted in anything. Most callers never had a clue where the shots had originated. That made the odds of finding a gunman, bullets, or a victim a crapshoot for any responding officers. A lot of the calls ended up just being fireworks, even when it wasn't the Fourth of July or New Year's.

Lord only knew what mess Gidion would have dealt with if Dad's car had been found in the park along with the two vampires he'd killed. Given how things had gone during the night, he felt karma owed him the break.

He and Ms. Aldgate recovered Dad's car before he drove Andrea to school. After that, she slept for two more hours and then threw herself into her assignment while he slept. She assembled a list of homes that sold in the Richmond area since he'd wiped out the local coven last fall. He'd given her some criteria to narrow her search. Most of all, he'd stressed the homes needed to be large and in nice areas. He didn't point out why. The size was partly because of the number of vampires Mom had working for her. The house had to accommodate all of them. As for the nice areas, that was all about Mom. More than once, Dad told him she'd wanted to live in some elaborate mansion, and he suspected she spent the past decade assembling enough cash to buy a place like that.

Ms. Aldgate organized her list in order of distance from the ambush site at the Willey Bridge. Her fingers shook from too much caffeine and too little sleep, which also made her talk faster than usual. He let her run through three pages worth of addresses, but in his gut, he knew the instant he saw the first home that she'd found his mother. He just prayed his instincts weren't delivering false hope.

She'd saved pictures and floor plans of the homes, and the house she'd located was just a mile west of the Willey Bridge. The backyard was right against the James River, perfect for disposing of dead bodies, if one had the knowledge of how to do it right. Cutting open the stomach would keep that sucker from ever reaching the surface.

He finished getting his gear together while Ms. Aldgate prepared some coffee and breakfast, which he took with him. He wanted a look at Mom's house while it was still daylight. Grandpa had long warned him about attacking a vampire's lair during the day. They woke super-pissed. Going after one during the day was risky enough, but a whole coven of them? He might as well walk in there and slit his wrists to save them the trouble.

That didn't mean he couldn't recon the exterior. One nice thing about vampires being flammable in daylight, they couldn't look out their windows. That didn't rule out human servants. The coven Gidion wiped out last year used half a dozen feeders, but Mom had passed on every opportunity, thus far, to use one.

Clear skies and lots of sunlight replaced last night's rain. He made good time to the house on Burnett Drive. Getting to the address forced him to navigate a series of twisted, narrow roads that followed the southern shoreline of the river. Even the smaller homes here must have cost a fortune.

He started to doubt the house on Burnett Drive would be the right one. The homes he saw as he got closer were jammed together, almost close enough to jump from one roof to the next, but as soon as he turned onto Burnett, he knew he'd hit paydirt. The houses not only got bigger, but the property sizes followed suit. The first house he passed was surrounded by a tall, wrought iron fence that sent an unspoken message of, "Stay out, but feel free to admire and envy our fabulous estate."

Not surprisingly, the address he'd come to see just emphasized the "Stay Out." A white, brick wall stood tall enough to prevent anyone driving by from seeing the house on the other side, but it wasn't so tall that he couldn't climb over it. He pulled his car onto the limited curb, which on this narrow road left half of his car sticking out in the roadway. This secluded an area wasn't likely to create a traffic issue, though. He crawled on top of his car. He had to stand to see anything.

From this angle, he realized the brick fence wasn't safe to climb. Jagged bits of glass were embedded into the top of the brickwork to slash any trespasser's hand to a bloody mess. Beyond the fence, tall evergreens covered the property and blocked most of the house from view. The two-story mansion was built from the same white brick as the fence, as if they'd constructed the outer wall from the house's leftovers. The trees formed a small forest that grew especially dense along the right and left sides of the property. He'd already guessed that from the satellite imagery he'd seen online. He used the camera on his phone to snap a few pictures.

From here, he could see enough of the house to know it matched the picture and floor plan Ms. Aldgate had supplied. Five bedrooms with a garage big enough to house three cars. More importantly, the garage provided a means to enter the house without going outside. Perfect for a vampire delivered during the day who needed to avoid sunlight. Also provided privacy for moving a body from a car into the house for dinner. The place contained all the little touches to make it a vampire's dream home.

A sign planted by the gate to the driveway warned to "Beware of Dog." Gidion decided to test that since dogs and vampires didn't mix. He climbed down from his car and popped open the trunk. He kept a bunch of sports-related equipment in there, which provided camouflage for his hunting gear and for transporting vampire bodies to the funeral home to cremate them. He pulled out one of his rattier looking baseballs and strolled down to the corner of the property. He whistled as loudly as he could manage and then threw the baseball over the fence as far as it would go. Climbing back on top of his car, he looked over the fence to see where his baseball landed. His toss went pretty far, but no dogs had rushed to see what had violated the fence line.

He considered pounding on the iron gate with one of his baseball bats as a secondary test. The gate bore an elaborate design of a lion and a dragon reared back to battle one another. The decorative design prevented the casual passerby from seeing onto the property without getting right up to it. A camera mounted on a tall pole on the other side of the gate pointed down at the outside of the gate, favoring a view of where the driver side of a car would be.

Not knowing how wide the lens of the camera was, he decided to avoid the gate. Even if vampires couldn't look out a window during the day, they could look at daytime video from a security camera. The camera might use a motion sensor to only record when something moved within its range. That meant someone could play back anything recorded later without having to search through hours of video. Not good for him.

Instead, he pulled two aluminum bats out of his car and pounded them against each other for almost half a minute. The racket got some dogs barking, but they weren't on his Mom's property. The dogs he heard were inside the fence of the house across the street. Their barking was just what he needed. He walked back to his trunk and put up his bats. He waited a little longer to see if the barking drew out any other dogs, but none answered from behind Mom's fence.

Verdict? No dogs.

Climbing back into his car, he typed a text for Blood.

'*Think I found them. Meet me at the hardware store at Forest Hill Avenue and Chippenham Parkway. Bring your wallet.*'

His thumb hovered over the "send" button. Once he sent this, he knew there was no turning back. He'd be ensuring his mother's end or his. Mom said Grandpa turned him into a murderer with a cause, and part of him worried she was right.

Could he just send Mom a text? He could warn her to let Dad go or else. Doing that might give away that he knew where she was. Hell, she might even lie to lure him into a trap.

He went back and forth on this, but what happened at the park last night settled the matter. Dad chose to move on to a life without her, and Mom answered by abducting him.

As soon as he parked in the lot of the Lowe's, he sent the text to Blood.

It was time to end this.

CHAPTER FORTY

The hardest thing about waiting was all the time it gave Gidion to question everything he was doing. Was he taking the nuclear option too fast? Was Mom really beyond redemption? Was Blood planning to betray him?

He'd decided to wait in his car in the parking lot of the Lowe's. At first, he kept the car running with the heat on, but he decided to save the gas and hope the cold would make him too uncomfortable to think about what really bothered him.

Every free moment of thought dragged him through each lie of the past decade. He was rewriting his life. Grandpa hated to sit at the kitchen table at home, because of mom's wedding portrait. He'd always assumed Grandpa just didn't like her. The time Gidion had seen the password Dad used for his laptop, Dad not only changed it but added a second password for the first time to keep him from getting on it. God only knew what other truths hid on that hard drive. Thanks to the laptops he'd taken from Bonnie and GQ Drac, he knew he could probably break into Dad's. He just wasn't sure he wanted to. Each thing he figured out only made him question three more things.

He liked the lie better. Did that make him a coward?

By the time Blood's silver Nissan pulled into the parking lot at about a quarter to six, Gidion muttered a sincere "Hallelujah." He flashed his headlights to draw her attention. Her car crawled into the space next to his, placing it so that their driver side doors faced each other.

He divided his attention between her and the entrance to the parking lot to make sure she wasn't followed.

When she rolled down her window, he did the same.

"Why here?" she asked.

"Some of us can't afford to buy our toys from Killers 'R' Us." He pointed towards the hardware store. "Welcome to the poor man's armory. You got a credit card?"

"Why should I pay for this?" Her all-too-human stinginess surprised him.

"Considering what you're getting paid to kill me, I'm sure you can spare the cash. Besides, it's not like we're buying stuff to build a house. We'll be tearing one down."

She rolled up her window and turned off her car.

They both stayed several steps apart as they walked side-by-side towards the store. He realized that might look weird once they got inside, so he moved closer to her. She reached into her jacket for God only knew what weapon as she stopped and pulled a step back.

He held up his hands. "Relax! If I wanted to saw you in half with a chainsaw, I certainly wouldn't do it here."

She stayed still a few seconds, but her hand fell back by her side without a weapon.

"We're here together." He lowered his voice and stepped closer to her again. "We just need to look like we're shopping, not having a domestic."

Her slow smile made him laugh. She'd dressed in all black. Even her light jacket was black, and while it looked nice, he could tell it had a certain practicality to it compared to what she wore to the Wawa last night. God and she only knew how many weapons she'd hidden in that jacket. Truth was, she could wear a pink t-shirt with a rainbow-striped unicorn on it and still look like a cold-blooded killer.

"Should we hold hands," the corner of her lips twitched with her sarcasm, "Honey?"

"So you're a bit of a smart ass, after all." So her lack of humor towards him last night wasn't caused by a language barrier, after all. She just didn't find him funny.

She nodded.

"All right, Muffin, let's go——"

"No."

"You can call me Honey, but I can't call you Muffin?"

Her silent glare offered him all the answer he needed.

"Baby? Darlin'? Puddin'? Love Beast?"

The brown of her eyes plummeted from freezing to sub-Arctic as he worked his way through the list of proposed nicknames.

"Maybe we should just go shopping," he said.

The way she stared back with an eyebrow arched silently called him a pea-brained idiot. He decided not to confirm his interpretation as they walked into the store together, managing to stay a little closer this time.

Her expression didn't change, but he felt her doubt choking him when they made it inside. Hard to blame her when the garden section greeted them on the left, ceiling lamps and fans straight ahead, and paint supplies to the right. This part of the store didn't really scream "vampire hunter armory."

"What items?" she asked.

"I have a few things in mind, but we need anything that will give us an advantage."

He led her straight to the tools. Her attitude improved dramatically as they stopped in front of a large display of hammers and axes.

"See anything you like?" he asked.

She surprised him by passing over the axes, none of which were very big and were more like hatchets. Instead, she lifted one of the hammers from its cradle. Unlike most of the hammers, this one didn't curve on the back end. Instead, the metal stayed straight and formed a vicious point perfect for stabbing it into something. Didn't take much imagination to envision it thrusting into a person's skull.

"Poor man's armory." She spun the hammer in her hand before placing it back on the display. "You did not come for hammers."

"No, but figured it was worth a look. Besides, we need to talk strategy."

"Goals dictate strategy." She formed the words with slow precision.

He nodded. "I know what my goals are. What's your goal?"

"Your father."

He stepped back and looked around to make sure they were out of earshot of anyone. "What does that mean?"

"First goal: retrieve your father."

He noticed she didn't say "rescue," but he let that go for the moment. "I know why he's a priority for me, but why for you?"

"Gives your mother leverage over you. I require you uncompromised."

That they both placed Dad at the top of the list didn't feel right. Gidion's instincts insisted she wasn't being straight with him about her motives, but he couldn't pin it down. He decided not to question it, though. They didn't have that kind of time if they wanted to move tonight.

He pointed down the aisle to a display with handheld blowtorches. A micro torch, the most portable looking of the batch, caught his attention. "Used something much more low tech to burn down the house for the last coven, but that could be handy."

She grunted in a way that left it unclear whether she approved. "Cannot burn their house while your father is inside. Dangerous to me, too."

"Vampires do tend to be a little more flammable." Grandpa said that applied to the older ones more than the newly-turned, like dried out firewood. He suspected none of the vampires they faced were older than Mom, and she was only working with about a dozen years.

Blood pointed to the price on the display, which showed it was just under thirty dollars. "Not too bad."

The way she coveted money made him curious. "How much are they paying you to kill me?"

"One hundred thousand dollars."

"Nice!" Gidion had to admit that his ego got a boost from that tidbit. "So, just how much is the price on your head?"

She shrugged. "Two million."

"Two million!" To say she just emasculated him didn't cover it.

She'd all but amputated his testicles with a dull spoon. He caught himself in time to lower his voice and look around once again to make sure no one was too close. "I wiped out a coven. What the hell did you do to earn a two million dollar bounty?"

She shrugged. "Why I need your mother's information."

He wondered how long her list of mayhem was, but he decided against pressing the matter.

"Let's get this anyway." He picked up the micro torch and gestured for her to follow.

"Just what made you so damn sure I'd side with you over my mother?" The bitterness to his question caught him off guard. By contrast, Blood looked as indifferent as always.

"Her portrait." She said that as if it explained everything.

He held his tongue as they passed a sales associate behind the counter of the paint section who was busy resting his chin in the palm of his hand and checking out Blood's ass. Idiot had a death wish and didn't even know it.

"So you get one look at my mom in a wedding dress, and that let you know which side I'd fall on?"

"Why did you start killing vampires?"

He knew the answer: Mom. "You didn't think I'd want to save her?"

"The thing you love corrupted by the thing you hate? I know how you plan to 'save' her." She smirked at him as they stopped in the middle of the aisle in front of the paint samples. "You are a killer. Killers are not complicated."

The need to strike her almost got the better of him. His fist shook from the effort to keep it at his side. He wanted to insist she was wrong, but they both knew better.

Instead, he said, "We should get some duct tape."

He turned his back to her as he went down the aisle past the paint supplies. The shelves with the duct tape contained a rainbow of options. Blood picked up a roll that came in zebra stripes.

"Kill vampires with this?"

"Welcome to America." He picked up a thick roll in the

traditional grey and tossed it to her. "That's enough to put the universe back together."

"What next?" Her voice had regained her initial skepticism. "Potted plants?"

"No, we need some flashlights."

She sighed, a long exhale of impatience. "I do not need help to see at night."

"Trust me. The flashlight won't be for you."

They spent another half hour in the store. That included a stop by all the house letters and numbers. Gidion went straight to a sticker for the number eight. He pulled out two of them, favoring a version of the number eight where the top and bottom of the number were identical.

Blood didn't bother filtering her opinion. "Stupid."

By the time they made it to the checkout line, Gidion felt Blood's irritation like a crazed velociraptor bearing down on him. The clerk, a woman who was probably only a few years older than Gidion, studied the two of them intently as she rang them up. At first, Gidion wondered if their purchases and demeanor had her suspicious, but then he realized she was just trying to figure out if they were boyfriend and girlfriend.

"That'll be one-twenty-eight and thirty five cents," she said.

"I believe you represent the treasury, Muffin." Gidion's grin dared her to protest the term of endearment with the clerk in front of them.

Even though she could have melted a polar cap with her glare, Blood kept silent and pulled out her wallet. Instead of a credit card, she handed over enough twenties to cover the purchase. Strangely enough, the exchange seemed to convince the sales clerk that they were a couple.

They discussed their plan as they walked to their cars. Blood summed up their strategy with one simple phrase about his mother.

"Offer what she wants."

CHAPTER FORTY-ONE

Gidion parked the Little Hearse behind Blood's Nissan. They'd chosen this spot along South Boston Circle, because this road didn't have any street lamps. Even though they were parked in front of some rather nice homes, the properties had high walls in front of them. No one in these houses would notice them unless they drove by, and even if they did, the cars were legally parked. If an officer investigated, the most he could do was suggest they leave. They didn't intend to overstay their welcome, but it still carried that risk.

Breath misted in front of Gidion as he climbed out of his Kia Soul. He grabbed his backpack from the back seat and locked the car. Like Blood, he'd opted for all black tonight and had limited his number of layers despite the cold. The only exception was to wear his t-shirt with the red bat symbol over his turtleneck. He needed freedom of movement, and once things got messy, he knew he'd be far too busy to feel the weather leeching his body heat. The shivers crawling through his skin had less to do with the weather. He kissed his fingertips and transferred the kiss to the red bat symbol on his shirt, hoping to ward off his fears.

Gidion walked to the Nissan and climbed into the front passenger seat. Blood kept the interior as cold as outside. He should have expected that. Not like Blood needed to worry about the weather.

"Thanks for keeping the car warm." His sarcasm didn't even make her blink. He rubbed his hands together, praying for enough friction to keep the chill away. Part of him wondered if the cold was intended as punishment for making her buy all that stuff inside the hardware store.

"Ready to call?" She didn't watch him. Her gaze focused on the intersecting street just thirty yards around the bend in the road.

"Almost." He reached into the backpack he'd placed on the floor of the car and pulled out the two stickers with the number "eight" in bold black font. He offered one to her.

Blood took the sticker and turned it over as if examining it for what possible use he could have in mind.

"Just put it on." He peeled off the rectangular sticker to demonstrate.

"It reflects light." She over-enunciated the words, but Gidion didn't think it was because she was having difficulty forming them.

"Inside of the jacket." He placed his sticker on the inside pocket on the left side of his jacket.

"But why?"

"For luck. Eight's considered a lucky number, so I figured this would help."

When she continued to stare at him like he was an idiot, he added, "If you put it on, I promise to never call you Muffin again."

She placed the sticker in the same place inside her jacket without another protest. "Ni naocan ma?" Well, at least not in English.

There was no mistaking her impatience as she said, "Call her."

He pulled out his phone. "Let's hope Mom has Dad's phone turned back on."

To his surprise, the line didn't go straight to voicemail.

"Gidion, I'm glad you called."

Mom's voice, even though he'd expected her to answer, hit him with all the force of a sucker punch. The way it offered false comfort both tempted and troubled him. He thought he was ready, but the fear that he might not have the will to take her head returned and heckled him. That fear could work to his advantage, though. For what he needed to do in this call, letting it show in his voice might be ideal.

"I think." He stopped, eyes twitching to his left. Having Blood here and listening made him uncomfortable, the way he felt when he'd have his friends over to play and they'd witness Dad barking at him for doing something wrong. "I want to talk," he said, "in person."

"I'd like that." The joy in her voice was impossible to miss. "I can have someone meet you, bring you here to me and your father. I know you'd like to see him. He'd like to see you, too."

"No, I'm not comfortable with that—not yet. Just you and me. We meet at the Capital Ale House downtown on Main Street."

She didn't answer right away, and he could just imagine the gears turning in her head. How easily did she think she could manipulate him? This would let him know.

"We can meet there at eleven."

He couldn't repress a nervous laugh. "I don't think so. That's a little too much time for you to make plans. I don't care to get hit over the head like Dad and tossed in a trunk."

"I promise it won't be like that. You have my word." Sincerity, thick as syrup, covered her promise.

He turned enough to hide his face from Blood. He wondered just how much added insight her heightened senses gave her. Did his heart racing make her hungry?

"If we're going to meet, we meet in a half hour."

"I'm willing to do that, but on one condition, we meet somewhere else."

"It needs to be public." He couldn't bend on that.

She sighed, the first cracks in her motherly façade starting to show. "Fine. Let's meet at Stony Point Mall, the water fountain in front of the teddy bear shop. I trust that will be public enough."

The minute Mom suggested Stony Point Mall, Blood turned to look at him. He felt her glare on his throat. If he'd doubted Blood's ability to hear and understand everything Mom said, that settled it.

"You plan to buy me a stuffed animal?" He didn't spare the sarcasm as he thought about that stuffed dragon she'd sent him all those years ago. "I'd prefer to meet downtown."

"I wouldn't."

"Then we compromise." He let his frustration show and hoped it would make him sound convincing. She'd never go for this if she thought he was happy with his suggestion. "We can meet in Carytown in front of the ticket office at the Byrd." He had to think the old movie palace would tempt her. Parking wasn't allowed directly in front of the theater. That made it an ideal place to have a car drive up, grab him, and go.

The silence that followed worried him. He wondered, just before she answered, if his phone had dropped the call.

"All right," she said. "We meet at the Byrd in an hour."

"8:30 at the Byrd. You got it." He wanted to hang up on her, but pissing her off wasn't the goal here.

"Gidion?"

He wished she'd quit saying his name. Hearing her say it, a whisper of regret from the past, felt like slow, tiny cuts.

"Yes?"

"I'm sorry it had to be like this, but I am looking forward to seeing you."

"I'll see you at 8:30," he shook as he forced out the last word, "Mom."

Then he hung up.

He stared out the window. This wasn't fair. He shouldn't feel like the monster in this, but all they were doing was trading lies.

"How much did you compromise?" Blood asked.

"Yes, I'm fine." He bit out the words as he turned to her indifferent gaze. "Thanks for asking."

"Stony Point is less than ten minutes away. How much did you compromise?"

He considered how far away the Byrd was. "Probably twenty minutes away."

"Not much time."

"Downtown was only going to be a half hour by comparison."

She turned her attention back to the intersection down the street. "Ten more minutes was better."

"Well, when it's your mom on the phone, you can make the call and plan the meet."

"My mother is dead."

"Join the club, Sweetheart."

Blood didn't press the matter after that, probably just satisfied that he hadn't called her "Muffin" again.

They waited in the dark and the cold, crouched in their seats to stay hidden. Blood pulled out a book from a compartment in her side door and cracked it open. Given her enhanced eyesight, reading in the dark didn't present a problem for her.

"What are you reading?"

She waited until she finished the page she was on and answered as she turned to the next. "*Hunger Games.*"

With the car turned off, the dashboard's display didn't offer the time. Gidion knew better than to check his phone. Boredom almost pushed him to start a conversation with Blood, but he thought better of it.

Blood looked up from her book. "Car coming. Two of them."

He kept low as he peered over the edge of the dashboard. A pair of headlights on the intersecting street drove by, followed by another pair.

He wished he had her keen eyesight. The twists of the streets along the James River made them almost as difficult to navigate as the river. The curve of the road they were on had helped hide them from view as the two cars drove by on the intersecting street, but it was near impossible for him to discern anything about the passing cars.

"Was it her?" His worst fear had been that he might have guessed wrong, that the house along the river wasn't hers. If that happened, then they'd done all this for nothing.

She sat up. "Shi," she said, which going by her nod, meant the same as "Yes."

"How many did she take with her?"

"Four."

"Four," he said to himself. The number tasted bitter.

He risked a check of the time on his phone. She'd left within fifteen minutes. She'd be in Carytown with plenty of time to let her guys position themselves and prepare an ambush.

"Plan worked." Blood sounded surprised.

"Like a charm," he muttered. Part of him was disappointed, and the realization that his mother hadn't proven him wrong, that part of him had hoped she would, angered him more.

"Leaves six."

"Actually, just three."

She slowly turned her head to fix her gaze on him. "When did you kill them?"

"Dad and I killed three at the park."

"You tell me now?"

He shrugged. "I was worried you wouldn't find dealing with seven intimidating enough. I would think you'd be happy."

She shrugged as he had. "When I said your mother had ten, I counted Pretty Boy."

"You lying, fanged piece of crap. Are you seriously telling me there are only two left?"

She smiled with obvious satisfaction as she opened her book to continue reading. "May the odds be ever in your favor."

Knowing only two vampires stood between him and Dad should have made Gidion happy. Unfortunately, all the past minute had accomplished was to make him wonder if the vampire to his left was the bigger threat.

CHAPTER FORTY-TWO

Gidion set the timer on his phone. "We'll give them fifteen minutes and then go."

"Good." Blood turned to the next page in her book. "Can finish this chapter."

He wondered if she was really that calm. Reading her wasn't as simple as the novel in her hands. Up until Blood, he thought he understood how vampires thought. For whatever reason, she didn't work the same as the others.

He sent a text to Ms. Aldgate. *'Getting ready to go in for Dad. If you don't hear back from me in three hours, call the police.'*

The reply was simple. *'Make certain I don't need to make that call. Be careful.'*

'10-4. No more texts or calls until after you see me or get a call from me.'

He considered texting Andrea, but he couldn't decide what to say that wouldn't just make her worry. Instead, he went through and purged all of his text messages. If he got caught or lost his phone, he didn't want to leave anything behind that might endanger Ms. Aldgate or Andrea. He wondered if Dad had done the same before the meeting at the park. The fact that Mom hadn't gone after Ms. Aldgate at her house suggested he probably had. Mom might not have gained total access to the phone, though. There were ways to gain partial access without knowing the user's pass code.

Gidion distracted himself by going to Tumblr and scrolling through his feed. He found a picture from the old cartoon *Gatchaman* and reblogged it. He wondered if Dad was still wearing the wristband he'd given him for his birthday. He hoped so. The memories of watching that show with Dad weren't tainted by what he'd learned in the past few days, and there was a comfort in that.

A few minutes later, his phone played Jimi Hendrix insisting there must be some way out of here. Seemed appropriate.

"You set?" Gidion asked.

She raised a finger to silence him as she stayed focused on her book. A few seconds later, she snapped the paperback shut. She shoved her book into the slot in the door and climbed out.

Even though Blood hadn't run the heat in the car, the wind caught Gidion unprepared, leeching what little warmth his body still had.

"Floor mat," Blood said as a reminder.

Gidion slid on his backpack and then grabbed the rectangular shaped piece of grey fabric from the floor of the car.

The privacy fences worked to their advantage. No one could see them from the houses as they ran down to the intersection and to the left. Mom's property was just three houses from here. The location also helped. This close to the river, they were far enough from any major roadway, so they weren't likely to have anyone randomly drive past them. Lord knows, they made a sight. As if he wouldn't look odd enough running down the street with a floor mat in his hands, neither Blood nor he bothered to hide their swords.

Once they reached the corner of the brick fence surrounding Mom's place, they paused just a second to make certain no one was watching, looking for any approaching cars, or someone out for a late night jog or walking their dog. The trees on the other side of Mom's fence hid them from view of anyone inside the house. Exploiting the vampires' lust for privacy gave Gidion and Blood their best advantage.

"Let's do this." He draped the floor mat over the top of the fence. He placed it with the carpet side of the mat face down. The fabric snagged on the bits of broken glass keeping it in place. The rubber side of the mat protected them from the glass, and its thick ridges provided them with something to grip as they climbed.

Getting over the fence turned out to be more awkward than Gidion expected because of his backpack. He carried most of their haul from the hardware store in there. He hoped that wouldn't put him too off-balance if he had to fight, which was certain to happen. Once they both made it over, Gidion pulled the mat down and left it on the ground. They weren't likely to leave this way, but they wanted the option. This was the easiest part of their plan, getting over the fence. Everything from this point forward was a viper-filled barrel of question marks.

They stayed in the cover of the trees as they worked their way towards the back of the property. They caught narrow views of the house. The front porch light was on, but none of the lights inside the front of the house had been left on.

"Probably in the back of the house," Gidion said. They'd studied the floor plans for the house that the real estate website had provided. The right side of the house was their best approach. The upstairs didn't have a single window, and even though the downstairs rooms did, they belonged to the master bedroom and master bath. None of Mom's guys were likely to be in those rooms. Of course, that assumed the master bedroom was being used for that purpose.

Blood led the way through the trees, since her eyes were better-suited for navigating in the dark. They headed towards the backyard so they could see the rear windows.

No lights were on in the back of the house either, except for the living room. The way that light flickered, it had to be a television.

"You sure about how many goons she has working for her?" Gidion asked.

She nodded. "Shi, a vampire betrayed her plans to the regional elder who herds nomads on the East Coast."

"Why did he betray her?"

"Because your mother is a fool."

"She's no fool, just driven by emotion." The desire to defend his mother surprised him, but Dad had talked about her enough for him to know something of what she was like. Dad worked with logic and precision. Mom drew him out of his shell as much as he'd tempered her. Wasn't surprising that they'd fallen into self-destructive lifestyles after they were forced apart.

"Emotions will end her and her followers." Blood led them deeper into the backyard.

Gidion still felt that urge to defend Mom, but he already knew the reasons Blood was being paid to finish her. Mom was far too young. At a minimum, bloodsuckers needed at least twenty-five years to qualify as an elder. Never mind that she was building a coven out of the nomadic vampires she'd met over the years, although she'd probably turned a few of them herself which would explain why some of them were shades.

Most male vampires were expected to travel, and only a few were welcomed within a coven. Nomadic vampires paid heavy tithes which were given to the covens and intended to finance safe houses. Judging from Bonnie and GQ Drac's emails, the covens were gouging the nomads. Mom's plans would turn Richmond into a haven for nomadic vampires outside of that system and deny the covens that revenue. In a strange way, he was proud of her, because her plans were intended to start a revolution. She'd assumed that once she had her coven in place, the other vampires wouldn't be willing to risk exposure for a war.

Mom hadn't counted on two things: Gidion being the hunter who took out the previous coven and Blood being hired to kill him. Once she found out about Gidion, it changed everything. If the vampires hadn't already brought in this assassin to finish him, they might not have considered the option to use her against Mom until it was too late. They would have had to acknowledge Mom's coven. That would be like the United States or China being forced to recognize an upstart dictatorship in some third world country as a legitimate government.

Mom's only hope was to take out Blood first and collect the bounty. With two million dollars, she could pay the East Coast elders enough to overlook her sins.

He pointed to a spot along the edge of the tree line that was equidistant between the house and the edge of the James River. From here, the river looked like warped, black glass. It was riding high, too, after all the recent rain. Blood led them through the dark, gnarled path of exposed roots and fallen branches to the place he'd indicated.

"This work for you?" he asked.

She smiled.

With that, he slipped off his backpack and zipped it open. "Keep an eye on the house." Among their purchases had been a small spray bottle. He sprayed the bottom of the selected tree trunk, and the scent of gasoline pushed Blood back a few steps. If that hadn't made him smile, the memory of how he'd used this same technique to burn down the previous coven's home did.

He pulled out a lighter, the kind that came with a long wand and a trigger, and offered it to Blood. She glared at him. "Where is my thirty dollar propane torch?"

"I got the torch for me. You thought it was a waste of money." He wiggled the lighter in his hand for her to take it. "Besides, this lighter keeps you farther from the flame. Given that you're more flammable than I am, I figured you'd prefer something that would make you less likely to go poof."

She snarled as she snatched it from his hand. "Plan had better work."

He winked at her and took off through the trees headed back towards the front of the house. Counting on the limited number of windows facing his direction, Gidion sprinted from the trees to the side of the house. From there, he moved cautiously towards the front. Azalea bushes, well-groomed into boxes, lined the edge of the house. The tallest bush was placed at the corner of the house and was shaped more like a Christmas tree. He sprayed the tallest bush with the bottle of gasoline. He hoped both of the vampires still here were watching TV together in the back of the house, or he might find himself attacked at any second. Their heightened sense of smell wouldn't miss this if they were anywhere near the front of the house, not to mention their heightened sense of hearing. The spray bottle wasn't loud, but it was probably loud enough for a vampire without any other sound in the room to distract him.

He looked in Blood's direction. Even with the moon out, he

couldn't see her. The blue flame of the micro torch hissed to life. He waved the torch in a slow arc to signal Blood to start her fire, too. Turning his attention to the tall bush, he pointed the flame at it making sure not to get too close. The gas probably wasn't necessary to set the bush or tree on fire, but given the recent, heavy rain, he didn't want to take any chances. Besides, they needed these fires to be big and easy to see from a distance. The gasoline ensured an impressive show.

The flame caught, the bush erupting with a loud gasp. Gidion jumped back, worried for a moment he might get burned. Satisfied with his act of arson, he checked on the second fire near Blood. Flames engulfed the base of the tree.

If the vampires were in that back room, it wouldn't matter what was on the TV. They wouldn't miss that tree going up in flames.

The fires got the desired reaction. He heard two voices, both men, yelling at each other. They came from the back of the house. Gidion crouched in front of the house. His position allowed him a slim bit of space between the corner of the house and the bush so that he could see what was happening. This was a case where the vampires' keen eyesight worked against them. Vampires were great at seeing in the dark, but the bright light of the fire would blind them and render Gidion little more than a shadow in the background. He saw them run towards the tree trunk, still together. They hadn't noticed Gidion's fire yet.

One of them yelled at the other to grab the hose. They'd expected that. Under normal circumstances, they might have been willing to call for the fire department. Vampires couldn't fool around where fire was concerned. Unfortunately, Gidion's fire right up against the outer wall all but ensured the fire department would check inside the house. Despite his careful application, some of the gas had made it onto the house and the flames jumped onto the wall. These vampires couldn't risk any humans going inside the house, not with Dad being held prisoner.

The shorter of the two ran for the back of the house again, but then he saw the fire Gidion had set and they both stopped. Both of them cursed. Gidion held in one of his own, because the tall one ordering the small guy around was already on his cell phone. Didn't take many guesses who was on the other end of the line, and it wasn't 911. He'd also hoped these guys would be shades like Mom. No such luck.

The good news was that the plan split up the two. The taller goon headed for Gidion's fire. The closer he got, the more Gidion realized this guy was really tall, close to six-and-a-half feet. Just great.

Gidion drew his sword and ran for the cover of another tall bush on the other side of the front door. There weren't many hiding places here, and no room for retreat. The three-car garage jutted out from the left side of the house. His hiding place positioned him almost right on the inside corner of the "L" formed by the garage and the front of the house.

Jesus, he hoped this worked, because he was going to need all the advantage of surprise he could manage, but his hiding place left more than twenty feet between him and where the vampire would be.

"What do you think I'm trying to do?" The Less-Than-Jolly-Fanged-Giant shouted into his phone as he rounded the corner. "Just hurry up and get here!"

Bushes rustled, followed by a shrill squeak as the vampire turned on the garden hose. The spout was just a few feet from the right side of the front door, the same side as the bush that was on fire. Water gushed from the hose. Then the sound of water spilling out changed. The vampire must have pressed his thumb to the spout to create the spray. Gidion assumed that required both of his hands. Even if it didn't, he'd be forced to use his gun one-handed while fighting the fire, and that didn't work as well as the movies suggested.

Gidion ran from his hiding place with his sword drawn. He kept his trap shut, but that didn't silence the clap of his feet on the brick driveway.

To his relief, the vampire used both hands to handle the hose, but he heard Gidion the second he launched from his hiding place.

Gidion worried about getting shot. What he hadn't expected was to get sprayed with the hose when the vampire turned to look in his direction. The blast of water was by chance at first, buy Jolly recognized the advantage and aimed the frigid water at Gidion's face. The attack blinded him for a split second. The spray went away, his vision restored, and he saw the vampire reach into his jacket. Already committed, Gidion finished the charge. He swung his sword, wishing he'd brought something longer than this wakizashi.

His swing caught the vampire's forearm before he could pull out the gun. The strike sliced deep into the arm, but it wasn't enough to sever it. Given how quickly vampires could heal, that made his attack little better than a paper cut. The vampire retreated, and without his gun. Gidion pressed the attack.

Jolly not only dodged his swings, but he reached past them to grab Gidion by his left forearm. He lifted Gidion off the ground one-handed and drew his gun. Gidion kicked with both feet into the guy's stomach. The strike caused Jolly to drop him and sent them both tumbling to the ground.

They landed on the grass and not the bricks. Gidion swung his sword before trying to get up, but Jolly rolled out of the way.

They scrambled to their feet. Gidion couldn't let this guy get off a shot. That meant staying in close and pressing his attack. He thrust forward, stabbing his sword deep into Jolly's stomach. He left it there and twisted it. Putting all of his limited weight into it, Gidion pushed the vampire back and into the burning bush. He'd hoped to send the vampire up in flames. That didn't go as planned, even though the back of the vampire's jacket smoked as they rolled off to the right. The only part that went in Gidion's favor was that Jolly lost his gun. Gidion ripped his sword out of the vampire as they pulled apart. The vampire hissed and bared his fangs.

A pair of gunshots cracked from the backyard, and brick shattered right behind Jolly as the bullets hit the side of the house.

Jolly flinched, glancing over his shoulder and then in the direction the shots had come from. Gidion resisted the urge to look and buried his sword in Jolly's thick neck. A second swing finished the job.

Only then did Gidion turn to look towards the backyard. Blood stared back at him as she tossed the gun to the ground. She picked up the hose and finished what the shorter vampire, now a head shorter than before, had failed to even start, which was putting out the tree.

Gidion did the same after he wiped the blood from his sword. If an officer or one of the neighbors saw these fires, first responders might pour into this place.

No sooner had Gidion put out the burning bush than he heard an alert tone coming from Jolly's headless body. Gidion pulled the phone out of the dead vampire's jacket pocket and saw the text message on the screen. The name on the screen "Caelan" let him know it was from Mom, and her message wasn't good news.

"Blood!" He ran to her as she dropped the hose next to the smoking tree and picked up her dead vampire's handgun. "We have ten minutes."

CHAPTER FORTY-THREE

The news that the fanged cavalry would arrive in ten minutes didn't receive the insult and gripe Gidion expected. Blood held her tongue and ran for the back porch of the mansion. He stayed with her. His body shivered now that he was no longer distracted by the fight with Jolly. Every stitch of clothing he wore was drenched, and when Blood paused just outside the door to the screened porch, he wanted to shove her out of the way and get inside the house.

"All of the first floor before the second," she said.

"I helped make the plan, you know." The last thing they wanted was to risk that another vampire was here and find themselves trapped upstairs while a guy with a gun blocked their path of escape.

They'd both taken the guns from their kills, but neither of them seemed eager to use them. Gidion had flipped on the gun's safety and placed it in his backpack. Handguns didn't do much good against vampires unless they were a heavy caliber hollow-point and the gunman's aim was near perfect. Gidion got damn lucky with the rifle against Blood back at his Grandpa's house.

He gestured for her to move, and she took them inside the screened porch which included a small bar. From there, they went through the back door into the kitchen and dining area. His wet tennis shoes squeaked on the tiled floor. A groan of disgust slipped out as they walked through the kitchen. He wondered what use, if any, a kitchen saw in a house full of vampires.

A cheer erupted from the living room, off to their left. Judging from the play-by-play of the announcer, their vampires were watching a hockey game. Sounded like the San Jose Sharks were chomping the mess out of the Carolina Hurricanes.

They went through the room with the TV. The master bedroom was on the other side with its door closed but not locked. Blood threw it open, glanced inside a moment and then moved to the right through the walk-in closet towards the master bath.

Gidion didn't follow her. The bedroom wasn't occupied, but they hadn't expected it would be. This space belonged to his mother. No question about that. The bedroom reminded him of Dad's, which he'd never bothered to update after she died.

A shut laptop rested on the night stand. A small light glowed to indicate it was in standby mode. The top of the case was purple, Mom's favorite color. He unplugged the laptop and slid it into his backpack.

Just as he was about to walk out, he saw several photographs framed and mounted on the wall. One included a picture of Mom and Dad holding him when he was a baby. Other frames contained his school pictures. He spotted his little league football photo. These were the extra five-by-sevens that Dad had claimed went into his locker. Then he saw the picture Dad took of him when he was eight and holding Windsor, his stuffed dragon. He pulled the picture off the wall.

"What are you doing?" Blood kept her voice low, but that didn't make it any less harsh.

He took a deep breath and blinked a few times to push back his emotions. "I was getting her laptop." He set the picture on the dresser.

"Downstairs is clear," she said. "We have six minutes." She took them to the foyer. The staircase to the second floor started there. That led to a landing and split to the right and left.

She pointed for him to go left while she went right. Naturally, that left him with more house to search. The first bedroom he came to faced the front of the house and contained three single beds. Mom's boys shared space to fit in this house. Only one of the beds was made, and they scattered all of their clothes throughout the room. The whole thing struck him as so damn domestic that it was weird. He checked the room's connecting bath and walk-in closet but found nothing.

He returned to the hallway. Blood emerged from the bedroom she'd checked. They exchanged shakes of their heads. Blood went for the rear bonus room, while he went to the bedroom to the left.

He was tempted to call out, but nothing guaranteed Dad was capable of answering him. Even worse, if the guy who had betrayed Mom fed Blood bad intel, they might run into more vampires. Shouting for Dad would give away their position, not that the hardwood floors throughout the house did anything to help with that. Their footsteps sounded far too loud.

The second bedroom he checked turned out to be just as empty as the first. Blood joined him from her section of the house. They only had one room left to check...the room over the garage. Next to the door, a narrow set of stairs led down. He glanced to make sure no one was there while he waited for Blood.

She held up three fingers to indicate how much time they had left. Gidion wanted to kick himself once he saw the door. This was it, without question. Unlike all the other doors that had been left open, the door was shut. Someone also installed two brass slide bolts on the outside of the door.

Gidion undid the bolts and threw the door open. The space wasn't finished. The blackout curtains blocked the moonlight and kept the room in total darkness. Gidion pulled out a short, stubby flashlight he'd gotten at the hardware store. He pressed the button on its base and 320 lumens flared to life. The light revealed a single bed, like the ones in the other rooms, placed in the center of the room. Dad was on top of the bed, stripped of his clothes and cuffed to the headboard.

Gidion had prepared himself for the poor conditions his father might have been forced to endure. He wasn't prepared for his father's reaction to his flashlight: an anguished cry and a hiss.

CHAPTER FORTY-FOUR

Gidion froze. The hiss sounded like a vampire. "That's not possible." He didn't know all the mechanics of the process, but he knew enough. "It's only been two nights."

"He is not turned." Blood gripped Gidion's arm and pushed the light to aim away from Dad and at the floor. "Bolt cutters. Hurry."

She marched up to the side of the bed and grabbed Dad by the head. Gidion went to the other side.

"Gidion?" Dad's voice came out slurred, hearing it like this reminded Gidion of how Grandpa sounded when he got drunk. "Who is this?"

"Call me Blood." Dad flinched back and gritted his teeth. Even with the light pointed at the floor, the glow revealed Dad's canines. They'd grown to sharp points, but still lacked the length.

"It's okay, Dad." The bolt cutters were heavy, and getting them placed on the chain was awkward. To Gidion's surprise, the vampires left on the *Gatchaman* wristband Gidion had given Dad, despite stripping the rest of his clothes. "I need you to stay still."

Blood turned Dad's head to examine his neck. "She has been with him twice."

Gidion grunted as he squeezed the bolt cutters to slice the link near Dad's wrist. They would need to wait until elsewhere to get the metal bracelets off of Dad's wrists, but they could at least free him. "What does that mean?"

"Bad for getting him out, but your mother will be weak from sharing her blood."

Dad lunged at Blood, reaching for her throat with his freed hand. Gidion shouted at him to stop, but Dad never got a grip on

Blood. She slapped his arm aside far too easily.

"Don't tell him." Dad's eyes had been glassy, but he focused when Blood mentioned Mom. He turned to Gidion.

"I already know."

Dad hid his face as Gidion snapped the chain of the handcuffs holding the right arm captive. Blood manhandled Dad into an upright position.

"There are more than a half dozen vampires and your mother," Dad said.

"We know." Gidion ran the light over the rest of the room, looking for Dad's clothes. "Only Mom and four others are left. They're gone, but we've only got a few minutes."

"Take from other rooms." Blood's glare warned Gidion to shut up and move. "Bathrobe, towel, just enough to reach the cars."

Gidion ran into the room across the hall. He grabbed some dark green sweats he'd seen earlier, hanging off the foot of a bed. Dad would have to go commando.

He went back into Dad's room and jerked to a halt. Dad was still sitting on the bed and Blood stood right in front of him. His head tilted back and his mouth gaped. Blood held the edge of a dagger against one of her fingertips.

"Get away from him!"

Blood glared at Gidion. "No time for anything else."

Dad raised a hand to keep him back. The hand shook from the effort to not collapse. "It's all right."

"He must walk, or we die." Blood sliced across her finger and several drops of her blood spilled into Dad's waiting mouth. His eyes rolled back in his head and his moan shook through the dusty air. She shared her blood, treating him like a feeder. The infusion gave him a brief high. Gidion knew how this worked, but he'd never witnessed it.

"Get dressed." Blood summoned Gidion with a gesture of her hand to give Dad the borrowed clothes.

Dad stood without any help. He slid the pants on and then the sweatshirt. "No shoes?"

Gidion shook his head.

"Don't suppose you have an extra sword?" Dad asked.

"Nope, but I've got this." Gidion reached into his backpack and pulled out the handgun.

"Where did you get this?" Dad looked like Gidion admitted to cheating his way through Ms. Aldgate's class.

"Took it from one of Mom's vampires."

Blood snapped her fingers at them. "Move!"

They didn't make it down the front stairs to the foyer. Light flared through the front windows. Dad cringed back and turned his entire body to place his back to the light.

The cars screeched as they stopped in the middle of the driveway. The headlights went dark.

"Wo cao!" She hissed and hit Gidion with the complaint he'd expected earlier. "Ten more minutes would have been better."

CHAPTER FORTY-FIVE

The vampires climbed out of the cars. They'd stopped halfway up the driveway. Even from inside the house, Gidion heard his mother yelling.

The irritation on Blood's face changed to a grin. "Arguing."

"Can you tell what they're arguing about?"

"Their guns," Dad said, clearly avoiding a look at Gidion, "and you. She doesn't want you shot, but they're losing patience with her."

Gidion hadn't considered how limited the loyalty of Mom's vampires might be. Vampires got stronger with age, harder to kill. Mom lacked the divide to make her position secure.

"Splitting up." Blood sounded pleased. "Two go for the back, one on each side."

Mom and the two still with her walked up the driveway to the front door.

"Other stairs." Gidion ran back towards the room where the vampires had kept Dad. "We go down that way, out of sight, and slip into the garage."

They raced down the narrow set of stairs, reaching the bottom just as the front door creaked open. Blood opened the door to the garage. Gidion and Dad got hung up trying to usher the other through the door first.

Blood grabbed Dad by his sweatshirt and jerked him into the garage. Gidion made a mental note that she was much stronger than she looked. That or the small feeding Blood gave him provided just enough energy to stay on his feet and little else.

Gidion shut the door with a click that echoed through the garage. He hoped it didn't sound as loud on the other side of the door.

A look around didn't offer Gidion the escape he'd anticipated. The floor plan they'd seen had suggested a door leading out the back of the garage, but someone had bricked up the door long ago. The only car in the garage, an army green Buick LeSabre that looked like a refugee from the seventies, was parked in front of the far garage door. A table with a large toolbox was placed against the wall flush to the house. A layer of dust muted the red of the toolbox, suggesting this was inherited from the previous owner. Blood went straight for the toolbox and pulled out a screwdriver and hammer.

Gidion found the control panels for the garage doors next to the house door. Each panel was dark grey with several buttons which were labeled.

"Soon as we open that door, they'll know where we are." Gidion glanced at Dad. He stood next to the door with his gun ready.

"Wait," Blood said as she walked towards the Buick.

"You know how to hotwire a car?"

She didn't answer as she climbed into the driver's seat.

"How is it you're working with this vampire?" Dad didn't take his eyes off the door as he asked.

"She was hired to kill me, but now she's getting paid to kill Mom."

Dad didn't say anything, but his face tightened. Whatever his thought was, he wasn't pleased. "Get in the car with her. Surely it has a garage door opener."

"Yes, but I'm in better shape than you."

Dad's jaw clenched. "Do as you're—"

The door flung open. Gidion saw one of Mom's vampires, not one of the shades. The vampire carried a gun in his hands, but he never got it up for a shot. He screamed just before Dad blasted three bullets dead center on the vampire's face. Gidion knew he'd never unsee the explosion of blood and gore. Definitely hollow-point bullets.

The car cranked to life.

"Get in!" Blood shouted. The garage door groaned and

screeched as she hit the opener on the visor.

Gidion and Dad ran for the car. Dad backed up, keeping his eyes on the house door. Gidion made it to the passenger side of the car, but he never got any further than to open the door.

"Cǎo nǐ zǔzōng shí bā dai!" Blood slammed her fist on the steering wheel. One of the vampires had moved their car in front of the garage to block them in, and two of Mom's remaining vampires stood on each side of the car with their guns ready.

So much for their escape route.

CHAPTER FORTY-SIX

One of the shades, who must have been the most recently turned, judging from the fact he still had a slight tan, aimed his gun at Dad.

"Put it down!" He hissed a slow threat to go with the spoken one. "Do it now, or we'll shoot you and your brats. I don't care what Caelan says."

"Matthew!" The shout came from the front of the house. Mom walked out the front door and strolled towards them. Seeing his mother move like one of these predators poured a cold sickness down his throat.

In some ways, she looked the same as always. Dad once described her fashion sense as eclectic. She wore a short, dark green velvet jacket that had a subtle military style to it. Along with her black pants and boots, she belonged in a Steampunk novel. She looked a little older than her wedding portrait, but not by much. She'd been turned when she was 29, and if the truth of what she'd become wasn't so horrifying, the irony of forever being that age would have been hysterical.

"Let's all relax." She smiled, the gracious hostess pretending her guests weren't held at gunpoint. She stopped next to Matthew and placed her hand on his arm. If Matthew's sunglasses hadn't been enough of a tip, Gidion would have recognized the show of ownership in how she touched him. She'd turned this guy herself. Given that the other two also wore sunglasses, they were probably all hers, which explained why she'd chosen them to go with her and left two non-shades behind.

Even with her eyes hidden, Gidion noticed how she looked from Blood to him. One of her eyebrows arched as her lips curled in amusement.

"Caelan, let our son leave, and I'll stay." Dad hadn't lowered his gun, and Gidion noticed the difference in how he held it compared to the three vampires working for Mom. He knew how to handle it. Grandpa had taken Gidion shooting, and while most of the experience dealt with rifles, he'd spent a lot of time pointing out the better shooters at the firing range. Only Matthew held his gun with both hands. He looked like he knew what he was doing, standing in a proper stance similar to Dad's. One of the guys, a short, hairy guy with a scruffy beard like Wolverine, had adopted a pose similar to the kind used in a duel. He held the gun in one hand. He probably thought this made him less of a target, but it would make his accuracy crap.

Mom patted Matthew's bicep and then placed herself between her pet and Dad. "I've always loved this side of you," she said with a smile that was equal parts sugar and sin, "my handsome white knight, but we both know it's too late for you to leave."

Judging from the pain in Dad's expression, he knew Mom was right.

Gidion pointed his sword at Mom as a threat. "We're leaving anyway."

"Then you're condemning your father to death." She walked in front of Blood's running car as if it presented no threat. Blood's eyes tracked Mom's movements the way a hungry cat follows a rodent. "I guess your school's sex ed classes left out the part on how you make a vampire. I've drained and fed your father twice. If he misses the third feeding, he'll die within a week, and he'll suffer the entire way."

The news hit him hard enough to make him stumble back. He glanced at Blood, who was staring at him. An impatient roll of her eyes and a single, firm nod confirmed Mom's warning wasn't a bluff.

"Gidion." Mom's voice pulled him back to her. "I was wondering if it was you who killed Teanna?"

The question left him confused for a moment, but then he remembered the vampires in the van outside the hotel. She was talking about "Bonnie," the vampire with the snuff videos on her laptop. The name on her driver's license had been Teanna.

"Yeah, I killed her. Why?"

"Did you like her?" She asked it like this was Christmas morning, and he'd just opened his presents. "I picked her for you."

"That's enough!" Dad moved in closer, his gun trained on Mom instead of Matthew.

"No!" Her snarl brought Dad to a stop next to Blood's driver side window. "You still don't understand. I'm doing this for us, so we can be together again. You have no idea how alone I've been."

Gidion remembered the email that was sent to Teanna about an opportunity here in Richmond. Now he understood. The opportunity wasn't to find the hunter killing all the nomads who traveled through Richmond. She'd planned for Bonnie to turn him, the same way she was turning Dad.

"You're wrong, Mom. He's been alone for a very long time. We both have, and I finally understand why."

Mom answered with a silent stare that belonged to the monster she'd become.

"Blood," he said, without taking his eyes off of Mom, "light 'em up."

CHAPTER FORTY-SEVEN

The headlights on the Buick flared to life, blinding Mom and her shades despite their sunglasses. Everything went to Hell after that.

Blood planted her foot on the accelerator, launching close to two tons of automobile at the vampires and their Hyundai.

Bullets fired both ways. Gidion heard them hiss past him and strike the cement floor and brick wall of the garage. Mom screamed, getting clipped by the front of the car as she tried to run out of the way. The vampires shouted and stumbled blindly as they retreated.

Metal smashed and screeched as the front of the Buick buried into the side of the Hyundai. With only ten feet to travel, it only managed so much damage.

Both Gidion and Blood, who abandoned the Buick, charged forward with their swords. Gidion reached the "duelist" first. The vampire tripped on one of the bricks as he fled. Even blinded, his keen hearing detected Gidion's approach. He raised his gun, pointing it towards the sound of footsteps, but he got the gun up too late. Gidion sent his head rolling across the bricks.

He wondered how long they had to finish this before the police showed. The two shots earlier wouldn't have drawn much attention. A car crash and a full-blown gunfight was a different story.

Mom ran for her car, but before she got halfway to it, two bullets from Dad's gun struck the black Mustang. Both hit the front tire. One shot ricocheted, whistling off the brick driveway. The other shot flattened the tire, deflating it in seconds.

Without missing a beat, Mom changed directions, running for the front door of the house. She pulled out her gun as she did it and shot in the direction the bullets had come from. The reaction must have been instinct, because she screamed as she realized she'd just hit Dad.

She stopped as he collapsed to the bricks. "Aric!" Gidion thought she might go to him, but she retreated into the house instead.

Blood was busy with Matthew. The driver of the Hyundai was still in the driver's seat of the car, but his head was now on the driveway where Blood had probably tossed it after slicing it off.

Even though Dad fell face down on the ground, a groan let Gidion know he was alive.

"Where are you hit?" Gidion asked as he rolled him onto his back.

"My hip." Dad winced as he laughed. "Your mom always did like my hips."

Gidion pulled out his phone to get an ambulance. Mom would have to wait. Dad grabbed his wrist to stop him.

"I'll be fine."

Was he nuts? "The big blood stain says otherwise. I'm calling. Now, shut up."

Dad didn't let go. "It's already healing."

The vampire blood Mom had fed him…. "What she said," Gidion glanced over his shoulder at Blood and Matthew to make sure things still weren't going Matthew's way. "Will you really die?"

Dad nodded. "Done deal."

"Then maybe we should let Mom finish it." Gidion laughed from nerves, but he was serious.

Dad grabbed him by the front of his jacket and pulled him in close. "That is not your mother. She's been gone a long time. I just didn't want to admit it." Dad took in a sharp breath as he sat up and leaned his head against Gidion's chest. "I've spent the past decade watching her slip away, because I couldn't bring myself to give her a quick end."

"It's all right." He lowered Dad to the driveway and stood.

"Gidion?"

"Because I'm gonna end it."

He didn't look back as he ran after Mom.

CHAPTER FORTY-EIGHT

Dad's shouts chased after Gidion just before he ran inside. He didn't doubt Dad felt obligated to finish this himself, but it was too late. If he didn't reach Mom before the police arrived, then this might never end.

The house was still dark and silent, except for the hockey game on the TV in the back. He glanced at the hardwood floor, hoping for a trail of blood to follow. No such luck. Mom's wounds, if she'd had any from Blood hitting her with the car, had healed.

Gidion patted his jacket just above the concealed "eight" which was also positioned above the red bat logo on his t-shirt. He moved through the house quickly. Mom had to hear him, but he'd long passed the need to keep quiet. Only the risk of ambush prevented him from running through the house.

He needn't have worried. He found her on the floor of her bedroom. She sat with her back to the door. Her gun rested next to her, just within reach. She held a picture in her hand, the one of her and Dad with him as a baby.

"I saw you play football when you were in fifth grade." She sounded like she was crying, but he couldn't decide if he should trust it. "It was the only evening game you had that season. Your Dad let me know ahead of time, so I could make it."

Gidion went into the room, but stayed just out of her reach. His hands ached from their grip on his sword.

"That was the last time I saw you." She ran her fingertips over him in the picture. "After that, I just couldn't bear to see you again, to be that close and never near enough."

Her body tensed. Then she launched from her spot. Her hands

dropped the picture and snatched the gun. Gidion darted to the right. He needed to get behind her and move in close enough to take her head before she could shoot him.

The gun fired before he could even rear his sword back for the strike.

The hiss of pain he heard didn't come from him or Mom. The bullets went towards the door and struck the same vampire Dad had shot in the garage. His face was only half-healed, a shattered mess of flesh with one eye obliterated. His body jerked back from the shots that went into his chest.

Before the vampire could recover, Gidion shoved him to the floor and sliced his head off in a single strike.

He looked back at Mom as she lowered the gun. The slide was locked back. She'd emptied every bullet to protect him. The gun slipped from her fingers and clattered to the hardwood floor.

She trembled as she removed her sunglasses. He expected to see his mother's blue eyes, the ones he'd always studied in her wedding picture, but they were vampire eyes, the eyes of a shade. The widened pupil all but hid her iris.

He followed her in here to kill her. She must know it, but she'd still prevented one of her own from attacking him.

"You're my son."

She reached out for him. He stepped back, and she whimpered at his revulsion. Something in him split apart to see her like that, to know even now when she was more monster than mother, he'd managed to hurt her.

"I just wanted things to be like they were." She kept her arms outstretched.

He went to her. A sob shuddered through her chest as she pulled him close. The hug didn't offer any warmth and only made him colder as she crushed herself against his body, still covered in damp clothes.

"I have a girlfriend," he said, struggling to get the words out. "You'd like her."

She laughed and sounded almost human again. "I wish I

could meet her."

"I made her a promise this morning." As he rested his forehead against Mom's shoulder, he noticed for the first time that he was taller. "I didn't realize until now that there was never any danger of not keeping it."

He still heard Andrea's voice, filled with all of her insistence and fear as she explained the old fable.

Mom stroked his hair and kissed him just above his ear. "What was the promise?"

"Not to be a frog."

Mom pulled back to look him in the eyes. Her face was twisted with confusion. "I don't understand."

He almost choked on his reply. "I know."

He'd always been the scorpion, and what came next had never been in doubt.

The strike of his sword was swift, arriving more than a decade late.

CHAPTER FORTY-NINE

Blood had already started the cleanup by the time Gidion rejoined her and Dad outside. Even if any of the neighbors had called the police and provided a detail to make it worth going lights and sirens, the twisted roads along the river probably slowed them.

The three of them managed to get the cars, except for Mom's Mustang, into the garage and slid the vampire bodies in there, too. From there, Gidion relied on a subtle bit of trickery to deal with the police.

Remembering Dad's comments about how most people can never tell the difference between fireworks and gunfire, Gidion had prepared for something like this long ago. This past New Year's, he gathered some previously set off fireworks that he'd found in his neighborhood. He tossed them over the fence and into the street.

If the officer stopped in front of the gate, he'd see them and assume some kids had set them off. Police expect citizens to get it wrong when it comes to gunfire and fireworks, just one of the reasons they don't go lights and sirens for those calls.

"Pretty clever," Dad said as they watched from inside the house. They waited upstairs, roughly in the same place on the stairs where they'd been when they spotted Mom and her vampires pull into the driveway. A patrol car crawled past the front gate. A bright light mounted on the top of the police cruiser flashed over the property, moving across Mom's car, but given the way the Mustang was parked and how far it was from the road, the flat tire was hidden from view. Dad didn't flinch this time. He'd borrowed Matthew's sunglasses, since he no longer needed them.

"Came up with the idea for the fireworks a long time ago,"

Gidion said. "Always wanted to surprise Grandpa with it, but I never got to use it until now."

"He'd have been impressed."

Gidion wasn't so sure about that, given how things had gotten between the two of them during Grandpa's last days.

"I need to call Ms. Aldgate," Gidion said, "and let her know we're not dead."

He didn't need to look at Dad to know the mention of Ms. Aldgate made him nervous. Dad's voice was cautious when he finally managed to speak. "What did you tell her—?"

"About Mom?" The words came out with more venom than he'd intended. He took a breath to get out the bitterness before he said more. "I didn't tell her anything. Just couldn't think of a way to do it. Didn't want to."

Blood appeared in the foyer below them.

"Find anything else useful?" Gidion asked.

She climbed the steps. "Not really."

Gidion reached into his backpack, resting on the steps beside him. He pulled out Mom's purple laptop and held it out to her. The entire time, he kept his right hand wrapped around the hilt of his sword, just in case she tried anything.

Blood eyed the laptop once she'd joined them on the stairs.

"My mom's," he said. "I suspect you'll find whatever information you need on here."

"Questioning her would have been better." Her complaint didn't prevent her from taking the laptop.

"So, how do you plan to provide them with proof I'm dead?" Gidion adjusted his grip on his sword.

"When you are ready," she said, looking past him at Dad, "call me."

Gidion didn't take his eyes off her as she headed for the front door. He wanted to cut her down for what she was suggesting, but part of him knew he should thank her.

She stopped at the door and smirked over her shoulder at Gidion.

"Remember, Honey." She waggled a finger at him. "No more killing."

"Sure thing, Muffin."

She didn't smile at the nickname he'd promised not to use, but she didn't complain either. Gidion watched her every step as she walked up the driveway to make sure she really left.

"Don't hate her for what she's going to do." Dad's voice was a whisper full of dread. "I'll be lucky if I last a week. Healing that gunshot probably used a lot of what your Mom gave me. Means I'll burn out a lot—"

"Shut up." Much as he didn't want to, Gidion glared up at his dad. "Grandpa's visitation is tomorrow, the funeral the day after. I'd rather save some tears for that."

Dad pulled him into a hug. Unlike the one from Mom, this one had the right warmth to it. She hadn't taken that from him yet.

CHAPTER FIFTY

Gidion spilled more tears at the visitation than he expected. In hindsight, he realized his backup plan to lure the vampires here would never have worked. He was drained, physically and emotionally.

The line of visitors for Grandpa went out the door of the funeral home. About half of them were people Dad knew from work, including some police officers in uniform who stopped by during their shift or on their way to work. Others were closer to Grandpa's age. A few of the older ones spoke about what a good man he'd been. Some would hesitate as if they wanted to say something more but were too scared to. A handful worked up the nerve to share a story of Grandpa saving them from a "mugger." Gidion wondered how many of them believed that was the truth and refused to believe it was a vampire? Maybe they didn't think Gidion or Dad would believe it.

Ms. Aldgate stayed at Dad's side the entire time. Seeing them together made Gidion smile. They held hands. Ms. Aldgate sometimes rested her head on Dad's shoulder.

Grandpa had insisted on a closed casket. While he didn't often discuss what his final wishes were, one thing he'd made clear was that he would never want his corpse put on display. Gidion and Dad had always known that, and even most of the funeral staff had known. During the funeral home's slower moments, the conversation would often turn to some of the more unusual requests they'd seen and what each of them would want at their own funerals.

The most awkward moment came early in the visitation. Seth, accompanied by his mother, came to pay his respects. They didn't hug or shake hands. That wasn't because they were angry with each other. They just never did that sort of thing.

While Seth's mom was busy talking to Gidion's Dad, Seth said in a lowered voice, "I messed up." He looked down at his feet. "You were right."

Gidion nodded. "I screwed up, too. I'm sorry if I got between you and Andrea."

Seth shook his head. "Problem was all me."

"Are you—"

"Andrea made it pretty clear we're done. I'm sorry if that means the same for us."

"She and I, uh." Gidion hesitated, unsure if saying this here was the best idea.

"Yeah, I know. Word got around fast at school." Seth smiled, which surprised Gidion. "I'm okay with it. Are we—I mean you and I—are we good?"

Gidion nodded. He meant it, and he didn't doubt Seth did, too. Later, he understood Andrea didn't kill their friendship. They'd started drifting in different directions long before she entered the picture. The night Gidion first learned vampires were real, that their existence had taken his mother from him, his childhood had ended. That night, he'd started to leave his friends behind to turn himself into a hunter.

He and Seth would still speak in the years to come. The conversations simply got shorter, and the time between them longer.

About halfway through the visitation, Andrea arrived. Gidion found it mildly ironic that she also came with her mother, but he didn't share the thought. He mentioned about Seth showing up earlier and left it at that.

The two of them went into the funeral home's garage with both their parents' blessings. Dad even suggested it. He must have known Gidion was well past his limits.

Andrea sat with him on the hood of one of the hearses. The stench of pipe tobacco lingered in the garage stronger than the odor of gas or oil. Gidion clung to Andrea, trying to bury his nose in her hair, hoping the smell of her shampoo might push away everything else.

She kissed him. "Do you want to talk about it?"

He shook his head, not wanting to fall apart on her, not yet. He knew worse things were waiting in the days ahead, but he wasn't able to say that. Just thinking about it was too much. Her silent support, the way she held him, stitched him back together.

Dad sold the funeral home that afternoon. The lawyer handling the transaction said they'd taken care of the paperwork in record time. Almost all of the money was going into a trust for Gidion. He'd explained it to the lawyer by simply saying, "College isn't cheap."

The rest of the money went to Ms. Aldgate. She'd offered to take Gidion into her home, and Dad didn't want her to struggle financially with the added burden. He'd said it better than that, but Gidion knew that's what it amounted to.

By the time Andrea left with her mother, it was well after sunset. Plenty of people were still filing through the funeral home, but Gidion knew he wasn't up for going back in the room with Grandpa's casket and all the frowns, handshakes, and hugs.

He went out to Dad's car. Only after he reached the car did he remember that Dad had locked it. Except, when he looked through the window, he saw it wasn't. Out of habit, Gidion reached into his front jacket pocket for the box cutter that wasn't there. Dad made him leave it at home. Gidion turned in a tight circle, looking for anyone or anything that was out of place. A group of mourners were gathered outside and chatting. If someone wanted to attack him now, they'd do it with an audience. He didn't think that was likely.

Turning back to the car, Gidion saw the light from a nearby street lamp hitting off of something metallic resting on the backseat. He opened the car door and climbed inside.

The light reflected off a four-inch deep metal box that was more than a foot long and nine inches wide. The box didn't have any details to it save for a small Templar cross engraved into the top.

A post-it note with some familiar handwriting on it was attached to the outside of the box.

Copied what I needed. You can have it back.

—Blood

He wondered if Blood had taken it from Grandpa's home or if she'd found it in Mom's mansion. Odds favored he'd never know. The lock on the top was broken. He opened it and found several photographs, almost all of them black and white, but the picture on top was the one that made Dad smile and cry when Gidion took it to him. It was the one of Grandpa with Grandma in Paris. The photograph was taken at night with the Eiffel Tower all lit up like some giant, metal Christmas tree. The carefree smile on Grandpa's face looked so foreign compared to the man he'd known that Gidion almost didn't recognize him.

The real find was a small journal bound in brown, weathered leather. At first, Gidion assumed it was Grandpa's, which seemed very unlike him. Only a few lines into it, he realized this was Grandma's. Maybe it would offer some answers about how Grandpa became a hunter and if there were others out there. Why else would Grandpa have hidden it?

Dad read it in his last days, and a few times it made him laugh.

Dad looked awful. His body lost weight, and the way his eyes had sunk in and his muscles shrunk, he resembled Grandpa more than ever. Dad explained it was the vampire blood feeding on him, because he had no way to feed himself. The first cup of coffee with toast he tried to eat sent him running to the bathroom to vomit. In a desperate experiment, they bought steaks and cooked Dad's rare. When that failed to stay down, Dad told them they needed to stop. All they were doing was costing him more blood and that meant he had less time. He was past the point of human food and not far enough along for blood.

Watching him fade made Gidion realize why Dad hadn't been able to kill Mom all those years ago. If a vampire had offered to give Dad the third feeding he needed, Gidion might have strapped his father to a bed to make it happen.

Dad lasted longer than they'd expected, but six days after Gidion had rescued him, the purging began. Nothing but blood came up. It was all his body had left, and in the absence of his third feeding, the human side of his body was rejecting the filth that invaded it. His immune system wasn't going to save him, though. That was the thing sure to kill him if he waited.

Dad made the call to Blood. Then he said his goodbyes.

Before Dad left, he slipped off his *Gatchaman* wristband.

"It did bring us luck," Dad said.

Gidion stared at it, hesitant to take it, because the longer he resisted, the longer Dad had to stay. "I didn't think you believed in luck."

"I've never needed it." He hugged Gidion for the last time, standing in the doorway of Ms. Aldgate's house the same as the night he'd left for the park. "Got all I needed when you were born on a Friday the 13th."

Dad placed the wristband in Gidion's hand after that.

The last Gidion saw of his father was as he drove away from Ms. Aldgate's house in his blue Corolla.

EPILOGUE

As much as Gidion fought against it, life settled into a routine within just a few weeks. He wore his one constant reminder on his left wrist. The only time he ever took off the wristband was to shower or bathe.

Ms. Aldgate had agreed to look after him, but they soon realized they were really looking after each other. By virtue of making sure one of them ate, the other did as well. The same proved true for school, sleep, and most anything mundane that life demanded.

Gidion's first few dates with Andrea helped him, too. They agreed that the night they'd shared after Proper Pie shouldn't count as their first.

They celebrated their first month anniversary on a Saturday night in March. He took her to Bottom's Up Pizza downtown. Since the weather was unseasonably warm, they strolled along the Canal Walk. He showed her where he'd once saved Ms. Aldgate from a vampire.

Not surprisingly, downtown was packed with people. They stopped inside Fountain Bookstore where Andrea splurged. They took her haul with them to a café a block up Cary Street where they drank café mochas. They sat next to one of the front windows and spent the next hour engaged in some serious people-watching as they sipped their drinks.

"Check out that lady." Andrea laughed as she pointed to a woman dressed in an obscenely short dress and even more absurdly high heels trying to cross the cobblestone street and doing a poor job of it. A less intoxicated friend in more sensible footwear helped her stay upright.

"How many points if she lands on her butt?" Andrea asked.

Gidion adopted a thoughtful pose, finger tapping his chin. "I'd call it a twenty-five pointer. Fifty if she takes her friend down, too."

No points were to be had, though. The ladies made it to the far side of the street without a tumble.

Andrea nestled against Gidion. He wrapped his arm across her shoulders. She pointed out the window at their next target. "Look at this guy. That dude is waaaaay too serious."

Gidion didn't laugh with her, having spotted the man before she did. He walked too smoothly to be human. His hungry blue eyes slid over each person on the street and connected through the window with Gidion's. That gaze left no doubt that the vampire recognized him as a fellow predator. His lips parted in a smile that kept his fangs hidden. Gidion glared at the vampire until he disappeared down the street in search of easier prey.

Blood had asked if he could stop hunting. She hadn't believed him when he said he could. Seeing that vampire walk by made his fingers flex to grip a weapon he no longer had, and in that moment, he knew Blood had been right.

ACKNOWLEDGEMENTS

Writing isn't a lonely art. At least, it isn't if you write for publication.

Joining James River Writers many years ago made a big difference in my writing and my life. I've met my best friends through JRW, fellow writers who push me to improve my craft and keep faith in it. I can't properly thank all the people within JRW I should, but I'd be remiss not to highlight Katharine Herndon and Kristi Tuck Austin. I've worked closely with both of them within JRW during the time I wrote this book. Like any best friends do, we keep each other sane enough to get stuff done, limit the bloodshed when possible, and occasionally help hide the bodies when necessary. I often think of Kristi as Gidion's godmother.

I need to thank Phil Hilliker for his beta reading on this book. He kept me honest with Gidion's second novel, saving me from myself in quite a few places. We've become fast friends during the past year, yet another friendship born from JRW.

Eveline Chao, a woman I've never met, provided an entertaining and useful resource in crafting the dialogue for Blood, the assassin pursuing Gidion. I'm grateful to my co-worker Elisabeth Moore, who also provided some insight into Blood's dialogue, for directing me to Eveline's book. *Niubi!* has proven an unexpectedly useful resource for this book and other projects.

Thanks to Piper J. Drake who provided some last-minute help translating the name of Grandpa's sword.

Kelly Justice, owner of Fountain Bookstore in Richmond, turned into a great supporter for my first book *Gidion's Hunt*. Her unwavering faith in that first book encouraged me to work that much harder to make the second book in this series the best novel it could be.

I also want to thank Matthew Plourde and Mike Boucher. Not only did they give me my start with Gidion at Fable Press, but their input in the early stages of writing *Gidion's Blood* made this a much better book.

The *Gidion Keep, Vampire Hunter* series has found a new home with Diversion Books. I can't thank my new editor Laura Duane enough for that. Working with the team at Diversion on this book, which includes Chris Mahon, Sarah Masterson Hally, and Beth Brown, has been a treat.

Writing a book always requires a sacrifice. For me, that sacrifice is the time I could spend with my wife and our children, time I can never make up. Sheri, Regan, and Liam have always supported me in my writing, but this book turned out to be the biggest challenge I've ever faced as a writer. Whenever I needed to take time to myself to get this book written, they never questioned it. At times, they even pushed me to get it done. If in reading this book you've wondered why a man would dedicate such a dark tale about Gidion's family to his loved ones, just know there was never a question the three of them deserved it. I couldn't have finished *Gidion's Blood* without them.